# Outrageous October

## A Novel

By

Barbara Levenson

ISBN: 1480093661

ISBN 13: 9781480093669

Also by Barbara Levenson

Fatal February
Justice In June

*This book is dedicated to the hard working strong Vermonters who populate the lovely villages of the Upper Valley.*

# Outrageous October

By

Barbara Levenson

# Prologue

Carolyn Brousseau was feeling sorry for herself. She had taken to her bed with a messy sick cold. Damn the changing Vermont weather. She should have found a warm hideaway after her husband died; maybe Florida or Arizona. But leaving her friends and charity work here in High Pines weighed on her psyche and seemed more than she could handle at her age.

She was supposed to be in Burlington at the symphony board meeting, a trip she always looked forward to. Instead she was alone with her stopped-up head and wheezing chest and only her Golden Retriever for company. Bridey was as old as Carolyn, ten in dog years and not any more energetic then her mistress.

She knew she needed to sleep but the Nyquil wasn't working. She poured a tumbler of brandy from the bottle on her nightstand and downed it in one gulp. Soon she was snoring in a sickly fog. Wind howled through her open windows as a new cold front approached.

A loud bang awakened her. She tried to sit up bracing herself on one elbow. She thought she heard rustling sounds. She wasn't sure where they were coming from in her brandy induced haze. From the open windows or inside the room? She felt a shiver run through her body.

"Bridey, come here girl," she called.

The flash of light blinded her for a moment. It dawned on her that it came from a flashlight. Then she heard a familiar voice.

"You're not supposed to be here. Thought you'd be up in Burlington giving away some of that money you never earned," the voice said.

"What – what are you doing here?" Carolyn stuttered, still fighting the fog in her brain.

"I'm here to get what's mine," the voice answered.

"Where's Bridey?" Carolyn was now fully awake. The chill she felt now was one of fear.

"We took care of Bridey, just like we'll take care of you."

That was the moment Carolyn saw the shiny metal of the gun caught in the glimmer of the flashlight.  She rolled to the far side of the bed and tried to roll to the floor, but the flash of the gun was the last thing Carolyn Brousseau ever saw.  .

# THE VALLEY NEWS
# SOCIALITE FOUND MURDERED

October 22
High Pines, Vermont

Local socialite and longtime resident, Carolyn Brousseau, was found dead in her home in the River Road area. She was discovered by her handyman, Al Shields.

Mr. Shields arrived at the Brousseau home early yesterday morning to plow the early winter snow that fell during the night. He saw no signs of life and did not see or hear Mrs. Brousseau's Golden Retriever. Several windows were open. He entered the house to check on the owner and discovered her body in the master bedroom.

Mrs. Brousseau was the widow of Maurice Brousseau, owner of Maurice Woolen Mill. The mill closed three years ago. She is survived by one son, Thomas, believed to reside in Boston. Funeral arrangements are pending.

Sheriff Jimmy Parsons is in charge of the investigation. "We are asking the public to report any suspicious activity observed in the area. There were no signs of a break-in, but few people in the area lock their doors or cars even though we have repeatedly warned them to lock up," the Sheriff said. Sheriff Parsons refused to reveal any details regarding the cause of death or evidence recovered, but stated that it was clear that Mrs. Brousseau had been murdered.

Al Shields was reached by telephone, but was reluctant to speak at length. "I am still quite shocked. I was able to tell the police that Mrs. Brousseau's 2001 white Lincoln Town Car was not in its usual place. Her Golden Retriever was nowhere on the property. "That dog is a real barker and should have alerted her to any strangers," according to Mr. Shields,

The Brousseaus were active in several charities in the state including the Vermont Symphony Orchestra and the Upper Valley Humane Society, but were known to be silent benefactors, keeping a low profile. Mrs. Brousseau traveled extensively and was often not in residence in her High Pines home.

Francie Wallace, former housekeeper in the Brousseau home, declined to be interviewed but did state that she left the employ of the family shortly after the mill closed. Mrs. Wallace's husband was employed at the Maurice Mill for many years. He committed suicide in 2002.

Anyone having information that would aid the police is asked to contact Sheriff Parsons at the main station in White River Junction, or the Vermont State Police in Montpelier.

# TWO

# One Year Later, Miami, Florida

It was the first day of October and I had an important court date. I'm always awake early when a trial is on my mind. My bungalow in Coral Gables was dark as I moved out of bed pushing Sam, my German Shepherd, onto the feet of my gorgeous Latin boyfriend Carlos.

Carlos yelled and sat up. "Hey, it's still dark out. What are you doing out of bed?"

He tried to pull me back next to him. I leaned over and kissed him lightly before stepping back into the reality of the work week ahead of me.

"This is the day I have to try your cousin's case. You must have forgotten."

I moved away quickly before I gave in and climbed back into bed. Then I would be totally late arriving at the office and at the courthouse.

As I threw on a long shirt belonging to Carlos, I thought back to the time before we bumped into each other, literally. It was only eight months ago that day in February when I went to the car wash and ended up being rear-ended by Carlos in his Corvette. I grinned as I thought about my first impression of him as a brash, rude, overly rich developer.

I fixed a pot of coffee for me and a special concoction of *café cubano* for Carlos, who was up and in the shower having given up on my returning to our warm bed, or really my warm bed. Carlos has his own house in the tony suburb of Pinecrest. He built his mega mansion on spec, but no one had opted to plunk down mega bucks for his starter castle so he moved in himself. I like my little house so we take turns staying with each other.

I gave Sam his kibble, walked him, and returned to the house and a quick shower. Carlos opened the shower curtain, I could smell his after-shave that filled me with regret for not returning to bed.

"Why didn't you join me in the shower?" He laughed and patted my behind. "See you later ," he called as he closed the curtain.

I couldn't wait until later. I realized we had spent too many mornings being late to business appointments in the last few months.

I returned to the bedroom to don my official attorney outfit; navy suit, white blouse, and very high-heeled uncomfortable pumps.


It wasn't even eight o'clock when I arrived at my office on Dixie Highway. I glanced at the sign outside my office as I hurried in, In the half light of day, the gold letters gleamed announcing MARY MAGRUDER KATZ, CRIMINAL DEFENSE ATTORNEY. I was enjoying my solo law practice and that was another thing that Carlos was responsible for.

I was engaged to and working for Franklin Fieldstone and his snooty civil law firm on the fateful day that Carlos and I made love for the first time. My only mistake regarding this happy occasion was that it occurred in my office at the Fieldstone firm. When Frank walked in on us, the engagement was over and so was my job. So now I was the sole attorney in my own practice and happier than I've ever been.

Catherine was already in the office booting up computers and listening to voice mail. Catherine is my amazing paralegal and guardian angel. She lives close to the office. She's a single mom with two handsome school age sons. Her ex-husband walked out on her when the kids were babies.

I guessed she had ridden her bike to work. Beads of sweat covered her forehead. October in Miami shows no sign of heat abatement until at least the end of the month

"Are you sure you're ready for trial? Are these all the files in Franco's case?" Catherine asked as she arranged the few thin files in my briefcase.

"I've been ready since July. It's the prosecutor who keeps asking for one continuance after another. Just because Franco is one of Carlos's innumerable cousins doesn't mean I'm not devoted to his case. He wouldn't have to defend criminal charges if he hadn't helped me get my car out of the Miami Police impound lot last June after the cops towed it away."

"That's what happens when you continue to park in those no parking spots. You never learn."

"I can't help it. I can't leave clients waiting in court without an attorney. Parking is a bummer."

"Not if you arrive on time or try being early for a change"

Catherine turned her back to answer the phone and I left the waiting room for the quiet of my office.

I went over Franco's case in my mind. Franco's profession is cars He knows everything about cars from fixing them to retrieving them from tow-away lots He spends most of his time repairing everybody's car in his extended family whether they need it or not. His car knowledge was the reason he was facing trial Last June he helped get my SUV back after it was towed. It was late in the evening. He gave the attendant cash and the car was released. He also repurchased the parts that the attendant had stolen from my car.

When the police made their monthly visit to Franco's house on a domestic call (Franco and wife, Lucinda, have a strange way of showing their love for each other) they served an arrest warrant charging him with bribing a city official and/or a police officer. This probably occurred because some officer had his eye on my Ford Explorer for himself and was pissed that the attendant let it go and pocketed the bucks Franco doled out.

Catherine came into my office with messages and e-mails to look at before I left for the courthouse. She frowned and fidgeted waiting for me to address the messages with her.

"Catherine, are you nervous because you think Franco will be convicted? I understand that your hot romance with Franco's brother makes you concerned. Whatever happens to Franco won't reflect on Marco. I know how much you care about Marco and his family. After all, you met him right here in this office when he helped us with some investigative work. I saw the sparks fly. What I can't understand is why you don't move in with him. I know he's asked you."

"I'm still kind of gun-shy after my marriage from hell. And I have my kids to think about. And Marco is very busy with his agency. Pit Bull Security is his life. Anyway, who are you to talk? You refuse to give up your house and move in with Carlos."

"Okay we're two independent girls. We might as well face it. We like the romance part, but not the forever part. I better get on the road or I'll be late again."

# C H A P T E R
# THREE

I carefully parked my car in a real parking place, not my usual 'Absolutely No Parking' labeled spot. For once I was early enough to stroll up the steps to the courthouse and arrive in Judge Johnny Lee Custis's third floor courtroom before nine o'clock.

The third floor courtrooms have bullet-proof glass separating the spectator section from the well of the court. No one has ever discovered why the glass was placed there, since the courtrooms on the third floor are the smallest in the building and never used for high profile cases.

Franco was already seated with his wife in the first row behind the glass.

"Franco, you need to come with me. You'll be next to me at the defense table." I said. "Lucinda, you can keep your seat here."

Lucinda gave Franco a hug and a huge wet kiss as Franco moved through the door. I assumed this was for the benefit of the court personnel.

"Mary, wait a minute." Lucinda grabbed my arm. "Will I get the bail money back as soon as this is over?" she asked. "If you lose, will Franco be going right to jail? How long do you think the sentence will be?"

"Lucinda, you ask me the same thing every time we've been in court. Yes, you'll get the bail money released. No, I don't expect to lose. Franco will be going home with you."

"Oh." Lucinda said. Disappointment covered her face like a heavy veil.

I made my way out of the public section and began unpacking my briefcase at the defense table. I glanced back at Lucinda and was surprised to see Carlos standing next to her, He waved when he saw that I noticed him. I felt my usual reaction when Carlos appeared unexpectedly. My heart quickened. I could feel its beat and I felt warmth wash over me. I wondered if that euphoric feeling would clothe me forever or would time mellow this relationship. I knew these were feelings I never had for Frank Fieldstone or even for my college boyfriends.

I turned my attention back to the courtroom and was surprised again although this time not pleasantly. Approaching the prosecutor's table was Assistant State Attorney Fred Mercer, the head of the public corruption unit. Fred never forgave me for proving that Judge Liz Maxwell was not guilty of fixing drug cases. He had been looking forward to prosecuting her and I spoiled his fun when I proved that she was squeaky clean.

"Fred, what a surprise. Your office brought you in on this teeny case? Are you taking over from the misdemeanor baby prosecutors?" I asked.

"Not completely, just to argue a brief motion," he mumbled.

"Really. I haven't received any new motions,"

Before Fred could reply, the bailiff called us to order. "All rise. The Honorable Johnny Lee Custis presiding. Turn off all cell phones and pagers or they will be confiscated. No talking or gum chewing. When your case is called come forward quickly or another case will be called. Be seated and have a pleasant morning," the bailiff concluded with a flourish.

Judge Custis was a large black man with a laid back approach. He was always cordial, never raised his voice, and best of all, he had been a public defender before becoming a judge.

"Good morning, ladies and gentlemen," Judge Custis said as he heaved his large frame into an even larger leather chair. "I'm going to call the trial docket cases first and then move on to the arraignments. The first case is *State vs. Franco Hernandez*. Are both sides ready to proceed? I've already called the jury pool to send a panel up here."

Fred and I both stood. "Yes, your honor, the defense is ready," I answered.

At the same time Fred spoke in a shaky voice. "Your honor, Fred Mercer, Division Chief of Public Corruption, for the state. Unfortunately, the state is not ready to proceed, and we are requesting a brief continuance." Fred looked down at his notes, unable to meet the judge's gaze.

"Judge," I said, but was immediately interrupted by Judge Custis who tipped back in his chair, hands behind his head.

"The state is not ready again? How many continuances have there been, Madam Clerk?"

The clerk was already shuffling through the court file. "Let's see, Judge, there was one in July, two in August and one in September, all requested by the state, over defense counsel's objection,"

"I believe I told you the last time you were here in September that there would be no more continuances granted to the state. Doesn't your file reflect that?" the judge asked.

"I wasn't the prosecutor here on that occasion, your honor. It was the regular division prosecutor," Fred said.

"Doesn't matter. Your file should have that notation. You prosecutors are fungible anyway. Just like dollar bills. Some are more wrinkled than others but they all have the same value." The judge chuckled at his own joke.

"Judge, I'm sure the reason that the state is never ready to go forward is their lack of an essential witness who is the alleged victim in this case. I tried to subpoena him for a deposition and he never showed up. I believe that their witness is permanently unavailable, like long-gone," I said and smiled at Judge Custis.

"Is that correct, Mr. Mercer?" Judge Custis asked.

"Well, he's not available right now, or, I mean, this week, your honor."

I interrupted. "He's never available. That's exactly my point. But there's more to this, Judge. My client is charged with bribing a police officer and/or city official. The man at the towing yard is just an employee of the towing service. He's not a police officer or even an employee of the city, let alone a city official. My client paid him the fee to release an automobile. If the tow yard employee asked for a payment that was more than the standard release payment, that's not my client's fault. He paid the amount requested. So even if this itinerant employee ever did show up, the state still couldn't meet its burden of proof. Therefore, your honor, I move for an immediate dismissal of this case." I watched Fred's scowl spread over his face.

"And I am granting defendant's motion based on the state's failure to ever provide the essential witness. Further, Mr. Mercer, the speedy trial rule will be kicking in shortly, and you'll be out of court anyway. Next case," Judge Custis shuffled through his files.

"But, Judge." Fred's whines sounded like an injured cat.

"What part of 'dismissed' don't you understand, Sir?" The judge's usual smile disappeared and was replaced by a small frown.

"Thank you, Judge," I said as I picked up my briefcase and motioned Franco to follow me from the courtroom.

# FOUR

Lucinda and Carlos were waiting in the lobby outside the courtroom. After giving instructions to Lucinda to retrieve the bond money, and cautioning her and Franco to stay out of trouble and removed from further domestic calls to police, I turned to Carlos.

"What a great surprise to see you here. You never said a word this morning about attending Franco's hearing," I said.

"I feel responsible for my various cousins taking up your time, besides, I love watching you in action. It makes me remember how you represented me when we first met and I conned you into helping me close a real estate deal. Watching you do your legal stuff turns me on."

"Well, please try to remember some of my legal advice. Don't pull anymore of those sort of legal deals of yours. Lying to clients isn't a good idea, and selling them land you didn't really own is an invitation to jail."

"That only happened once," Carlos said.

"Once that I know about."

"I do listen to you, but I enjoy more looking at you." Carlos pulled me close and kissed me.

As I pulled away, I saw people staring at us. They were probably think-ing that I was saying goodbye to someone on his way to prison. I really didn't care. Carlos has erased most of my inhibitions.

"Let me walk you to your car," Carlos said as he slipped his arm around my waist.

"I have to make sure that the order of dismissal in Franco's case gets signed, so I can't leave yet. Why don't we just meet at my house this eve-ning? I'd really like to go out to dinner to celebrate the end of Franco's case. Maybe we could meet at that bistro on the Miracle Mile."

Carlos looked away. "No can do tonight. I have a dinner meeting with some new investors. How about tomorrow night instead?"

"Can't you postpone the meeting? Or maybe I should go with you to make sure you have legal advice right next to you at the table."

"I can't change these plans and I promise not to do anything that you wouldn't approve. You go have a nice evening and we'll do something together tomorrow."

"Well, if that's your final answer, I guess I'll just have to look for another dinner date for tonight."

"I'm sorry Mary. I may be late tonight so I'll go back to Pinecrest. I don't want to wake you."

"Is everything okay, Carlos?"

"Of course, why wouldn't it be?" Carlos walked away without his usual goodbye kiss.

# FIVE

In a few minutes I was on my way back to the office to share the court victory with Catherine. She hugged me and screamed her congratulations, Then raced to her desk to phone Marco with the good news that his brother would not be a state prisoner.

A minute later Catherine walked into my office with the mail. "You look disgusted. What's the matter?"

"I really feel like going out tonight and Carlos has some dumb meeting. What are you doing tonight?"

"Oh, Mary, I'm sorry. Tonight is the meeting at school for the soccer parents and I have to go."

"Okay, I understand. No one wants my company for dinner tonight.

Undaunted, I reached for the phone again and dialed

"Boutique de Luis. How may I help you?" The sensuous voice of Celia Martin, a.k.a. Chicky answered.

Chicky is Carlos's sister who returned from her stint as a club bum in Buenos Aires to help Luis Corona open the Corona family shop in Coral Gables. Carlos's father is Argentine and his mother is Cuban. But if you think that's a mixed up family, mine is more so.

My father is Jewish and my mother is Southern Baptist. That's the Magruder Katz in my name.

Angelina, Carlos's mother, is ecstatic to have her baby girl home again, and credits me for getting Chicky back. She's sure that if I hadn't freed Luis from the clutches of the U.S. government after his arrest last June, Chicky would still be spending her youth dancing the tango in smoky Argentine bars. Much to my surprise, I really like Celia who is nothing like her mother.

"Chicky, it's me, Mary. Is this a busy time? Can you talk?"

"It is busy, but I can always make time for you. We're having our sale of last year's things and getting ready for our winter lines. I thought you were going to stop in and try on some of these sale creations."

"I meant to, but I've been so busy. Today I finally got Franco's case dismissed. That's why I'm calling."

Well, you don't need me to pat you on the back. You are the best. I'm sure everyone of your clients tells you that. Never mind about the sale. I'll pick out some things for you and put them away. You'll try them on whenever."

"I wasn't calling for praise. I want to go to dinner somewhere fun tonight to celebrate. Can you go?"

"With you and Carlos?"

"No, no Carlos. Just us girls. He's tied up on some business dinner."

"Oh, I'd love to have a girls' night out, but I can't."

"Bet you've got a big date."

"I've got inventory here. That's my date, and I can't leave Luis to do it alone or it'll be all screwed up."

"Okay. Chicky, turned down by another member of the Martin family. Happy inventory." I clicked off.

I wandered out to Catherine's desk. "No one wants to have dinner with me. Should I change my deodorant?" I asked. "Sam would probably go, but he tends to bark at the other diners."

"What about your friend Lucy? Have you tried her?"

"No. Brilliant idea! Why didn't I think of that?"

"That's why you pay me the big bucks." Catherine went back to her typing and I went back to the phone.

Lucy has been my best friend since third grade. She and her husband, Steve, and their three kids live in Miami Beach a few blocks from where we both grew up.

"Lucy, it's Mary. I know this is last minute, but could you possibly get away to have dinner with me tonight? I got rid of that case against Franco, Carlos's cousin today. I'm dying to go out for a leisurely dinner with much wine. I'll even pay."

"Why aren't you going with Carlos? Don't tell me you split with him."

"No, he's tied up in a business meeting tonight."

"Dinner sounds great. Steve is working late and to be honest, I wasn't all that thrilled about pizza with the kids, but can you come over to the Beach? I'll have to get a sitter and it's a school night. They all have to be home early."

"Sure, I like coming to the Beach and driving down memory lane.. I'll pick you up around seven."

So, the die was cast setting up the dinner that changed my life..

# High Pines, Vermont, October 26<sup>th</sup>
## One year Ago

Dash Mellman and Tom Brousseau went back to Dash's law office as soon as they could extract themselves from the villagers who assembled at the community church for the lavish funeral of Carolyn Brousseau.

The cold rainy afternoon was an appropriate backdrop for the sober crowd at the church. Several dignitaries spoke about the Brousseau family's place in Vermont history. Tom opted not to be one of the speakers. This caused much whispering among the gathered audience while the choir sang a group of Carolyn's favorite hymns selected by the Vermont Symphony conductor. A goodly number of cars, SUV's and trucks made the trip from the church to the family plot in the cemetery that overlooked Old Main Street and the hills beyond.

The mood was melancholy, not because of Carolyn's demise, but because the village gossip mongers had finished chewing over the facts about a murder in their home town, and craved new revelations. Some of the facts were actually facts, others grew from rumor and guesswork. Dash was asked whether it was true that Mafia figures from Boston were tied to Tom. Someone started a story that Carolyn had a secret "boyfriend" who was staying with her.

Most of the gossip centered on Tom and his lack of mourning for his mother. Throughout the days of planning for the funeral and the actual service, Tom maintained a business-like appearance. New Englanders are known for reticence. Tom's demeanor ran more to lack of emotion.

The crowd returned to the church for a potluck meal put together by the caring committee. Hot casseroles and coffee took the chill off the wet group, many of whom slipped into the kitchen to savor several bottles of scotch and bourbon.

The Brousseau house was still surrounded by yellow evidence tape and sealed off. Dash, Tom and Sheriff Jimmy Parsons did a quick walk-through to identify any missing property. Tom claimed he couldn't remember any particular items among the hundreds of souvenirs, figurines and bric-a-brac that covered the tables and shelves in all the rooms.

It was 4:30 by the time Tom and Dash arrived back in Dash's office. Dash took a bottle of scotch out of his desk drawer and poured two shot glasses. He handed one to Tom.

Tom downed the scotch without even taking a seat or removing his wet raincoat. "Why did you insist that I come back here with you?" he asked.

"We need to discuss how you want to handle the house. Do you want to sell it? Will you want me to hire some folks to oversee the upkeep? And then there are the financial matters, the insurance policies and the stock certificates and bonds. Will you be returning to Boston?"

"I guess so, since I don't seem to be under arrest."

Tom's sarcasm was as thick as the rainclouds still visible through the sheets of water covering the office windows. Dash thought about Tom's interview with Sheriff Parsons. Jimmy had been brief, zeroing in on questions regarding Tom's last visit to High Pines, and his relationship with his mother. Tom answered in terse sentences as if words needed to be conserved. He said he hadn't been back to High Pines in nine months. Nothing he said incriminated him, but on the other hand, nothing he said erased the sense that Tom knew something more.

Dash realized that Tom was shifting uncomfortably and eyeing the door.

"Look, Dash, I know half the people here think I actually killed my mother. I don't know who did this or why. I can't figure out if anything is missing. Mother's jewelry was kept in the safe deposit box along with the stock certificates and deeds that you and I found when we went through everything yesterday."

Dash thought this was the most he had heard Tom say in the last three days

"I think people in High Pines knew that you and your parents didn't get along too well. I know they shouldn't mind each other's business, but this is such a small village that it's bound to happen."

"No, I didn't get along with my parents. Dad kept pushing me to go into the business, but he ended up selling the mill anyway. He just couldn't stand the thought that his only offspring wanted to be an artist. Mother was of the 'old school'. She went along with whatever Dad wanted. She never approved of my friends or lifestyle, never called me anything but Thomas. She acted like we were part of some royal family. If it hadn't been so damn annoying it might have been funny. I couldn't wait to get out of here and get a life."

"That's why Jimmy questioned you. He has nothing to go on, not a clue, so of course he turned to you, hoping to uncover some theory. And then there was the disappearance of Bridey. Whoever came in must have known the dog."

"People came and went from the house all the time. The handyman that found Mother walked right in. There was the housekeeper too. And you came and went on many occasions. Did Jimmy question you or anyone else?"

"I don't know who he questioned. He's trying to do his job."

"You know that a lot of people hated our family. When the mill closed, they blamed Dad for selling out to a foreign company. I can't blame the workers for being angry. There aren't many places for jobs in this state. Taxes are high so businesses don't want to locate here, and the winters are long and hard. If Jimmy doesn't have the brains to figure out that there are plenty of suspects right here in the Upper Valley, and he wastes all his time trying to make me the murderer, then he should be voted out of his job, and you can tell him I said so."

Tom began buttoning his drenched raincoat and moving toward the door.

"Wait, Tom, I'm not your enemy. Don't walk out. We haven't even gone over the details about your property here. I don't even know how to reach you."

"Here's a card with the post office box to forward any papers. I'll think about the house. In the meantime, I'll take care of hiring a property manager. The house is mine, so I'll take care of it. I don't need any help from anyone in this village."

Tom threw the card down on the desk and slammed the front door as he left

Dash realized that Tom had a volatile temper triggered by what appeared to be hatred for his family and High Pines. It hadn't taken much to unleash those feelings. Tom was the perfect target for Jimmy Parson's suspicions. Dash decided that the sheriff wouldn't look any further to solve this murder. He sighed and settled comfortably into his chair, propped his feet on the desk and retrieved the bottle of scotch from the drawer.

# SEVEN

# One year later, Miami, Florida

I fought my way through the evening rush hour on the causeway to Miami Beach. Even though it was crawling along, I still felt a sense of ease. The causeway surrounded by the aqua water of Biscayne Bay has a tranquil effect. Small pleasure boats darted by. The view of the receding Miami downtown skyline sparkled in the waning sunlight making the high-rise buildings look like so many crown jewels. The causeway ended as I inched through familiar territory. My old high school, the Katz Kosher Super Market where I stopped after school with my friends for candy treats from my grandfather. It all looked the same.

Then I turned down Fiftieth Street. The second lot from the corner is where our old house should be standing. Instead there were two town-houses squished onto the lot I slowed to view it all. The yard where my two brothers, William and Jonathan, and I played endless hours of football and soccer was filled with the faux Spanish architecture that has become the new Miami look. I stared in bewilderment as I recalled mother's garden that decorated the front of the house. Now the front of the new buildings consisted of a brick courtyard without a bit of grass or a tree.

I sped up again still wondering why my parents had sold the old place when Dad and Uncle Max sold Katz Kosher Super Market that my grandfather started.. Now they lived seventy miles away in a gated community with a golf course and clubhouse, amid a sea of cloned houses lacking even a modicum of the character of our old place that met its demise with a few scoops of a bulldozer.

Lucy's house is one of the old Spanish style original Miami Beach homes. It is warm and inviting, like stepping back in time; especially since Lucy has a few pieces of furniture that were her mother's.

Lucy was waiting for her neighbor's daughter to arrive to babysit. She had poured two glasses of wine. We sat in the family room while the two older boys watched TV and Lucy's ten month old daughter slept in her playpen.

"Where do you want to go for dinner?" I asked. I really felt hungry.

"I made a reservation for seven-thirty at Tony's Fish House. It's sort of new and it has a water view. It's in the Majestic Condo building."

"I know that building. Carlos built it right before I met him."

We finished our wine just as the babysitter arrived. Lucy said she was fifteen, but she looked more like twenty-five, wearing a figure revealing dress that appeared to be made out of spandex.

We piled into the Explorer and pulled into the condo building in a matter of minutes. Valet parking was jammed, cars lined up two deep. I waited in line and finally inched up to the attendant. "Look at that parking attendant who just jumped into that Corvette. He's driving off like he's at the Homestead Speedway," Lucy said pointing out the window.

"That's a car just like Carlos's. He'd kill someone that drove his car like that," I said.

We went up the elevator to the seventh floor and made our way to the restaurant. It smelled delicious. Lucy gave the hostess her name and we waited to be seated. The hostess was dressed in a spandex dress much like the babysitter's . I felt out of style in my staid courtroom attire.

The hostess returned to her podium after checking out the available tables. "This way, please," she said as she led us through the aisles of tables.

"Right here please," she said as she pointed to a small empty table adjoining several other tables.

"We'll never be able to have a conversation here," I said "The noise level is awful."

I glanced around and spotted a booth across the aisle. The banquettes had high backs. Why can't we have that booth? I'm sure it's less noisy."

"That booth is occupied. This is the only table available right now," the hostess answered.

"No, it's not occupied. I moved to the side of the booth and that's when my heart stopped beating. I clutched Lucy's arm to steady myself. The noisy room spun for a minute.

"What's wrong, Mary? Are you ill?" Lucy put her hand on my shoulder. Then she saw what I saw and her only comment was, "Oh no."

"We won't be staying." I said as I moved back through the maze of tables to the entrance, to the elevator, and away from the moment I felt my heart break.

Outside the breeze from the ocean swept away the sticky feeling from my face, but the picture of the occupants of that booth couldn't be moved by the breeze. The picture of Carlos and his ex-wife, Margarita, half hidden in that cozy booth was indelibly painted in my brain. My eyes were filled with that image even as the first of many tears rained down from it.

I moved at a run through the front portico of the building. Lucy raced behind me trying to keep up. My car was still in front. I threw a ten dollar bill at the attendant and jumped into the driver's seat. Lucy barely had time to close the passenger door as I hit the gas and roared away from the building and the dinner that changed my life..

I drove along the ocean instead of turning back toward Lucy's house. I opened the windows and felt the wind filling the car, but still I couldn't erase the picture of Carlos and Margarita.

Lucy was quiet for a while. Finally she closed her window and asked if she could drive. I pulled onto the shoulder of the road and switched places with my forever best friend who eased the car back to the traffic of Miami Beach. She stopped in her driveway and led me into her house.

After the babysitter was dispatched and the two older boys sent to their room, Lucy poured two glasses of brandy and set them on the coffee table in front of us. She sat on the sofa next to me.

"Oh, God, Lucy what am I going to do? I thought Carlos was the one right guy at the right time in my life. I thought I knew him, but I must have closed my eyes to his ability to lie so smoothly. He told me, right to my face, that he was going to a business meeting. Now I wonder how many other times he pulled this crap."

"Mary, I am so sorry. Why did I have to pick that restaurant? I feel awful."

"It's not your fault. I would have found out eventually and that might have been worse. It's just a shock. It's better to know where I stand now. I feel like such a fool. I thought I was a better judge of people. That's what I get for mistaking lust for love. I'll get rid of this rock of a ring and make a clean break."

"Maybe there's some explanation of why he was with her. You need to give yourself some time to think, like a time-out that I make my kids take."

"I do need some time away, but not to think. I have to break this off with Carlos. The one thing I can't forgive is being lied to; that, and being part of a triangle. I guess that's two things I can't forgive."

"Listen, you're exhausted. You work without a break or a vacation. I've got a great idea. Why don't you go up to Vermont for a couple of weeks and use my house there? I've been trying to get you to go ever since my grandmother left me the house. You'll love it, especially right now with the leaves changing colors, and the crisp autumn days. We'd be up there ourselves if Steve wasn't getting ready for a big trial."

"Maybe it would be good to get out of here for a while. Where is it exactly?"

"It's in the Upper Connecticut River Valley near a cute village called High Pines, and you can take Sam. I know you never go anywhere without that dog. Trust me. It'll be totally relaxing. Absolutely nothing ever happens in High Pines."

# CHAPTER NINE

I tried to go to sleep but I tossed and turned, My bed felt alien with the smell of Carlos surrounding me.. Finally I got up and changed the sheets. I tried again but I was fully awake. I gave up and raided the fridge where I found a leftover slice of pizza and a half eaten, fully forgotten carton of Moo Goo Guy Pan from the Chinese carryout near the office. I nuked them both in the microwave and ate a few bites. The strange meal made me nauseous to look at it. I couldn't remember the last time I didn't want to eat.

I settled in the living room and tried to focus on the plan to leave for Vermont. Sam jumped up on the sofa and nestled his head in my lap. At least I still had one loyal male in my life.

I tried to count the good things in my life like Mother always told me to do when I was unhappy. I still had my family, my dog, my law practice, a few friends and then I looked down at my hand. I was still wearing my humongous emerald and diamond engagement ring. I was filled with rage as it shined in my eyes as if it were taunting me.

I had to figure out what to do. I went to the desk and pulled out a yellow pad and a pen. I would use my organization skills and make a plan.

First, I wrote: 1. call the messenger service as soon as I get to the office and ship Carlos's ring back to him with a letter. I rewrote the letter several times and finally decided on:

Carlos,

I am returning your ring. I saw you and Margarita at the restaurant last night. You lied to me. I can forgive many things, but not total lies. Any relationship that we had is over, ended, finished. Do not phone me, e-mail me, or attempt to see me at the office or anywhere else.

Next I outlined everything I had to do to leave quickly for Vermont. I made a list of work things to do and house things to do. The clock read five-thirty a.m. when I finished the paper work. Time to shower, and feed and walk Sam, who was thrilled that he was partaking of an early breakfast, My appetite began to return. I downed toast and two cups of strong coffee.

I was seated at my desk by seven-thirty and had already called the messenger service when Catherine arrived.

"What are you doing here so early?" she asked,

"I had a bad night. What's your excuse?"

"I had to have the boys at school early for soccer practice so I came here instead of going back home."

Catherine had a sixth sense when it came to detecting troubles. "What's going on? Is it Carlos?"

"Oh, yes, it's that lying untrustworthy Carlos. I caught him having dinner with Margarita last night. His business dinner turned out to be a cozy fling with the ever-present ex. Listen, Catherine, I've called the messenger service. I'm sending back his ring. I'm really through with him. And do not discuss this with Marco, or you'll be looking for a new job."

"Mary, you know I'd never do anything you didn't want me to do. You know I will always take your side. I understand about cheating partners. I lived it with my ex."

"I guess you do understand after your ex, that louse, Brady, walked out on you and the two babies and ended up with some bimbo in Ft. Lauderdale."

"Sure, I know the whole feeling; blaming yourself, blaming him, but at least you never made things permanent."

"Lucy has offered me her house in Vermont. I need to get away, so I'm taking her up on it. I'm going to get out of here as fast as I can."

"What can I do to help? What about the office?"

"I want you to keep it open. Get Joe Fineberg on the phone. He can take over my cases and interview any new clients for a couple of weeks. He owes me a favor now that he and Liz Maxwell have finally tied the knot. And I'll want you to check my house from time to time. Sam and I will be out of here in a day or two."

"Of course. Anything else?"

"Yes, do not tell Carlos where I am. I need time to let this broken heart heal."

"Mary, I'll miss you. Please, don't stay away too long."

"I can't leave my work for too long or I'll have no practice to return to. I just need some quiet time, and Lucy tells me nothing ever happens in High Pines."

# CHAPTER TEN

Two days after the disaster dinner. I had the Ford almost packed. Keys to the house were left with Catherine and my neighbor, Mrs. Armando, who didn't believe that I was just going on vacation. She probably thought I was being run out of town because of my colorful clients.

Sam was bathed and brushed. My files were left in Joe's capable hands and Catherine had a list of instructions for every kind of office disaster imaginable and even a few unimaginable, like a hurricane and a tsunami both aimed directly at my office.

Only one thing was left to do. I went to the phone. "Hi Mother. Would it be okay if I came up there for dinner and spent the night?" I'll tell you why when I see you."

"Well, of course it's great, but your dad won't be home until late. It's his poker night."

"Good. It'll be just us girls. See you later."

I finished loading the car with water and Sam's food. I threw in a blanket and the few cold weather clothes I had packed away for trips up north in winter to depose witnesses. I loaded Sam's crate in last and whistled for him to jump in. He loved riding and the crate was a sign that this was a longer ride, not just to the cleaners or grocery store.

The house was as cleaned up as it had ever been. I made one last round through the rooms checking windows and doors. The checklist for Catherine and my neighbor was pinned up on the refrigerator. All systems were go. There was nothing left to do but start the SUV and say goodbye to the Carlos era in my life.


The trip up to Boynton Beach to inform my parents of life's turn of events was necessary to keep them from calling out the state police and the FBI to find their missing daughter. Besides it was on the way and it would be easy to start from their place in the early morning.

The usual traffic filled the turnpike even in midafternoon. The report on the radio warned of a tractor trailer rollover accident closing all but one lane. Just the usual, but the report allowed me to change routes and arrive at the gated community a little before five. And I was two hours further north.

The guard came out of his little house. He was wearing his usual uniform; a cross between a ship captain and a high school band member.

"What is your destination, please?" he asked.

"I'm here to visit my parents. I'm Mary Katz, Abe and Hope Katz's daughter. You've seen me many times."

"Your name, please?"

"I just told you. I'm Mary Magruder Katz."

"Let me see some ID."

"You've got to be kidding."

"No, I'm serious. My job is to keep outsiders out."

"Look, I'm in no mood to be hassled. Get on your phone and call Hope Katz and tell her Mary, her daughter is here. Do it," I barked. That caused Sam to stand up in his crate and give out an ominous real bark.

Captain Courageous shot into his guard shack and dialed the phone. In a minute he returned, handed me my visitor's placard and opened the gate..

I have never understood why a group of elderly retirees whose main occupations are golf and bridge need to be secured from their relatives. Maybe some of them don't want to be disturbed by the real world of their grown children.

Mother was waiting in the doorway. She came out to the car as I drove up the red brick driveway.

"Mary, all this for an overnight?" she said as she looked inside the car.

I opened Sam's crate and he bounded into the house. He loved visiting his "grandparents" who were good for lots of snacks from the dinner table.

"No, I'm headed on a little vacation. Let's go inside so we can talk."

"What's wrong, honey? You look like you've been crying." Mother put her arm around my shoulder as we walked inside.

I was trying not to turn on the waterworks again. I thought I was all cried out. When Mother put her arm around me the flood began .

Mother handed me a Kleenex from her pocket as I collapsed onto the family room sofa.

I blew my nose and a torrent of words rushed out at the same time. "I have returned Carlos's ring. He's a lying bastard. He lied to me that he had a business dinner he couldn't cancel and I caught him having a cozy dinner with Margarita, his ex."

"I can't believe that. What do you mean you caught him? Were you following him?"

"Of course not. Lucy and I went out to dinner and he was in that same restaurant, the rat."

"Well, what was his explanation? He's so crazy about you, Mary. There must have been a good reason."

"If he had a good reason, he could have told me instead of lying to me. I didn't wait for some fairy tale explanation. I sent the ring back by messenger. He tried to call me and to get into the office to see me, but Catherine got rid of him for me, and I'm not taking his calls or text messages or e-mails. I just made the decision to take a couple of weeks of vacation. I'm burned out anyway. I just need to get away and think."

"Well, where are you going?"

"Please, don't be angry. I'm keeping my destination totally secret from everyone except Catherine. She'll be speaking to me every day to keep the office going, so if you need me, let her know and I'll call you or you can call my cell."

"I'm not just anyone. I'm your mother."

"If you know where I am, you'll let Carlos wheedle it out of you. I know you really like him."

"Correction. I did like him, but if he's upset you this much, I have to review my opinion of him. Maybe Abe was right about him from the start; he never trusted Carlos. Do Angie and J.C. know that you've sent Carlos's ring back? You know we've become very friendly with Carlos's parents. I really do like them, so this is going to be awkward. They were hoping you two were going to get married."

Angie will probably be relieved. She wanted Carlos to find a nice Hispanic girlfriend. I don't care if you remain friends with them as long as they leave me alone." I fought back more tears. Who was I kidding? I missed Carlos already and his big noisy family.

"Mary, you should think this through before you rush off like this. You're not thinking clearly. Stay here for a few days."

"No, my mind is made up. Please don't worry about me. I'm going someplace quiet and safe and I'll be back as soon as I get my head together"

"Well, I'll pray for you. But for now, come in the kitchen. I've got your favorite, meatloaf and mashed potatoes, and chocolate pudding for dessert."

It sounded wonderful and it also felt like I was ten years old again, and had just come home from school after having a fist fight with the class bully.

# ELEVEN

I was packed up and ready to hit the road by six the next morning. Mother and Dad were outside in their robes to wave me off. I had a complete picnic lunch prepared by Mother and Dad's parting hug and advice. "It's good that you found out about that *schtunck* Carlos. You'll find a nice Jewish boy, a beautiful girl like you."

I had mapped out my itinerary to include a stop in South Carolina with my cousin, Celeste, daughter of mother's sister, Faith. Celeste lived in the low country in a small town whose claim to fame was the largest Baptist Church in the area with a steeple that could be seen for miles, considering the flatness of the area.

Celeste's parents were killed in a traffic accident a few years ago in Haiti where they were serving as missionaries. For some reason, Celeste felt the need to continue their church work. Celeste's husband was a "born again" preacher and Celeste ran the day school at the church.

We hadn't seen each other for a few years. I was shocked to see beautiful Celeste turned into an overweight, frumpy woman who looked ten years older than her real age of forty. It was just an overnight visit, but there was enough time to see that Celeste still was beautiful under the extra weight.

As we sat and talked late in the evening, I asked the question that my mother would have asked and I was surprised to hear myself prying into Celeste's life. "Is your life turning out the way you had imagined it? Are you happy with your marriage?"

Celeste looked down at her hands and turned the plain gold band on her ring finger. I had a flashing thought of the rock of a ring I no longer possessed while I waited for Celeste to say something.

"The reason I asked," I said, "is that I remember one summer when I was fourteen and you were nineteen or twenty. I was visiting Aunt Faith and you came home from summer school. You told your folks that you wanted to be an actress. I think you had the lead in a musical at your college. You looked so glamorous. Your parents threw a fit. You said you were going to New York as soon as you had enough money. Do you remember that?"

"Oh, yes, we fought on and off for the rest of the summer."

"So what happened? That's why I was asking if you were happy, because I just broke off a relationship. I guess I'm just trying to see my disappointments in comparison to how you've coped with yours."

"Those silly teenage dreams were just that. I grew up. No marriage is perfect, if that's what you're asking, but Lincoln and I have so much in common. We are always busy with our parish members and their children and problems, and we're planning for a mission in a year to carry on the work of Mom and Dad."

"I wondered why you didn't pursue the driver who caused that accident. Mother was so horrified losing her sister. She and Aunt Faith were very close in spite of their different life styles. I know she was hoping you would pursue some court action."

As I spoke, I saw Celeste looking behind me. I turned to see Lincoln standing in the doorway. He frowned at us.

"I'm sorry, Lincoln, were we keeping you up?" I asked.

"Please, don't come breezing into our home, filling Celeste's head with all your lawyer talk. It was God's will that took her parents. The courts are an ugly place. I don't want my wife upset. Nothing she can do will bring them back. Celeste, shouldn't you be coming to bed? It's late, and I know Mary will want to get an early start." Lincoln stared at me.

"Of course, I'll be leaving early tomorrow," I assured Lincoln. I hugged Celeste and Sam and I headed for the tiny guest room behind the kitchen.

How could my cousin stand to be bullied by Lincoln?. One more reason I was glad I wasn't married. You can erase an errant boyfriend by letter, but getting rid of the wrong choice in spouses might take a lifetime.

# TWELVE

The drive to South Carolina had taken nine hours and I did not have a restful night thinking about Celeste and Lincoln and the death of Aunt Faith,

I had no set agenda for the second day. I decided to make some stops in Virginia and Pennsylvania to see some of the Civil War monuments. By the time I reached Gettysburg, the day was nearly gone. Sam and I found a dog-friendly motel. After checking in and examining our clean but Spartan room, I decided to haul Sam's crate into the room, although I was sure he'd opt for sleeping on the bed. I gave him a heaping bowl of his favorite chow and then we took a leisurely walk along the street filled with fast food joints, and tourist shops with tee shirts touting "See Historic Gettysburg" and pictures of Honest Abe.

I took Sam back to our motel room and secured him in his crate. After a quick face wash and a clean shirt, I prepared to get some people chow for me. I rummaged in the overnight bag for a sweater. As we drove north, the weather had begun to change. We left the heat and humidity behind. It was early October but Pennsylvania was swept with the cool breeze that ushers in autumn and hints at winter. It felt amazingly refreshing, like it was blowing away all my problems.

I left the TV blaring in case Sam decided to howl over being left behind. Sam was a good traveling companion. He hadn't complained about the accommodations at Celeste's. He didn't offer any negative opinions about my choice of motel. Well, who needed a spouse when a girl has a great German Shepherd for company?

Walking back down the tourist street, I spotted the Chamber of Commerce office and ventured in for advice about what to see in the morning. I found maps and brochures for self-guided tours of the battlefield and directions to a Gettysburg museum. Armed with my reading material and directions to an honest-to-goodness diner, I was feeling relaxed for the first time in a long time.

Two hours later, I returned to the motel food logged from pot roast and real apple pie, made by an Amish farmer's wife in the area. I expected to hear howls of welcome from Sam. Instead I found the door to my room ajar and a broken door hanging abruptly to the side of Sam's crate. What I didn't find was Sam.

CHAPTER

# THIRTEEN

Panic enveloped me. I felt like I was having a nightmare but I was wide awake. My first instinct was to call Carlos and ask what he thought I should do. I had gotten into the habit of relying too much on him whenever bad events came my way. Now I realized that I would be relying on myself. The feeling of loss enveloped me. There was no more Carlos in my life and now I'd lost Sam.

I walked completely around the motel, yelling "Sam, come" to no avail. I went to the front office, but the desk clerk who looked all of sixteen years old, was busy talking on her cell phone and glared at me for interrupting her.

"I haven't seen no dog. The rules say, keep your dog confined at all times."

She turned back to her cell phone.

I walked up and down the route that I had walked with Sam just a few hours ago. It was completely dark now and the street was only two blocks from the Interstate. I kept yelling for Sam. The wind carried my voice away. I stopped the few people still walking about. No one had noticed a large German Shepherd. Sam would be hard to miss.

I leaned against one of the stores and called again. Guilt over dragging Sam and me a thousand miles from home overwhelmed my ability to think what to do next. I felt hot tears start down my cheeks. Just then a police car pulled up to the curb.

"Everything okay, Miss?" One of the cops leaned out the window to ask.

"No, I've lost my dog," I said. I walked over to the cop car. Why hadn't I thought about contacting the police?

"I left him in his crate at the motel a few blocks from here and went to dinner. When I got back, he had broken out. I'm so afraid he's been stolen or gotten hurt or something. We're from Miami and he doesn't have any idea where to go,"

I paused for breath and heard, "Is he a very big German Shepherd?"

"Yes, have you seen him?"

"No, but we got a report a little while ago. Someone has him. He wandered into a restaurant near here. Hop in and we'll take you over there."

So that's how I happened to be riding in the back seat of a squad car in Gettysburg, Pennsylvania, in the space usually reserved for prisoners. I hardly noticed the drunk snoring gently in the seat next to me. In a minute, we pulled up outside the diner with the delicious pie. We all got out, except for the drunk. I opened the door to the diner and Sam threw himself on me, knocking me into the cop who I could now see was a cute young guy. He took his time picking me up and standing me in front of the owner who was patting Sam.

"No need to ask for proof that he's yours," Mrs. Gallogly, the owner, said. "Come on back here, all of you, while I get some pie and coffee for you."

"Sam, you bad boy," I said as I hugged my dog.

"That'll teach him," the young cop said.

"But he found the place I went for dinner. I forgot that German Shepherds are great tracking dogs." I couldn't stop hugging Sam.

We all sat down in a booth and Sam and I had a new bunch of friends.

# FOURTEEN

The next day was spent looking at the history of the Civil War. Miami has very little history. When a building reaches thirty years or so, it's considered ancient and is promptly torn down in favor of the newest fad in architecture. Our real historic background in south Florida resides in the lore of the Seminole Indian Tribes that once inhabited all of South Florida. Our other claim to a history is the art deco buildings of South Beach which aren't really old at all. Viewing real history whet my appetite for more.

I kept Sam close by and started the next leg in our journey by midafternoon. My father's brother's daughter lived in Elkins Park, a suburb of Philadelphia. Uncle Max's daughter, Madeline, and I grew up together in Miami Beach. We were close in age and shared friends, family, and school until Madeline won a full scholarship to the University of Pennsylvania. She graduated with an MBA, found a husband from Philadelphia where they both have jobs in banking or finance or one of those fields based on numbers.

Madeline also has two children, Nancy aged seven, and Martin aged nine. She has the suburban house to go with the husband, job, and kids.

I pulled into the long driveway lined with a tall privet hedge. The house was an English Tudor model. It fit the rolling landscape and looked like the set in the movie *The Philadelphia Story*.

A Lexus SUV pulled in behind me. Two kids and Madeline spilled out and rushed over to my car.

"Have you been sitting out here long? My God, I was sure I'd beat you here. Soccer practice was too long." Madeline practically yanked me out of the car and hugged me hard. She was still dressed in her dark work suit and heels. The years between us slipped away and we began to gab as if high school just ended.

Nancy and Martin grabbed Sam's leash and led him onto the lawn where they all proceeded to roll around in the grass. So began forty-eight hours of pure fun for Sam and me. The overnight stop stretched into two nights and by the time I was loaded back into the Explorer with Sam now occupying the front passenger seat, I felt full of good food, good conversation, and a brighter outlook.

"Remember," Madeline said as she leaned into my car window, "You'll know who the right guy is when he comes along, but anyway you can take care of yourself. You always have."

As I headed to the interstate, my mind swirled around my two cousins. They were so different; a reflection of the differing backgrounds of my parents. Somehow Hope Magruder and Abe Katz had melded those differences into a successful family life for my brothers and me. I wondered if Carlos and I could have done as well. That led me to think about Carlos's many cousins, but I knew I had to put everything about Carlos out of my mind and move ahead.

"We're moving on," I said to Sam. "Next stop is High Pines, Vermont, Lucy's house, and real peace."

# FIFTEEN

Sam and I were finally on the last hundred miles to High Pines. I slowed our pace as we crossed into Vermont. The further north I drove, the more riotous the leaf colors became, ranging from deep scarlet to orange and yellow.

Each side of the road looked as if Chagall had painted canvases on the landscape. We stopped at a rest area high on a hillside. I took numerous photos with my phone and Sam took care of his dog business. We breathed the fresh brisk air. The thermometer on the dashboard read 55 degrees. When we pulled out of Miami, it had read 89. I told Sam he shouldn't have shed so much coat which now covered much of the interior of the Explorer. He answered by shivering.

I decided to check in with Catherine before we got back on the road, but all I got was "out of service area." Lucy warned me that the mountains cut off transmission from the few cell towers in the state. It wasn't a tragedy not being bothered by cell phone interruptions. I realized I was not home-sick for the stress of court appearances, traffic, excessive heat. However, I couldn't rationalize that I wasn't missing Carlos. A month ago, I would have called him to share the scenery I was observing.

I urged Sam back into the car. The sun was getting lower in the sky. We needed to move on. Soon it would be hard to follow Lucy's strange directions. "When you near the village, take the turn under the covered bridge. Stop at the general store for groceries. Then proceed through the village past the golf course. Keep following the river until you come to the third dirt road. It winds up a hill and you won't see anything but woods. Then you'll come to a meadow. Ahead of you will be a driveway. Turn there and the house will be at the top of the hill. The caretaker will have the house unlocked. I instructed him to leave some lights on for you. Hardly anyone locks up their houses, so don't worry about carrying keys around, if the caretaker leaves any keys for you."

"Don't these roads have any names?" I had asked Lucy. "Aren't there street signs?"

"Everyone knows the names of the roads, so why would signs be needed?" Lucy laughed. "You'll see how easy it is."

We did as directed. The climb up the main road led us to the High Pines Village Green. It was green alright; an oval of inviting grass surrounded by shimmering hills. The general store and post office were really white clapboard houses facing the green.

"We were just about to close," the man behind the counter said glancing at his watch. His long frame was wrapped in a white apron which said "Welcome to the Upper Valley." A name tag pinned to the apron told me he was Hal.

"Hi, Hal, I'm Lucy Stern's friend from Miami. I'm on my way up to her house to spend a week or so. Sorry to keep you from closing." I sniffed the great smells in the little store. "Boy does it smell delicious in here."

Hal came out from behind the counter and extended his hand. "So you're Mary. Al Shields told us to expect you. He's got Lucy's place all ready for you. We'll get you squared away with some supplies. I do the baking and cooking here early every morning so you can stop by for coffee and cinnamon rolls anytime. I've got some left so I'll just box those up for you, and some of this carrot soup I made fresh today. Hal started loading bags and boxes just as a round white-haired woman came in through a side door. She had rosy cheeks and wore a long skirt and what looked like a hand crocheted sweater.

"Margaret, this is Mary, Lucy's friend. We're just getting her ready to go up to the house."

"We've heard all about you. You're the lady lawyer from Miami. Welcome. Where's that dog I heard you were bringing?" Margaret extended her hand and gave me a firm handshake. "I run the post office right next door. Will you be getting mail while you're here?"

"Probably not. The dog's in the car. Thanks for asking," I said. I couldn't believe these people knew more about me than some of my neighbors in Miami did.

"I'll help you get these packages loaded in your car. I don't mean to rush you, but you still have a bit of a ride ahead and it's almost dark out. The roads are pretty dark up here and you don't want to meet a deer or a moose. They can do you a lot of damage."

Hal and Margaret followed me out to the SUV and loaded the groceries. They both patted Sam. Hal gave him a doggy treat which Margaret said she baked herself. They pointed me back to the River Road, and we were underway again.

As the darkness quickly settled over us, I realized just how far I was from my comfort zone. I knew how to cope with rude drivers who signaled left and turned right. I knew to count two cars after the light turned green before venturing through an intersection. Those were Miami rules. I wasn't prepared to watch for deer and moose and to find my way through a maze of dark roads that contained neither lights nor signs.

"Well, Toto. It looks like we're not in Kansas anymore." I said to Sam quoting my favorite *Wizard of Oz* saying. The road was a series of sharp twists and turns. Once I almost hit a tree. Thank goodness there was hardly another car in sight. I counted the dirt roads that came into view as I passed them.. I missed the third road. With no one else in sight, I backed up and took the turn. Trees loomed over the car on both sides of the narrow gravel road. The friendly village seemed more like a horror movie. My heart was pumping hard as I climbed to the top of the hill. Suddenly the white farmhouse loomed in front of us. A gravel driveway led to the side and stopped in front of a red barn. A wooded area stretched from the left side of the house. A deck or a porch hugged the front and sides of the house. A row of rocking chairs dotted the porch.

Lights shone through the front windows. Sam jumped out and followed me to the front door. It was unlocked just as Lucy had said. We walked into a large living room. The stone fireplace that dominated the room welcomed us with the heady aroma of a wood fire. I warmed my hands for a minute while Sam eyed the fire with suspicion.

We walked through the dining room that contained a mahogany table and eight chairs. Through a swinging door we found the kitchen. A butcher block table was set for one with a glass of red wine in front of the checkered placemat.

"What a great caretaker the Sterns have. He's thought of everything to make us feel welcome," I said to Sam who had begun sniffing the floor for any hidden crumbs of food. "You must be hungry, Sam. Wait here," I said.

I returned to the Explorer and began to unload, starting with Sam's dish and food bag. I filled the dish and led Sam out the back door. Sam ate on the concrete stoop while I sat on the steps leading to a backyard or meadow. It was too dark to see more than a few feet. Then I saw twinkling lights and realized that I was looking out into the valley. I couldn't wait to see the whole view in the morning.

After several trips to unload the car, I began to walk through the other rooms on the first floor. There was a bedroom and bath at the end of a long corridor. It had a luggage rack and some fresh towels stacked in the bathroom. I decided this must be the guest room and dropped my suitcase on the rack.

Back in the kitchen, I unpacked the groceries from the general store. There was a newspaper tucked into one of the bags. The Valley News said its banner. I warmed the soup and unpacked a sandwich. While I dined on the delicious food and drank the dry perfect wine, I thumbed through the paper. There was a calendar of events and places to visit; a hike through a Gorge called the little Grand Canyon, a bird sanctuary, a flea market on Sunday. It all sounded peaceful.

On the front of the local section a story caught my eye. "Nearing the first anniversary of the murder of a matriarch and still no killer is found. Carolyn Brousseau's killer still at large." The story outlined a bizarre murder of a woman in her own home. Lucy said nothing much ever happens up here. She must have missed this.

My stomach was full. Now I began to feel a little restless, so I whistled for Sam and we began to explore the rest of the house. I thought I'd check out some television, but there wasn't a TV on the whole first floor. This surprised me since Lucy had kids. Well, good for the Sterns, I thought.

They must want the children to enjoy nature without interruptions from cartoons and Play Station.

There was a telephone on a table in the long hall. I picked up the receiver but it was disconnected. I thought Lucy had told me the land line in the house was operative. I must have misunderstood. I went back in the bedroom and tried my cell phone but all I got was "out of service area." The peaceful feeling of a few minutes ago receded and I wondered what I would do if there was an emergency and here I was with no phone in a strange house, in a strange place.

Sam and I went up the steep steps adjacent to the living room. There was another flight of steps behind the kitchen. I though how much fun Lucy's kids must have hiding and chasing each other from the front stairs to the back. It made me wish I was a kid again.

There were four bedrooms and two more bathrooms. Everything looked as if the original furnishings of Lucy's grandmother were in place: flowered wallpaper, patchwork quilts, chenille bedspreads, maple furniture. I was surprised Lucy hadn't redecorated.

Inside one of the bedrooms we came to a door with a step in front of it. I tried the door but it was locked. Sam growled a low growl at first and then an excited bark. The hair on his back stood up. He looked exactly like he does when he spies a squirrel in the backyard.

"Come away Sam. It must lead to an attic or storage room. You probably smell a mouse or something worse like a rat or a possum."

I dragged Sam away and down the back steps. The wine and the drive made me sleepy so I quickly unpacked the suitcase, shut the bedroom, door and hit the bed. I pointed to the rug beside the bed but Sam leaped on to the bed and settled down. Just as I dozed off we heard a loud bump. Sam went into full bark mode. We walked back to the kitchen, listened at the back door, and checked the living room. All was quiet, so once again I hit the bed. The next thing I knew sunlight streaked through the open window.

# SIXTEEN

I threw on jeans and a sweatshirt. I took Sam's food and my coffee, made in a stove percolator and definitely not Starbucks, out to one of the rocking chairs. The air was cold and fresh. The mountains looming ahead of me looked purple in the morning sun. Why were they called the Green Mountains, I wondered? The woods on the side of the house were deep and covered in leaves of all colors from green to scarlet. The only thing I could compare it to, were the colors on the wild macaws that circle my backyard in Coral Gables.

Sam and I walked out to the barn at the end of the driveway. The heavy door was not locked. It slid back to reveal a huge space. It was cool and moist inside and smelled of newly mowed grass.

There was a black Subaru SUV parked in the front section of the barn along with an array of garden tools. Against one wall was a large worktable and woodworking tools. A stairway led to a loft.

What a great time Lucy and her family must have up here. She never mentioned that they kept a car up here, but it would make sense for them to have ready transportation.

Back in the house, I stacked the dinner and breakfast dishes in the sink and grabbed the Valley News with all the good tourist info. Sam and I were off for a day of sightseeing.

Once we reached the village, I stopped at the local filling station to gas up. They also had delicious pumpkin flavored coffee and blueberry muffins in the mini-mart. I never met coffee and muffins that I could pass up. The girl behind the counter was as attractive as a South Beach model. She was tall and wore her long hair in a thick braid.

"Haven't seen you before. Are you one of the leaf peepers?" She smiled as she handed me my change.

"A leaf what?" I asked

"A leaf peeper. That's what we call the tourists that come to view the leaves in October. By Columbus Day, it'll be wall to wall tour buses and RV's out there on Route four. It's not a mean expression. We love the tourists; for our economy you know."

"I guess you might say I'm a peeper. I'm visiting from Miami, staying at Lucy Stern's house. I'm Mary Katz."

"Well, hi, I'm Riley Simmons. I've known Lucy's family for years. How are they?"

"They're great. She has three kids now."

"Excuse me a minute," Riley said as she looked over my head.

I realized there were people waiting to pay for coffee and papers. I moved to one side.

"Don't leave, Mary," Riley said. "Hi, Norman," she held out her hand to the man standing behind me. "If you want to see Dad, he's over at the gift shop."

"No, I just want a word with you," Norman said lowering his voice. "As the newest member of the Select Board, I want to know whether you think we should keep Sheriff Parsons on or what. The unsolved Brousseau murder makes a lot of us uncomfortable."

"I haven't been on the board too long. Not long enough to start firing people. Besides I've known Jimmy forever. He's the one rescued me out of the river when I almost drowned."

"Geez, Riley. You were eight years old then. Aren't you worried that no one was ever arrested in the murder?"

"This isn't the best time to discuss town business. It's real busy right now. Call me later." Riley turned to the next people in line.

I decided to try my cell phone from here while Riley was busy. I wanted to wait 'til Riley was free. Maybe I could find out more about the murder she was discussing. It must be the same one I read about in the paper. My lawyer curiosity was aroused.

The cell phone worked from here where the land was flat.

"Hi, Catherine, it's me. How's everything? I'll bet it's restful with me out of your hair," I said.

"Are you kidding?" Just a minute. I need to take this call in Ms. Katz's office."

"What?" I shouted while the connection faded and returned. There was a pause. Then I heard Catherine although she was speaking softly.

"I couldn't talk to you out at my desk. I'm in your office with the door closed."

"Why not?"

"Because Carlos is out there for the third time since you left. And when he's not here in person, he's on the phone. He's driving me crazy. He just threw an envelope with your season tickets to the Panthers hockey team on my desk. He said, and I quote, 'tell Mary I'm giving her these tickets. She wanted them. I couldn't stand to use them without her.' I looked at them and they're great, six rows off the ice. Can I use some of them?"

"Have you let anything slip about where I am?"

"Of course not. But you should see him. He looks like he's going to cry."

"I wish he really felt that sad, as sad as I do about how things ended between us. I just can't trust him again after that terrible lie. I can't count the times he told me how unhappy he was married to Margarita. Then I catch him having a secret cozy dinner with her when he told me he had a business meeting. How can I ever believe him again?"

"I hear you," Catherine said. "It's just hard to think that there isn't a good reason for his actions."

"I can't imagine what that could be except another lie. I just don't want to talk about this anymore. What else is new?"

"Well, your mother has called several times to see if I've heard from you. And both your brothers called. Then Chicky called and said she wanted to talk to you. I said I didn't know how to reach you."

."What about client calls?"

"You've got some new referrals that I sent on to Joe Fineberg. He said to tell you he accepted two new cases for you. One concerns some athlete. I think he said a football player who got arrested for rape or something. He'll handle it 'til you get back. Aren't you reading your e-mails? I've been sending you these updates."

"I haven't even opened my laptop in three days. I'm really trying to get away from the pressure-cooker I've been living in. Anyway, sounds like you're doing great. Call my cell if you need me. It doesn't always work so just leave a voice-mail, and the phone at Lucy's isn't connected. I'll keep checking in with you, and I promise to start looking at the e-mails."

"Mary, I miss you. It's not so much fun without you to laugh with. I'm beginning to feel sorry for Carlos. Maybe you should come home and hear him out."

"I miss you, too, but Carlos is not in my future. Gotta go. Bye.".

My heart was pounding just hearing about Carlos. Talking to Catherine brought back all the pain of seeing Carlos with Margarita. I stood staring out the window of the store.

"Mary, are you okay?"

I turned back to the counter, now free of new customers. Riley came around the counter and perched on a wooden stool "Mary, I'm glad you waited. Is everything okay?"

"Oh, sure, just office problems."

How long will you be visiting? I'd be glad to show you around over the weekend. As you can see, I'm pretty tied up here at the store during the week. My dad owns this and the gift shop down by the Gorge, so he keeps me busy."

"I really don't know how long I'm going to stay. I've needed a vacation from work and stuff at home. I'd love to have you show me around. By the way, I couldn't help overhearing your conversation before. What's the Select Board?"

"Oh, it's like a town council. See every town is made up of a group of villages. I was elected to represent the village of High Pines."

"That sounds different. But I guess it's like our County Commission in Miami-Dade County. Each area has a commissioner and then there's a mayor from any district."

"Oh, we don't have a mayor; just one member who kind of runs our meetings, but we Vermonters aren't shy about speaking up. As the saying goes, 'put two Vermonters in a room and get three opinions.'"

"That sounds like lawyers. I'm curious about the murder you were talking about. Is it the one in the headline in yesterday's paper?"

"Well, of course. We don't usually have more than one murder to talk about. Carolyn Brousseau was murdered last October. It's been almost one year and no one's been arrested. Our sheriff questioned a lot of folks but nothing's ever come of it. People in the Upper Valley are concerned that someone will strike again. It looked like a robbery, but I've talked to Jimmy, that's our sheriff, and he believes that it was Carolyn's son who did it. Don't repeat that. I shouldn't be telling you something told to me in confidence."

"Don't worry, Riley. I don't know anyone here to talk to."

"You will. It's a very friendly place. You'll meet lots of people in no time. Meanwhile, if you're lonesome you know where to find me. Stop in at the end of the week and we'll make a plan for the weekend."

"I drove to the visitor's center, and parked at the entrance to the trails leading to the Gorge. Standing on the bridge above it, it looked like the hike would be a tough descent and an even harder climb back to the road. I put Sam on his leash and decided to get some guidance inside the center.

Two people were behind the counter which was covered in maps of the area. Both looked to be in their seventies or older. The woman turned to the man and said, "I'll take this one, Henry. You can take a break."

Henry moved from behind the counter. He leaned heavily on a walker.

"What can I do for you?" the woman turned to me.

"I need some information about the hike into the Gorge. How difficult is it?"

"My land, it's so easy little kids do it all the time. Your dog can do this hike with no effort," she said.

"I guess it just looks so deep. I come from Miami, Florida. We don't have any hills except Mt. Trashmore. That's our landfill."

"You really are a 'flatlander'. No offense, that's what we call you people from away. If you weren't born here, you're a 'flatlander'. I guess the gorge is deep enough for us to have at least one suicide jump every year. We're about due for one. Say, did you say Miami? Are you Lucy Morgan's friend?"

Yes, I'm Mary Katz. I haven't heard Lucy called Morgan for a while. She's been Lucy Stern for at least twelve years."

"I'm Harriet McIntosh. We heard you were coming to visit. Good to meet you. Lucy was one of our favorites. Her grandma was a great lady. We all miss her. Now let me get you some trail maps, and I'll draw some easy hikes for you." She produced a yellow marking pen. "And, let me suggest that you invest in some hiking boots and a good fleece jacket, if you're going to stay for a while. You can go over to Bradford to the Farmway Store. They're always having a sale. I'll show you how to get there on this map. Those sneakers won't feel so good if they get wet."

I glanced at the maps. "How far is it to Hanover, New Hampshire? That's where Dartmouth College is, isn't it?"

"Oh, that's just a hop and a skip from here. Not more than fifteen minutes. Maybe ten, depending how fast you drive. It's a pretty drive and a beautiful campus especially at this time of the year with the leaves changing. You got friends over there?"

"The son and daughter of one of my clients go to school there. Do cell phones work in this area? Maybe I'll call them"

"Sure do. At least most of the time. Now you stop in anytime and we'll be glad to help you. And tell Lucy we all send our love." Harriet turned to assist a family that had just walked in.

I walked back to my car, and fished out my little address book in my backpack. I still hadn't transferred most of the numbers into my cell. I found the address and phone number for Sherry Yarmouth.

Sherry and Brett Yarmouth are the offspring of Gary and Lillian Yarmouth. Lillian was accused of stabbing Gary to death with her silver letter opener. I am the lawyer who got the charge dismissed.

Lillian seemed like a shy fearful person that needed my protection until her case was dismissed. Then she turned into a hard-charging business executive. She grabbed the reins of her family business and she consumed the lives of her children I got to know Sherry and Brett during Lillian's case and still get e-mails and notes from Sherry.

I pulled out my phone, hoping for cell service, and dialed Sherry's number. I glanced at my watch. It was ten a.m. She probably would be in class at this hour. To my surprise she answered on the second ring.

"Sherry? It's Mary Katz. I didn't think I'd find you in your dorm at this hour."

"Mary, is something wrong with my mother?"

"No. I'm not in Miami. Actually I'm in Vermont, in High Pines, just a few minutes from you. I thought maybe we could make a plan to get together, maybe for lunch or dinner while I'm here."

"Mary, this is great. You're just the person I want to talk to. Where are you right now? I don't have classes 'til two this afternoon. Can you come up here for lunch? Or are you here on business?"

"This is actually the first vacation I've had in ages, so no business. I was just about to start a hike into the Gorge, but that can wait. I have Sam with me. You know, my German Shepherd. Can I bring him? Is everything okay with you?"

"Absolutely. I've never been better. I just need someone for some girl talk. Bring Sam. Everyone takes their dogs everywhere here and it's all casual. Meet me in front of the Dartmouth Book Store. It's right in the middle of town on Main Street. You can't miss it. There are parking meters behind it. Come right away and I'll walk you around town before lunch."

# EIGHTEEN

It was a beautiful drive to Hanover. The granite formations on either side of Interstate 91 looked like a study in geology or ancient history or both. Sunlight shimmered off the mountains. There was no traffic at all; this freeway and Interstate 95, my normal Miami route, have nothing in common except that they're both freeways.

Once off the freeway we crossed a huge bridge over the Connecticut River. Rowers were practicing on the river and a few guys and gals were stretched out on a dock enjoying the sun. At the top of a hill the town stretched to my right and what appeared to be the college campus spread out to my left.

I turned right and saw the book store along with shops and restaurants. It looked like a backdrop for a movie about New England. I pulled down an alley and found a parking meter behind the store. Sam and I strolled back to the main drag, Every person we passed smiled and said "good morning" or "great dog." Now I began to feel like I was in the movie *The Stepford Wives.*

A large table sat in front of the store filled with all kinds of books on sale. I began to browse just as Sherry came from somewhere and tapped me on the shoulder. I automatically jumped and whirled around, fists clenched and Sam pulled close.

"Hey, take it down a notch. This isn't downtown Miami. This is safe and sound Hanover, New Hampshire." Sherry laughed and hugged me. She was wearing a Dartmouth sweatshirt and jeans. With her hair pulled back and without makeup she looked fifteen years old.

"I am so glad to see you. You look great," I said. It's good to see you relaxed and without the tension when your dad died."

"It was such an awful time, but we've all managed to get on with our lives. I know Brett will be disappointed not to see you. He's doing an internship with a wine distributor in New York, so he won't be back at school until after Thanksgiving. So tell me, what are you doing here?"

She took my arm and we started walking toward the campus. "This is the Dartmouth green right ahead of us, and over there is the Hanover Inn, very old, at least by Miami standards, and that big building is the Hopkins Center where there are all sorts of plays and concerts and an art gallery."

"Sherry, let me ask a favor of you. Please don't tell your mother that I'm up here. I guess you could say that I've run away from home. I broke up with Carlos and I just felt burnt out. One of my friends owns a house in High Pines and she insisted that I come up here and give myself some peace and quiet. But I don't want anyone to tell Carlos where I am. I don't want him following me and breaking down my decision to end things. You understand, don't you?"

"Why did you and Carlos break up? I thought he was so nice and so good-looking. You seemed like the perfect couple when we all had dinner after you won my mother's case."

"It's hard for me to talk about it. Please try to understand."

"Sure I understand. You can trust me because I'm going to ask you not to tell my mother something. Let's turn back to town. I'll tell you when we sit down to lunch."

We circled the campus. Sherry pointed out her dorm, Baker Library, the football stadium which looked like a miniature compared to the Orange Bowl, and the hockey arena. I filed away the information about the men's and women's hockey games. Maybe I would still be here when they began playing.

Back in town, we stopped at a cute bakery and sandwich shop. Sherry went in to order for us while Sam and I held onto a table on the patio. In a few minutes, she returned with grilled cheese sandwiches and mugs of hot chocolate and a cup of water for Sam. We were both quiet while we devoured the gooey Vermont cheddar sandwiches.

"Okay, Sherry, don't keep me in suspense any longer. What's up? What can't I tell Lillian?" I asked.

Sherry's cheeks were crimson. I wasn't sure whether that was from the cold or from her excitement as she leaned forward across the table.

"I think I'm in love or at least in heavy lust. I just need to talk to someone about it," Sherry said.

"That's great, I guess, but why can't you talk to your roommate or your friends?"

"He and I agreed to keep this to ourselves for a while. See he's not from Dartmouth."

"Where is he from? Is he older or, Sherry, tell me he's not married." I was getting a bad picture.

"Carson, that's his name, isn't married. Don't worry. After what happened to my family I'm smarter than that. He is a little older. He lives in this area. He's a dairy farmer and he makes cheese. I think he doesn't have much money."

"How did you meet him?"

"Some of my friends and I drove over to Hartland to Skunk Hollow one weekend."

"Where's that, and what in the world is Skunk Hollow?"

"It's a bar with local beer and a band. It's fun. That's where I met Carson. We had some drinks and I ended up giving him my cell phone number and we started texting and talking. He's so cute." Sherry looked like she was going to burst with excitement.

"I still don't get it. Why can't you tell anyone about him?"

"We just thought that, you know, because we're from different backgrounds that maybe it'd be best to just see where this was going before we upset anyone."

"Why would anyone be upset?"

"Well, Mother married Dad who was pretty poor and brought him into the family business and things turned out so bad for her. You know what I mean. We all found out that he cheated on her for years. She was devoted to him. If I told her about Carson, I know she'd try to protect me or even forbid me from seeing Carson. I just knew she'd be upset. And Carson feels like he'd be uncomfortable hanging out with my college friends. He never got to go to college, just technical school for a few months."

"Maybe we should run a background check on him. What's his last name You know, Sherry, you'll be coming into a lot of money in a few years. Maybe your mother isn't wrong to try to protect you."

"Sherry glared at me and started to get up from the table. " I thought you'd understand. I'm sorry I told you about him. I didn't ask you as my lawyer. Just as a friend, but you sound like you're my lawyer."

I pulled Sherry's arm and she sat down again. "I am your friend. I just don't want you to get hurt. I understand how physical attractions can sometimes get in the way of reality. Please don't think I'm judging you, but how far has this relationship gone?"

"If you mean are we having sex, the answer is yes. I'm not a little kid. I'm almost twenty."

"Have you been to his home, met his family?"

"His parents are dead. They left him the farm. I'm planning on going down there over the weekend, so I'll give you a report when I get back. Please, promise me you'll keep all this confidential."

"Okay, Sherry, but please, call me when you get back. I'll be here for at least a week, so we can get together again and you can tell me all about the farm."

We left the little shop. Sherry waved as she headed back to campus. Sam and I decided to do a bit of shopping, something I never have time for. I had a mental picture of Sherry in her sports car and expensive wardrobe helping to milk the cows or muck out the barn. Maybe the best thing to end this unlikely affair was a visit to Carson's farm.

CHAPTER
# NINETEEN

It was after three o'clock when we returned to Lucy's house. I had acquired two mystery novels from the Dartmouth Bookstore where I found more books than I'd ever seen under one roof. I had also purchased an expensive pair of Ugg boots and a warm leather jacket. The credit card slips in the bags made me aware that I had just spent more money on myself than my usual twice a year sale shopping. This is a vacation so a little extravagance won't kill me, I rationalized.

As Sam and I entered the kitchen, I realized that the dirty dishes in the sink were gone. They had been placed back in the cupboard.

"Maybe Lucy's caretaker doubles as a maid," I said to Sam "Lucy never mentioned anything about someone coming in to clean the house. I certainly wasn't expecting maid service. I guess Lucy remembered about our sloppy habits." Sam looked disinterested and I realized that I was doing more conversing with my dog lately, sort of like an old maid cat lady.

I went to the hall phone to try to call Lucy, but it still had no dial tone. My cell phone showed no service as well.

Now I can't communicate with Lucy or anyone else until I go back down to the village tomorrow, I thought. I glanced down on the hall table and saw a stack of mail next to the phone. There were several letters and bills. The top one was addressed to Carolyn Brousseau. The next one was addressed to The Brousseau Family. My heart jumped. Why wasn't the mail addressed to the Sterns? Wasn't Brousseau the name of the woman who was murdered? What was mail addressed to a murder victim doing in Lucy Stern's house? My heart raced into panic mode.

Sam and I heard a loud thump, like a door slamming. Sam's ears shot up and he bolted up the front stairway, barking loudly. He stopped in front of the locked door, his hair on end. Then he went into full bark and growl attack, pawing at the door. He looked exactly like he does when the Florida Power and Light guy comes to read the meter.

I grabbed Sam's collar and dragged him away from the door before he left his scratch marks imbedded in the old wood. I tripped as we tussled down the front stairway. Back in the front hall, I remembered the stack of mail and picked it up. There was an electric bill, a statement from a brokerage house, and two ads. I stood there trying to figure out how that mail got into this house. Then I heard footsteps on the back stairs.

I grabbed the stack of mail and grabbed Sam by his collar. Sam pulled me through the front door .The mail, Sam, and I tumbled into the SUV. Lucy had told me that all the village mail was picked up at the post office. There is no delivery on the mountain roads. Margaret, the post office person, needed to explain where this mail came from and I had to escape from the house of strange noises.

# TWENTY

I left Sam in the car, grabbed the mail and entered the post office. One side contained all the mail boxes for the village. The other side had a high counter and the usual post office signs and stamp pictures.

Margaret was busy dispensing stamps and chit-chat to an older couple. She looked over at me.

"Hi, Mary, is everything okay? You're as white as a newly fallen snow."

"I'm not sure. I have a question for you, but I'll wait 'til you're free."

"No problem the woman said. Go ahead and help her, Margaret."

"Mary, meet John and Emma Collins. They live up the hill from the Sterns' house."

"Oh, you must be the visitor Jack was opening the house for. You're from Miami where Lucy lives, right?"

I couldn't get used to everyone knowing who I was and where I was staying,

"I don't mean to intrude on you but I found this mail in Lucy's front hall and when I saw the Brousseau name, well, isn't that the woman who was murdered last year? Why would this be in the Sterns' house?"

The Collins and Margaret looked at the letters and looked at each other.

"What would the Sterns be doing with the Brousseau mail? " Margaret looked over her glasses at me as if I were a suspect in a mail theft.

"I don't know. That's why I'm here asking you," I said.

"Just a minute. Tell me what house you're staying in," Emma Collins said.

"Lucy Stern's house," I answered.

"No, I mean describe the house. How did you get to it?"

"I went up the River Road. I counted the driveways after I left the village. When I got to the third one I turned right and followed it up the hill 'til I came to the house. It's a white farm house with a big porch around three sides, and there's a red barn on the side."

Margaret and the Collins looked at each other. John Collins shook his head. Margaret was trying to stifle a laugh.

Emma finally turned to me. "Honey, you're in the wrong house. You've been staying in the old Brousseau place. Lucy's house is up the next dirt road from where you turned. Lucy's house is a two story federal style house with an attached garage."

The two women stared at me. I guessed they thought I was some flakey airhead like they see on TV shows about South Beach.

There was a long silence. Then John Collins spoke up. "Don't feel bad. It's easy to miss Sugar Hill. That's the road to Lucy's house. Those sharp turns on River Road can throw you. But no harm done. No one stays in Carolyn's house since the murder."

"This just isn't possible. Lucy told me the house would be all ready for me, and when I got there, there was a fire in the fireplace and wine on the table."

"Well, Tom Brousseau owns that house now. That's Carolyn's son, but he left here right after the funeral and no one's seen him around here since. He's got some caretaker, but it isn't one of us. He hired some fancy agency, I hear. Serves him right if his caretaker is using his house," John said.

"Oh my God, are you telling me I've been staying in the house where Carolyn Brousseau was murdered?" I'm not squeamish about the details of a murder. I hear plenty of that, courtesy of my clients. But when it comes to paying overnight visits to murder scenes, my stomach lurches.

"Is there some other family around here that uses the house? I've been hearing a lot of strange noises."

"Nope, no other family exists. Carolyn's husband died a few years before her. They only had the one son, Thomas. He lives somewhere around Boston, I hear," John said.

"Well, he was at the funeral," Margaret interrupted.

"Yeah, well he hasn't been seen since. Folks say he's just disappeared. He and Carolyn had a falling out right after he quit Dartmouth. I heard he was going to some art institute down in Boston. He never came up to see his ma before the murder. Of course, some folks think he's the one that did it."

"John, you are a terrible gossip. And they talk about women." Emma scowled at him. "You shouldn't be spreading rumors to this poor girl. She looks upset enough."

Emma took John's arm and started moving him toward the door.

"Maybe the place is haunted. Carolyn's ghost roaming around her house," John said, as Emma shoved him through the post office door.

I felt a chill run through my body. Maybe all those house noises hadn't been mice in the attic.

"Maybe someone rents the house. How would the son take care of everything from down in Boston?" I said trying to use my practical lawyer's mind.

"If anyone knows about the house it'd be the lawyer who handled Carolyn's affairs," Margaret said.

"Who is that?" I asked

"Only two lawyers in the village, Dash Mellman and Leroy Poston. Has to be one or the other. Dash's office is right down the road in the yellow house with the rocking chairs on the front porch."

"I've got to get my stuff out of that Brousseau house right away, but maybe I can catch the lawyer down the road as long as I'm here."

"Sure. Maybe he knows what's going on in the Brousseau house and it'll set your mind at ease. Let me know what you find out. What about that mail? Shouldn't you give it to me?"

"I will later, but if this Mellman guy is the lawyer for the Brousseau family, maybe he needs to see it."

I gathered an impatient Sam out of the car and we walked down the road to the yellow house.

# TWENTY-ONE

The sign on the porch of the yellow house said "Daniel 'Dash' Mellman, Attorney at Law."

I opened the front door and stepped into what once must have been the entry hall of a Victorian house. Now it was a reception area. A woman with grey hair done in what used to be called a beehive hairdo was on the phone.

I waited as patiently as I could, tapping my foot and eyeing the woman who had no intention of pausing in her conversation. "I told her no one makes blueberry jam like Edith. She grows those berries on her own property, some special plants she originated and she said—"

Sam decided not to wait for a further introduction. He put his front paws on the phone blabber's desk. That got her to notice us at once. She stood up. Sam transferred his paws to her shoulders. She wasn't a very tall woman. She let out a small scream.

"Can I help you? You don't have an appointment, do you? she asked accusingly trying to regain her composure.

I hauled hard on Sam's leash and he released the woman.

"I was just hoping to catch Mr. Mellman. I'm an attorney from Miami, Florida, and I'm in need of some information." I smiled at Mrs. Beehive, hoping to repair Sam's intrusive introduction.

"Well, why didn't you say so? Welcome to Vermont. I'm Daisy Mellman, Dash's mother. We're always happy to help a colleague." She turned toward a door at the end of the hall and shouted, "Dash, come out here. We've got a guest."

The door opened and a man of about forty strode out. He was dressed in khakis, a golf shirt and some kind of boots. He was tall, muscular, and suntanned; the outdoorsy type, but not bad looking.

He held out a big hand and shook mine. I introduced myself and pulled out a card from my backpack.

"What brings you all the way up here?" he asked.

"It's a long story, but mainly I'm on vacation. I'm trying to find out about Carolyn Brousseau and her house. Did you handle the estate?"

"The house isn't for sale, if that's what you want to know. I did handle the estate."

"Believe me, I don't want to buy that house. I have some other questions."

"Let's step into my office," Dash said. He pointed to a door at the end of the hall. I followed him and Daisy followed me, but Dash shut the door firmly.

"My mother is my receptionist, secretary and all around good helper but she has a lot of curiosity. She never has understood attorney-client confidentiality." Dash pointed to the chair next to his desk and I sat down. Sam settled on the hooked rug that covered part of the pegged wooden floor.

"I understand. I have a mother, too. I'm afraid Sam scared your mother. I apologize for bringing him along, but he gets tired of being left in the car."

"He's no problem. Everyone has dogs around here. Now how can I help you? Are you investigating Carolyn's murder?"

"Oh, no, I'm not a private investigator. I'm a criminal defense attorney."

"Have you been retained by someone who claims to be an heir to the Brousseau estate? I carefully researched for any missing heirs before I closed the estate."

"I'm not here in any professional capacity. I really came up here to forget about clients or crimes for a while. I just stumbled into this whole thing. I'm a good friend of Lucy Stern. Her grandmother, Mrs. Morgan, left her the Morgan house and Lucy offered it to me for a place to relax for a while. I guess I jumbled up her directions. Anyway, I've been staying in the Brousseau house for the last two days. It was my mistake. I took a wrong turn and ended up at a murder scene. I guess this will seem hilarious someday, but right now I feel like an idiot."

Dash smiled and then laughed. He had a nice smile; not a heartbreaker smile like Carlos. It showed the crinkles around his eyes and it kind of made you relax. I sat back in my chair and smiled back.

"The way I discovered my huge mistake was when I found this stack of mail in the front hall." I pulled the mail out of my backpack and handed it across the desk.

Dash looked through the letters and frowned. "This is strange. Some of these letters were sent to a post office box in Rutland. The owner of the house is. Mrs. Brousseau's son and only heir, Tom Brousseau, but I forward any papers to him at a post office box on Cape Cod, outside of Boston."

"The house is in excellent condition. I think someone has been living there. Maybe a caretaker is taking advantage of a nice empty house and getting paid at the same time."

"Maybe in Miami, but not in High Pines." Dash looked indignant.

"Well, do you know who the caretaker is for the house?"

"Tom told me he hired some real estate agency. He e-mailed me the information in case I needed to contact someone. I'll have to search my file."

"I've taken up enough of your time. I need to get back to the Brousseau place and get packed up and out of there before I get arrested for trespassing, and I want to find my real vacation house before it gets dark again. If you find out anything about who has been hanging out in that house, give me a call. I'm really curious."

"Sorry I haven't been more help. Why don't I follow you back to the Brousseau place and take a look around. I can help you get your stuff moved over to Lucy's house and make sure you don't get lost again."

"I couldn't impose on you and drag you out of your office. You probably have more appointments or paper work."

"Nothing that can't wait 'til tomorrow."

"Okay, I'd like some company while I get packed up. Fred Collins suggested the place may be haunted, not that I believe in ghosts. But there have been a lot of strange noises there."

"I don't know. There are a lot of stories about ghosts in these old houses. Where's your car?" Dash ushered me past Daisy who was immersed in another phone conversation.

# TWENTY-TWO

Dash followed my SUV in a Subaru sports wagon. We entered the house together with Sam leading the way.

"The night I got here there was a fire in the fireplace and a glass of wine poured and waiting on the kitchen table. I figured that Lucy's caretaker had gotten everything ready for me. Now that I know I wasn't expected at this house, I have to believe that someone has been using this house." I started packing my few groceries in a bag in the kitchen.

"It does seem strange. I'll check out the rest of the house while you pack up." Dash went up the back stairs while I hurried into the bedroom and began throwing clothes into my suitcase.

I carried the groceries and Sam's food bag and dish out to my car. That was when I glanced at Dash's Subaru. It was black just like the one I found in the barn. I finished loading my car and went back inside. Dash was standing in the living room examining the contents of the bookshelves.

"Dash, I just remembered something else. There's a car parked in the barn. It's a black Subaru just like yours. Did Carolyn have a Subaru?"

Dash paused for a minute and looked away. "No, not Carolyn. Lots of us drive them up here. They're good in the snow with four wheel drive, but

Carolyn had a white Lincoln Town Car. It was missing after the murder, but it was found a few weeks later abandoned on a dirt road over in New Hampshire."

"Want to check out the barn?"

"I guess so. I couldn't find anything upstairs that looked like signs of a resident. Everything is neat and clean, just like you said."

We tramped out to the barn and I slid back the big door. In front of us was nothing but empty space undisturbed except for a bird circling in the rafters.

"Where is it?" Dash asked. "Where's the car?"

"It was here this morning," I said as I walked the length of the place. "I know I saw it."

Dash gave me a funny look. Maybe he thought I was some kind of crazy lady who had escaped from a mental institution. "Well there's no car in here now."

"I can see that, but I know what I saw." I marched out of the barn and headed to my SUV. "You don't have to go with me to Lucy's. Just point me in the right direction."

"I'm happy to go over there with you," Dash said. Her house is just on the other side of these woods, but to drive there you have to go back to River Road, turn right and then turn right again into the next gravel drive. Please just follow me and I'll help you get your things inside. It's getting cold and it looks like rain."

"Thanks. I don't want to get into the wrong house again."

Sam jumped in the car as soon as I opened the door. I followed close behind Dash as we rounded a big turn and then turned immediately into the gravel road. It wound up a hill just like the drive into Carolyn's house. The wooded area was on my right. Then we passed a sprawling meadow and finally pulled up into a circular drive in front of a magnificent two story white house with green shutters. A large flagstone terrace sat in front of the house.

Dash got out and tried the front door which he held open as Sam and I got out of my car. We entered a foyer with a black and white tile floor and a circular stairway. Light streamed in from the stained glass window at the top of the stairs.

"This looks nothing like the Brousseaus'. What a gorgeous house," I said. I put a firm hand on Sam's collar before he could go exploring on his own.

"This is one of the nicest houses in High Pines. I remember Lucy coming here in the summer to visit her grandparents. She's a few years younger than I am but all the high school kids hung out together. She was very pretty. "

"She still is, even after three kids." I glanced to my right and saw a Great Room with a stone fireplace and a huge flat screen TV.

"Let me help you bring your things in," Dash said. He went back out to my car without waiting for an answer. In a couple of minutes he was back, carrying the suitcase, grocery bag and Sam's supplies. He carried all of it as easily as if he was bringing in the morning newspapers.

"I think I've got it all," he said.

"I grabbed the groceries out of his hand and looked for the kitchen.

"It's down at the end of the hall," he said. "Wow, Lucy must have had all this remodeled."

I was looking at granite countertops, stainless steel appliances, and walls of oak cabinets. "This is about the size of my whole house in Miami," I said. I opened the fridge and saw that it was stocked with beer, white wine, and bottles of every sort of condiment. I grabbed two beers and handed one to Dash.

"Here's your reward for hauling my junk in here."

Dash popped the top and sat down at the long table in the center of the room.

"So what are you really doing up here?" Dash asked

"I told you, taking a little vacation."

"A vacation might mean a cruise with a boyfriend or a spa in Mexico with a girlfriend; not a quiet village in a lonely house where you don't know anyone. I guess you're running away from someone or something."

I stared at Dash. Either he was very perceptive, or he had spoken to Lucy. An uncomfortable silence filled the space in the immaculate kitchen.

"You don't have to tell me anything," Dash broke the silence. "After practicing law for a lot of years, I'm a pretty good judge of people."

"I thought I was too, but even lawyers make judgments that don't reflect their brains. I came up here to try to erase a bad relationship, so I guess running away is the right label to pin on this trip."

"I'd be glad to be part of your R. and R. How about I take you out to dinner tomorrow evening? We have some great restaurants in the Upper

Valley, and you haven't had much chance to see the other villages in the area. We can compare notes about law practice in different environments."

I looked at Dash. He was nice looking and I would enjoy hearing about a country law practice. Well, what the hell, I thought.

"That's really nice of you, Dash. It sounds like fun. Everyone is so friendly here. I met Riley Simmons at the mini-mart and she offered to take me sightseeing too."

"You can go with her on Sunday. Tomorrow night is Saturday night. She's probably busy then anyway. She has a boyfriend."

"Okay. Shall I meet you somewhere?"

"I'll pick you up around seven. This is right on the way over to Woodstock. Will Sam be okay by himself? He seems glued to your side."

# TWENTY-THREE

I spent Saturday visiting the VINS center, the Vermont Institute of Nature. It was on a glorious site with trees surrounding it. The center cares for injured birds and tries to restore them to health. Those that can't be returned to the wild are placed in holding areas made to resemble their usual habitat.

Sam stayed in the car while I got a look at a snowy owl, several hawks, and a bald eagle. There was even an educational show where the predator birds were brought out for picture taking and close up views. I was as much in awe as the group of school kids seated around me.

I retrieved Sam from his perch on the driver's seat of my SUV. This is where he waits for my return. Several hiking trails led from the center and we spent some time looking at wild flowers, shimmering leaves, and hilly terrain. Finally we arrived at the gorge and climbed down behind a family with several kids in tow. It was worth the climb down and back up to see what the locals call their "little Grand Canyon."

I knew my legs would ache tomorrow. They aren't geared to climbing considering that they live at sea level.

We stopped back on the main road for hotdogs, one for Sam and two for me. I spotted the gift shop that Riley mentioned and decided to pick up some things to take back for Catherine and her kids. To my surprise, Riley was behind the counter.

"Aren't you in the wrong place?" I asked.

"I got pressed into service over here. Dad's short of help and I know the inventory. My cousin is manning the mini-mart. How are you doing?"

"Aside from the fact that I found out I was staying in the wrong house, just fine, thanks."

Riley looked at me like I had two heads.

"It's a long story. I'll fill you in when we get together. Are you free on Sunday?" I asked.

"Sure, Sunday is fine, but what about this evening? My boyfriend and I are going to the Salt Hill Pub to listen to some jazz. You are welcome to join us," Riley said.

"Thanks, that's so nice of you, but I have a dinner plan for tonight. Does your boyfriend live in the village?"

"No, he lives up in Hanover. He's the high school hockey coach. Who are you having dinner with? I didn't know you had friends around here."

"I don't except for two kids at Dartmouth who belong to one of my clients. I met a local lawyer yesterday and he asked me to dinner. I love hockey. When does the high school play?"

"Don't change the subject. Which local attorney?"

"Dash Mellman. Do you know him?"

"Well, you are the foxy girl, finding one of our eligible bachelors before the week is out. Everyone knows everyone here. Dash is kind of quiet, but he's okay and not too bad to look at. Meet me in front of the mini-mart tomorrow around noon, and I want to hear all about your date."

"It's not really a date, Riley; just two lawyers comparing notes. See you tomorrow."

# TWENTY-FOUR

I returned to Lucy's comfortable house and settled in front of a cozy fire that I started all by myself. I settled on the sofa and started one of the books I bought. When I looked up it was five o'clock. I haven't felt this relaxed since I once played hooky and stayed home in bed with a little cold. Then I remembered a few months ago when Carlos and I had spent the weekend at his parents beach condo on Marco Island. We had laid on the warm sand and let all our office stress float away on the waves from the Gulf. I wished I could get rid of all those memories.

Keeping busy was what I needed right now. I fed Sam and ran him around the back yard. Then I showered and dressed in slacks, my one cashmere sweater and full makeup including eye shadow and mascara. The new leather jacket looked fashionable and felt warm. I whistled for Sam to put him in his crate. I didn't want him running loose in Lucy's perfect house. He is prone to eating any available cushion containing foam.

That was when I realized that the crate was nowhere in the house or car. I remembered that in my haste to be out of the Brousseau murder house, I left the crate sitting in the bedroom.

I glanced at the clock. I had thirty minutes before Dash was picking me up. I put Sam on his leash and tried to decide whether to walk through the woods between the two houses or drive. I opted for the walk. It seemed quicker.

As soon as we came through the stand of oak trees, I could actually see the Brousseau house. I sprinted down the semi-cleared area and approached the side of the house. The barn door was partially open and the Black Subaru was visible. It was back.

"Someone must be staying in this house," I said to Sam.

We marched up the porch to the front door. I decided to knock. No one answered and Sam was pulling hard on his leash. I opened the unlocked door and yelled "hello" several times. My voice echoed up the stairs. Then Sam began to bark.

I pulled him with me down the hall to the guest room and there was the crate, just where I left it. I pulled the crate by its handle along behind me. Sam struggled and tried to go up the stairs.

I shoved open the front door and managed to get the crate, Sam and me to the driveway. Dog crates aren't really crates. They are holding cages. Dogs feel safe in them, sort of like a traveling bed and breakfast. They aren't heavy, just very bulky.

We started back toward the woods. Darkness was fast approaching. The trees rattled in the wind. Their branches looked like tentacles on a giant animal. Some birds flew toward us shrieking a warning that announced our presence. As we started down the path, a branch touched my face and I let out a screech too.

That was when I saw something or someone running behind a stand of white birch trees, their white bark illuminating a figure. The sun was almost completely down I stopped to stare at the disappearing figure. Sam barked loudly. His bark echoed and more birds answered in alarm.

Sam barked again and again. He gave one gigantic pull on his leash which broke away leaving me holding a piece of leather. I fell back against the crate. "Sam, get back here," I screamed. All I heard was rustling in the underbrush and running footsteps.

I picked myself up and began running down the makeshift path, pulling the crate behind me and screaming for Sam. My quickly hatched plan was to get back to the house, get the car and start searching for my dog, and hope that whoever was running in the woods was scared away.

When I reached the cluster of oak trees, Sam came limping out of the brush, tongue hanging out and looking exhausted. He fell in step with me and the crate.

We reached the house and sat down in the front hall. "You bad boy," I said to Sam as I checked his paws. His back left paw had a cut. In a kitchen cupboard I found a first aid kit. I cleaned the cut with alcohol and Neosporin. Sam was too exhausted to protest.

I put him in the crate with a full bucket of water. Then I went to the nearest mirror and saw a sweaty woman with leaves and twigs in her hair. Of course, that's when the doorbell rang.

Dash stood on the doorstep with a package under his arm.

"Come in please, Dash. I'm sorry I'm not quite ready to leave. I've just had a fright night experience," I said as I tried to pick the twigs out of my hair.

"You do look slightly undone," he said. "What's wrong?"

"I had to go back to the Brousseau house because I forgot Sam's crate. I decided to walk over, and when I started back, someone must have seen us and started running away, and Sam broke his leash and chased the guy, and I couldn't find Sam and I was dragging that crate along." I stopped to take a breath.

"Slow down. Did you find Sam?"

"He actually found me. He's in his crate in the kitchen. And I have half the woods in my hair. I'm sure someone is living in that house and saw us and ran away. By the way, the Subaru was back in the barn."

"There are deer and coyotes in these wooded areas all the time. Once in a while someone spots a bear. Kids play in the woods, too. It could have been some kids or an animal. About the car, maybe Tom is renting the garage space to someone. Lots of summer folks rent space for their cars and golf carts over the winter." Dash looked at me like I was an out of control client.

"I'm pretty sure it was a man, not an animal. Too bad Sam can't tell us who he chased. Give me two minutes to get cleaned up."

"Sure. No problem. I'm a little winded myself. I got a call from a distressed client this afternoon and had to ride out to her farm. I'll tell you about it at dinner. Oh, here," Dash held out the package he was carrying. "One of my clients makes maple syrup and this is from his spring batch. He paid my fee with a case of this syrup."

# TWENTY-FIVE

I brushed my hair and washed my face and was ready to climb into Dash's Subaru. I couldn't help noticing that it had a lot of leaves and dirt on the floor.

Dash saw me looking at the mess. "Sorry about my car. I have so many clients who are farm people and sometimes I have to go out to see them. This is nothing compared to what this looks like after hunting season."

"You hunt? You mean you shoot animals?"

"That's what hunting is about," Dash laughed. Everyone hunts here. If we didn't, the deer population and the Canadian Geese would take over. I guess hunting isn't much of a hobby in Miami."

"True. People just shoot each other there."

Dash looked over at me with a frown and then he got my joke and laughed.

We were headed west on the River Road. In a few minutes we entered the village of Woodstock. It looked like a picture of a New England village painted by Norman Rockwell. White clapboard houses, churches, and small shops dotted the streets. We pulled into a parking place in front of a general store that advertised fresh produce, garden supplies, hardware, and fishing licenses. I tried to detour into the store, but it was closed.

Dash took my elbow and led me down a tiny alleyway and into a door-way whose sign read "The Prince and the Pauper". The cozy restaurant was warm and smelled delicious. I realized that I was starved after my fresh air hikes and my disturbing experience in the woods.

"Good evening, Dash," the man inside the front door greeted us. "Your table is ready. Just follow me. How is your mother? Still working in your office?"

We were seated in a booth at the back of the restaurant. "That's the owner," Dash explained. "And he's highly curious about who my very attractive dinner companion is."

"Thanks for the compliment. Why not just tell him that I'm the nutty attorney from Miami who came into your office after staying in the wrong house?"

"I'm sure you've noticed that everyone knows everyone and everything about them here. So it's fun to have a mystery date. I'll bet he'll be on the phone to my mother by tomorrow morning, if not sooner," Dash said.

We opened our menus filled with wonderful choices. In a few minutes, a young man appeared with a bottle of wine and two glasses.

"I hope you don't mind that I have a standing order for this special bottle of wine. It's a great drink in cold weather, but if you don't like it, please order one that you enjoy. This is a red from Argentina."

I looked at the label and thought of Carlos at once.

"Is something wrong?" Dash asked

"I guess I don't have a poker face. Not a good trait for a trial lawyer," I said. "It's just that the guy I just broke up with was half Argentine, and this is the same wine his father always ordered at dinner. But it's a very good wine. I'd enjoy a glass."

"Like the song says, 'breaking up is hard to do.' I understand. I was divorced a few years ago, and sometimes some small thing brings back hurtful memories."

"Were you married long?" I couldn't believe I was turning into a nosy questioner. Chalk it up to my love of cross examination.

"Almost three years. We were both practicing in Burlington at the time. She was a prosecutor and I was working for a land use firm. I wanted to come back to High Pines to practice and Melanie wanted to move on to a bigger city. We were on different wave lengths."

"Are you happy back here with your own practice?"

"Yeah, I am. The Mellmans have lived in the Upper Valley for several generations. My grandfather owned a small department store in Lebanon. That's on the New Hampshire side of the river. My dad was the editor of a bi-weekly paper. I like being my own boss and getting out to fish and hunt and ski in the winter. It's all at our doorstep without driving miles through traffic."

A pleasant waitress took our orders. She asked Dash if he wanted his usual.

"The crab cakes are very good this evening," she said. She stared at me, I guess wondering why she had never seen me before, or maybe she had a thing for Dash.

I ordered the scallops. The waitress was young and athletic looking. She tried to hang around longer, but finally left when someone at the next table beckoned her.

"You said you had to see a client this afternoon. Is it a new case?" I asked.

"No, it's an old one that I thought was settled. It was in the paper all last year. My client is a widow trying to hang on to her sheep farm. The farm next door to her is a dairy farm. My client and her neighbor have been feuding over her sheep coming on to the dairy farm and grazing all the grass. The dairy farmer sued my client and after numerous court hearings, my client decided to put her farm up for sale and move into the village."

"So why did you have to go there today?"

"The farm hasn't sold and the dairy guy is jerking her around, threatening to shoot her animals, so I had to go out there and defuse the situation."

"Well, I've never had a case like that. Mine are more about drugs and domestic violence and bribes."

"Things aren't so different here. There are a lot of drug and alcohol related cases and domestic violence occurs a lot in the long winters here. People get cabin fever and they go after each other." Dash paused while two servers brought our dinner orders.

We ate in silence for a few minutes. The food was as good as any fine restaurant in Miami or New York. Everything tasted fresh. The vegetables were crisp and steamed perfectly; probably right out of the many farms in the area.

"Mary, are you interested in doing any legal work while you're here?" Dash asked.

"You mean like a busman's holiday? I really never considered doing that. I'm not sure how long I'm going to be here. I have an office that I need to get back to, or I may not have an income."

"I was just thinking that maybe you would like to get admitted to the bar here as an added credential. You can be admitted by applying as an active litigator and all you have to do is serve a four month apprenticeship with a lawyer in good standing."

"Hey, slow down. I'm not spending four months here. I'm a sun-belt girl, for one thing. For another, I have a house and a practice and parents and brothers in Miami."

"You don't have to do all four months right now. You're here anyway and I need some help. I have more than I can handle by myself. The courts are spread out here, so if I'm covering a case in White River Junction, I can't be at the courthouse in Barre at the same time."

"Why don't you hire another attorney, maybe someone just out of law school?"

"That's just it. I have a lot of work right now, but when there's a slow down, I can't keep paying a full time person. Just think about it. You could appear *pro hoc vice* out of my office, and if you ever decided to come back here, the time could be applied to the four month apprenticeship." Dash put his fork down and took a long swallow of wine. He looked at me like Sam does when he wants some of his liver treats.

"I'll think about it," I said. What would you want me to do?"

"Take over a case that's sort of this year's neighborhood feud."

"What's it about?" I asked.

"It'd be a piece of cake for you. You're probably in court all the time. I actually like transactional work. You know, drawing wills, estate planning, and contracts. Anyway, my client, Ken Upham, owns a two acre lot with a nice new house. He moved in a year ago from New Haven. It's his retirement house. The property behind him is owned by Roland Behr.

"Roland has lived up here for at least forty years. Roland claims that Ken cut down trees and brush that ran between the two properties and he's pissed because he alleges that his privacy has been invaded. He also is some kind of a tree nut. There are a lot of Vermonters like that. They think no tree should ever be cut down. So he says Ken has decimated living trees against some state law."

"I don't know, Dash. This really isn't my kind of case. Where do court hearings come into this?"

"Roland has filed suit against Ken for damages of ten thousand dollars, claiming that's the amount he will have to spend to restore privacy landscape to his property. He also wants a judge to make a finding that Ken has violated public policy by removing two trees."

I looked at Dash for a minute thinking this was some kind of joke, but he didn't even crack a smile.

"Are you serious?" I asked. "If everything Ken removed was on his own property, there is no case. Surely a busy judge will grant a motion to dismiss in about ten seconds time."

"It might be decided by a side judge." Dash said.

"What in God's name is a side judge? "

"It's unique to Vermont. They are elected office holders who assist the trial judges," Dash said.

"You mean like a magistrate? We have those in Florida. They hold preliminary hearings in certain family law cases."

"No I don't think magistrates are like side judges. Are magistrates lawyers?"

'Of course they are."

"Well, side judges aren't lawyers. They can be anything; plumbers, farmers, whatever. And they also plan county and court budgets."

How can they assist judges if they have no familiarity with the law?"

"Well, they do assist them and they can push judges to make some decisions. That's why I'm telling you Ken's case is not a onetime hearing kind of case. Ken is a new resident and Roland has been here for years. Maybe I shouldn't have asked you to help. It just seemed like a great idea. I thought it might be fun for you and a good help."

Dash looked so disappointed. He really was a good looking guy and had a laidback relaxed kind of personality. Everything about him was different from Carlos, not that I was in the market for another boyfriend. Still, the thought of going back to Miami right now left me with an aching feeling somewhere between my heart and my stomach. Maybe getting back into some legal work here would make the transition back to Miami easier. Or was I just using this as an excuse to stay away longer? I realized Dash was staring at me. I could always make up my mind later about whether accepting Dash's offer was an excuse to sidestep facing the changes in my life.

"Well, say something, Mary, or I'll begin to think I'm boring you," Dash said.

"Well, how about this? Ken might not want some strange out-of-state attorney handling his case. Why don't you talk to him on Monday and if he wants to meet with me, I'll come over to your office and interview him."

Dash smiled broadly. "Oh, he'll want you for his lawyer once he meets you. I'm sure he'd much rather spend time with a great looking lawyer instead of one of his golf partners."

"Oh you play golf?"

"Yes, do you? The Upper Valley is loaded with golf courses."

"No, I don't play, but my dad adores the game." I thought how much Dad would like Dash Mellman.

# TWENTY-SIX

Sunday morning arrived all too soon. The sun streamed through the windows, but I had no urge to get out of bed. The bedroom was freezing. I pulled the down comforter up to my chin and was about to lapse back into a dreamless sleep when a strange sound re-awakened me. It was a ringing telephone.

I ran downstairs, remembering that I had seen a landline phone in the kitchen. Thank goodness there was caller ID. I saw Lucy's name print out.

"Lucy, hi. What time is it? Is everything okay there?"

"It's nine o'clock. Were you still sleeping? My God, you're turning into Ms. Lazy. I'm jealous. I've been up for hours with the baby. How is it going up there? Catherine said something about a house mix-up. Are you okay?"

This was typical Lucy, asking a slew of questions before I could answer the first one.

"Yes, I was sleeping. Everything is fine now. Your house is wonderful. You won't believe what a jerky thing I did. I got a little lost and thought Carolyn Brousseau's house was yours and I ended up staying there for two days before I found out where I should have been."

"I guess Carolyn was out of town."

"Not exactly. Carolyn was murdered a year ago, right in her house. Maybe even in the bed I was sleeping in".

"Murdered? How awful. I didn't know anything about that. Who did it?"

"No one's ever been caught. Some people think it was her son, Tom. Did you know him?"

"I knew Carolyn and her husband. They were friends of my grandmother. Tom must be ten years younger than I am. I just remember him as a very little boy."

"Anyway, I love your house and this gorgeous place and I am relaxing. Do you know Dash Mellman?"

"Yes, I do. Is he part of your relaxation?"

"Not exactly, but he did help me find your house and he took me to dinner last night. He wants me to help him with a case in his office while I'm here. So what do you think of him?"

"He's older than I am, but he was always friendly and cute. Wasn't he engaged or something?"

"He was married briefly but got divorced."

"Mary, don't start a relationship on the rebound, which reminds me why I was calling you. Carlos has called me three times asking if I know where you are or if I've been in touch with you. I acted surprised that you had broken up and I said I didn't know you weren't around. He sounded just awful. Maybe you should give him a chance to explain. You know, clear the air. If you don't like what he says, you can still end things."

"I don't care what he has to say. It'll just be more lies. That night at dinner with Margarita wasn't the first time Carlos was hanging out with Margarita. I never told you that she was at his house once when I arrived unannounced. He said she was collecting an alimony check. He was probably lying then too. Please, don't tell him I'm up here."

"I won't. I'm sorry I brought up the subject. Keep in touch so I won't worry about you."

After a quiet morning with a quick trip to the village store, I settled in with the Sunday papers and more of Hal's delicious cinnamon rolls.

At noon I drove back to the village to meet Riley at the mini-mart. She looked dazzling in a warm-up outfit and her hair loose from its long braid.

"Riley, you look like a high fashion model. Did you ever consider modeling?" I asked.

"When I was at the university, I was interviewed on campus by an agency. I don't know why I even went to the interview, but the agent invited me to come to New York for a further interview and some pictures. I spent three days down there going through the process. They wanted to sign me."

"So what happened?"

"For one thing, I met some of the models. They all smoked and looked emaciated. I had a hunch some of them were taking uppers or downers or something. I also would have had to quit school and I was having a great time. I played basketball. I also didn't want to move to New York, so here I am tending to my dad's stores and dabbling in politics which I'm finding I really like."

"Vermont seems to have a magic hold on people who grow up here. Dash told me how he couldn't wait to get back here and start his law practice," I said.

"How did your evening go? Come on, let's get in my car, and we can go to a Farmers' Market and to the Flea Market. It's a gorgeous day to take in the sights." Riley started toward a white Subaru.

"Do you mind if we go in my car? I have Sam waiting in the back seat."

"No, he's waiting in the driver's seat." Riley laughed. "You didn't answer. How was your dinner date?"

We climbed into the Explorer after coaxing Sam back to his passenger area. Riley gave me directions to the Farmers Market, and we drove through two tiny villages and ended up in a field dotted with booths and awnings, each displaying a wealth of vegetables, meats, cheeses, and crafts. In the center of the field, three musicians were playing a lively song and singing in French.

"They're from Quebec. It isn't all that far from here. Everything sold here is from this area or made in this area. So stock up and you can have a great lunch or dinner when you get home," Riley explained.

While I loaded a canvas bag furnished by Riley, I purchased a croissant, goat cheese, apples, tomatoes, jam, and a small pumpkin pie. My mouth watered thinking about my evening feast.

"If I keep this up, no one will know me when I get back to Miami. I'll be the fat lawyer whose clothes don't fit."

We sat under a tree and listened to the music. Sam stretched out between us and lapped up some sun. He must have missed his Miami naps in the back yard.

I told Riley about my wrong house adventure.

Riley laughed so hard that other shoppers turned to stare. "But you still haven't told me about your evening with Dash."

"It was fun. He's relaxing to be around, but honestly, I'm not looking for a boyfriend. I just broke up with someone who I thought was my soul mate. What is interesting is that Dash invited me to do some legal work for him while I'm here. He wants me to take over a case of his. It doesn't sound like my kind of criminal case, just two neighbors fighting."

"Oh, that must be Roland's case." Riley grimaced.

"Wow, Riley you know everyone and everything going on around here. How did you know that was the case?"

"This neighborhood argument is taking on a life of its own. Roland claims that Ken Upham has violated an ordinance from 1830 stating that no tree could be removed without permission of the village council. It was all because Vermont was shorn of most of its trees during the farming surge of the late 1700's when the land was cleared for cultivation. Roland even came before our select board to complain."

"It's kind of funny. My religious background is mixed. One parent is Jewish and the other is Baptist, so I always tell people that I'm of the Druid faith; they worship trees. I think I've just discovered the lost tribe of Druids."

"Mary, this case could become criminal. I think these two guys are going to become violent if someone doesn't intercede soon. Maybe you can do everyone a favor and make this whole thing disappear. If nothing else, you'll get famous in the Upper Valley. The newspaper has been covering this fight every week."

"I'm a lawyer, not a magician, but I can try to negotiate a peaceful solution. Not to change the subject but I'll bet you can answer a question for me, Riley. How did Dash get that nickname? No one calls him Daniel, his real name."

"Dash loved to run. He was a track star in junior high and in high school he broke some track records in the state. I don't know if it was his parents or his friends, but everyone has called him Dash forever. We better get moving if we're going to see some more of the valley today."

We loaded Sam and our goodies back in the car and headed for the flea market back in High Pines.

As we drove, Riley asked me what else I had seen. I told her about my trip to Dartmouth.

"Riley, you know everyone around here. Do you know a young dairy farmer whose first name is Conrad?"

"Not off hand. What does that have to do with your visit to Dartmouth?"

"My client's daughter, Sherry, who I went to see, seems to be having a secret love affair with some farmer. She wouldn't tell me anything other than his first name. I'm worried about her. She doesn't want her friends to know anything about this guy. She met him in a bar and now she's gone off to his farm for the weekend."

"Well, won't she be back at school tomorrow? You can phone her then and hear all the hot details. I wouldn't worry too much. This isn't a big city, like Miami. Everyone's pretty mellow here."

"I met my former serious boyfriend at a car wash and that didn't turn out too well. I guess that's why I'm worried."

Riley told me to turn in to an area of shops with a large field surrounding it.

The flea market wasn't what I expected. I was thinking of the ones in South Florida, where convicted felons sell stuff they've hijacked off of trucks, or where they're selling knockoffs of Gucci handbags for ten dollars.

The High Pines flea market consisted of tables filled with beautiful china, glassware, linens, and old kitchen ware. All of it looked like things my Grandmother Katz gave away when she moved to California. But that's another story.

I found a hooked rug like the one in my living room made by my Magruder grandmother. Riley explained that I had to bargain over the price or the seller would have his feelings hurt. I did as told and carried my bargain to the back of the SUV where Sam snuggled down in it as if we'd always owned it.

I dropped Riley back at her car and promised to call her when I had an evening to fill, so I could see her boyfriend's hockey team in action.

The day had been fun and carefree. This Vermont life wasn't at all boring. In fact, I never felt so energized.. Maybe representing Dash's client wasn't such a bad idea. Maybe I was missing out on what the wide world had to offer while I sat around having a pity party about the loss of Carlos.

Monday morning was colder than the weekend mornings. The TV news said there had been a light frost so I was in no hurry to rush outdoors.

I decided to start some loads of laundry, mainly because everything I brought with me was dirty. Bras and panties had been worn more than once. Of course, there wasn't anyone to see them except Sam and me but even Sam was beginning to sniff in areas where his nose shouldn't be.

The sun finally warmed the air enough for me to venture out on Sam's morning walk. We walked along the river. The leaves were almost all in color and their reflection on the water was hypnotic. I backed up in the road to try a photo from my cell phone.

Just as I took the first photo shot, I heard a loud bang. In a second, I realized it was a gun shot. I grabbed Sam's leash and stepped behind a large oak tree just off the edge of the road. A car passed us so close to our location that gravel and dust from the shoulder sprayed over us. I raced into the road to see a small black SUV careening down the road.

"My God, is that where the shot came from?" I asked out loud. Sam pulled on his leash, and I turned and ran back up the long dirt road to Lucy's house. As I reached the front door, my cell phone rang.

I was so startled that I dropped the phone which continued ringing. "I thought there wasn't cell service up here," I said into the phone.

"Mary, is that you?" a male voice said. Then it faded out.

When I plunked down in the great room, I read the caller ID which said "Mellman Law."

My cell phone said "out of service area" again so I picked up the land line and dialed the number on the caller ID.

"Dash Mellman," the male voice answered.

"Dash, it's Mary Katz. Did you just call my cell?"

"Yeah, I did. Is everything okay? I guess we lost our connection. I'm in the car on the way to the bank, but I wanted to let you know that I spoke to Ken Upham this morning and he'd be pleased to meet with you and discuss his case. I told him to come over to the office around three this afternoon. You can meet with him in the conference room. If the time is okay, I'll have the file ready for you so you can read it before he gets here."

"I guess it'll be okay. I'm just a little shaky right now. I think someone took a shot at me and then almost ran me over."

"Where are you?"

"I'm in the house now on the land line. My cell said 'no service' again. How are you able to get service if you're in the car? I was out walking along the river on the path next to the road."

"It was probably a hunter. It's not deer season yet, but farmers go after coyotes all the time. You need to wear bright colors when it is hunting season."

"You might be right but I had the distinct feeling that the shot came from behind me and then that car roared by."

"Did you get the license number? What did the car look like?"

"It was a small black SUV like the one in the Brousseau barn and the one you drive. It was too fast for me to see the license number."

"Everyone up here drives Subaru SUV's. Are you okay or would you like me to swing by there?"

"No, I'm okay. I'll see you at your office a little before three. You never answered me about how you have such good cell phone service."

"I have a satellite phone in the car. I got tired of not being able to return client calls while I was out. See you this afternoon and thanks for agreeing to talk to Ken."

I clicked off and went to pour a cup of coffee. My hands were shaking. Just what I needed, a drive-by shooting, and I wasn't even in Miami.

I went down to the basement laundry room to finish what I had begun that seemed like hours ago. I looked through the laundry basket for a blouse that could go to a client meeting. I picked up a white long sleeved blouse and remembered how many times I had worn that with a variety of suits during the Lillian Yarmouth murder hearings and then I remembered that I wanted to hear how Sherry was after her weekend on the farm. I kept hearing the theme song from *Green Acres* every time I thought about Sherry hanging out with a herd of cows.

My brothers and I used to watch those reruns when we were little kids, and laugh hilariously until Mother would come and shoo us outside to play.

I ran upstairs and found Sherry's number in my address book and dialed from the phone in the kitchen. A female voice answered on the first ring.

"Hi Sherry, it's Mary Katz."

"No, it's not Sherry. This is her roommate, Madison. Sherry's not here."

"Could you tell her I called and she can call me this evening when she's through with classes?"

"Are you the lawyer she had lunch with last week?"

"Yes, that's right."

"Do you happen to know where Sherry is?"

"What do you mean? Isn't she in class?"

"No, she went away for the weekend and she isn't back. I think she went to Boston. It just isn't like her to miss class and not to call or anything. She said she'd be back around dinner time last night."

"Why do you think she went to Boston?"

"She didn't take her car and she said she was going to take the Dartmouth Coach. That's the bus that stops on the campus and goes in to Boston several times a day."

"I might have some idea where she was going, Madison. Will you please let me know if you hear from her or if she gets back, have her call me right away. I'll give you my cell and the number where I'm staying."

"Do you think I should call the campus security or the Hanover Police?"

"Let's give her a little time," I said.

I had that uneasy feeling as I clicked off, like when you've done something wrong but you aren't sure you can fix it. I should have tried to get Sherry to call her mother, or I should have forced her to tell me where the farm was located. What if she had eloped, or what if the farmer was a serial killer. I had to stop imagining the worst case scenario about everything. But isn't that what lawyers are supposed to do?

# TWENTY-EIGHT

I arrived at Dash's office at two thirty. Daisy was, as usual, on the phone, but this time she interrupted her gossip spiel immediately.

"Call you later. Hello, Mary, so good to see you again. Dash tells me you're going to give us some help. Everything's ready for you in the conference room and if there's anything you need, you just tell me. I'm so glad that you can help out. Dash is working too hard," Daisy said. She took my arm and led me to the room behind the reception room.

The room was small with a bay window looking out to a garden. There was a fireplace on one wall and in the middle of the room a round maple table with four chairs around it. I guessed that this had been the dining room of the old house at one time.

A file sat on the table along with a legal pad and some pens, a carafe of water and two glasses.

"Thanks, Daisy, this is fine."

"Dash will be here in a few minutes to introduce you to Ken Upham. I'll leave you to read the file." Daisy shut the heavy wood sliding door.

The file had a history of the controversy between the two neighbors. There were pictures of Ken's property before the tree and weed removal and after showing a pleasant garden area. There was a survey showing the property line abutting Roland Behr's property. There was a copy of the lawsuit filed by an attorney named Christian Berger on behalf of Roland and the paper showing service of process on Ken.

Apparently, no answer had been filed by Dash and I noted that the time to answer was about to run in five days. .

Just as I finished reading the file, Dash came in with Daisy hurrying in behind him. She was carrying a coffee pot and Dash had a tray of cups.

"Thanks, Mom, just put everything on the tea cart," Dash said. He was dressed casually in khakis and a plaid shirt.

"Can I help with anything?" Daisy asked. She didn't catch Dash's hint for her to leave.

"Yes, you can," I said. Is there a place with a computer where I can work?" I'll need to draft an answer to this complaint and file some affirmative defenses as soon as I talk to Ken."

"Of course, I'll get an office set up for you." Daisy bustled out, happy to have an assignment.

"You're good, figuring out how to move Mom out of this conference," Dash said.

"It's not busy work. I really will need to get something drafted right away. We only have a few days left for the time to file, if I'm going to take over this case."

"Oh, don't worry about those deadlines. You can usually get an agreed order for an extension of time. Sometimes time heals these arguments between neighbors."

"Or time can escalate them, too. I've heard that this thing could get ugly and violent."

"Well, well, you've joined the Upper Valley gossip hotline. Keep this up and we'll have to award you honorary citizenship." Dash laughed. "How are you feeling? Over your scare about the gunshot?"

Just then Daisy opened the sliding door. Standing next to her was a heavy-set man, probably in his sixties. His hair was thinning. He had a well- muscled look, sort of like a retired wrestler. Something about him shouted cop.

"Mary, let me introduce Ken Upham. Ken, this is Mary Magruder Katz, our visiting attorney from Miami," Daisy said.

I extended my hand and Ken shook it with a firm grip.

"We'll leave you two alone to get acquainted," Dash took Daisy's arm and they moved to the door. "If you need me, just pick up the phone and dial one on the intercom line." The door slid shut.

"Please, have a seat, Ken. I just want you to know that if you would rather that Dash continue in this case, I will completely understand. Of course, Dash will continue to be involved in whatever is happening in the case."

"Actually, Mary, I Googled you after Dash told me about you. You've had a very interesting career. I think you're over-qualified for my little annoyance of a case."

"Thanks, but I always feel that every case is important to the people involved, so let's talk about your position. Do you mind if I take some notes?"

"That's fine."

"First, let me get a little background about you. How long have you been in High Pines? I believe Dash told me that you're retired. What kind of work did you do?"

I retired a little over a year ago from the New Haven, Connecticut Police Department. My last job there was as chief of the detective bureau. I see you are smiling."

"It's just that I thought of you as a cop the minute you walked in here."

"Once a cop, always a cop," Ken answered.

"I was pretty sure when you took the seat facing the door. Never turn your back on points of entry. True?"

"You've got it. My wife and I and our kids have come up here to ski for years. I usually rented a condo in High Pines for the winter months. We always talked about coming up here permanently when I retired. Right before my retirement date, the house that we bought came on the market. It was built by a couple around our age who never got to live in it. The man passed away, and his widow didn't want to come up here alone, so we got a great deal. Property values are pretty low here compared to big cities like where you're from."

"Was the house complete when you bought it?"

"Mostly. I finished a few things myself. No landscaping had been done and the backyard was a jungle."

"I saw the pictures in the file. Tell me what you removed and where these trees were located."

"Okay. I hired a garden expert to help me with a landscape plan. Actually, the guy is an arborist. He took the pictures in the file. That's how I happened to have them. He suggested that we get rid of all the underbrush and take out two white pine trees near the backyard property line. White pines are pretty much weeds. They crop up on their own and choke out the better trees like the young maple. Let me show you in the pictures."

We looked at the photos together. Ken pointed out the difference in the before and after photos. Instead of the wild look in the first photo, there was a long garden bed along the fence line. At the corner, stood the young maple tree. Ken pointed out the new pear tree he had planted on the other corner. There were masses of purple asters and yellow mums. It looked peaceful and gracious.

"When did you meet your neighbor, Roland?"

"Most of the people around us came over to welcome us, but Roland wasn't among them. The first I saw of him was when he came over while the removal work was being done. I later learned that he questioned the workmen about what they were doing. They told him to talk with me, so he knocked on the door. My wife called me to talk to the guy. He was very rude to her. He started asking me all kinds of questions like didn't I have any regard for nature and did I know I was killing living things; a bunch of garbage about how people from away, that's how they refer to new people, are trying to wreck the environment. I tried to tell him that I was improving the looks of things, but he kept ranting. Finally, I told him to go home; that this is my property and I have a right to improve it."

"What do you know about Roland? What's his background?"

"He's lived up here for fifty years. He's from Detroit, I think, but he has a bit of a foreign accent, or a speech impediment or something. He keeps to himself except for some group he belongs to having to do with trees or nature or something. You'll have to come over to see my place and we can walk around and see the front of his place which is completely overgrown."

"Ken, according to this complaint, he's asking you for $10,000 to plant a privacy hedge. Have you ever tried to negotiate with him? Offer him a few bucks so he'll go away?"

"Sure, he came over again after a few days. This time he griped about how his privacy was destroyed. I asked him why he didn't plant some things in his own yard, and he said he couldn't afford to, so I offered him $500. He said it'd take a lot more than that. He started screaming about laws prohibiting the killing of trees. The whole thing is bizarre. I never thought he'd actually sue me."

"Who are the other people in this group he belongs to. What's it called?"

"I'm not sure. One of the other neighbors said the members are from various places around the area; Bridgewater, I think, and Rutland. I'll try to find out more. I call him the 'tree Nazi'."

"Okay, I think I've got enough background. I'll file an answer and affirmative defenses and set this down for a hearing for a motion to dismiss. I'll let you know the court date, and I will come by and see your yard and Roland's, if you're comfortable with my handling this for you."

"I sure am. You're a hell of a lot better looking than Dash, and you ask smart questions too."

After Ken left, I got busy drafting the pleadings. Dash came into the library and I told him he had a new helper. He was so pleased that he asked me to have dinner with him when I finished my work.

"We could run by the courthouse and file the papers and then have a quick dinner.

Tonight is a playoff game on TV. This is Red Sox Country, so everyone will be glued to their TV's. That means I'll have you home early," Dash said.

"I have to go home to feed Sam and walk him anyway, so why don't you come over? I can stop at the village store and get a few things. Then I'll watch the game with you at my place," I suggested.

"Great," Dash said. I'll take the stuff to the courthouse and pick up a couple of steaks at a market near there. You can provide the fixings."

"It's a deal," I said.

As I turned my attention back to the computer, I asked myself again if I was using this legal work to stall returning to Miami. I contemplated how easily I accepted another dinner with Dash. Was I using him to fill a void in my life? Lucy was right when she said not to jump into a new relationship.

# TWENTY-NINE

I really had planned to stop at the village store and gossip mill anyway. I thought Hal and Margaret might shed some light on this Roland character and his 'hug a tree' society.

When I walked out of Dash's office I could see the weather had changed. The sun was setting but it was partially obscured by gathering clouds. A damp chill accompanied a whipping wind.

I moved the car down the road and parked on the green at the store. The warm smell of fresh bread enveloped me as I came through the door.

"Well, if it isn't wrong house Miami Mary," Hal greeted me. Three older men were gathered around the counter. I recognized John Collins from my last visit to the store. All three laughed heartily.

"I guess everyone has heard about my lack of sense of direction. Well, one empty house is as good as another as long as they've got furniture," I countered, and joined in the laughter.

"How's it going?" Hal asked. "I hear you're going to give the courts a whirl here helping Dash Mellman,"

"How'd you find that out so fast?" I asked.

"Daisy stopped in today," John said. "She hopes you're gonna stay a while. I think she's got her matchmaker's hat on."

"Well, sooner or later I have to get back to my real world, so I think Daisy better change her hat," I said. "What's the soup of the day today?"

"It's my hottest chili. I heard that the weather was going to get blustery," Hal said.

"Give me a container and some of that potato salad and a loaf of that great smelling bread. Do any of you guys know Roland Behr, or anything about the club he belongs to? Something to do with the environment?"

"He's lived up here forever, but he keeps to himself. His wife died a few years ago. She used to be involved in the Community Church, but Roland doesn't participate in much except hunting. He loves to shoot; practices in his yard all the time. At least that's what I hear," Hal said.

"He's the guy suing Ken Upham, isn't he?" John Collins asked. "Isn't it about Ken's trees? Hey, Hal, how would anyone know what old Roland is doing in his yard? It's so overgrown you can't see a damn thing. I hear Ken started calling him the 'tree Nazi'."

"What about this club or organization of Roland's? Anyone here belong to it?" I asked.

"I don't know what it is. Just that they meet at Roland's; a lot of guys from other towns. Sometimes some of them stop in the store for coffee, but they don't talk much. There are a lot of different groups around here that preserve land. There's the Vermont Land Trust, and other small land trust groups that work to keep developers from buying up the farm and timber land. There are groups that try to keep timber companies from taking out too many trees. You name it and there's some group for it," Hal said.

I gathered up my food purchases and headed for the car. By the time I pulled into Lucy's driveway, rain had started pelting the windshield. I dashed for the house, started a fire in the fireplace, walked Sam around the yard as fast as possible and set the table in front of the sofa for dinner for two.

# THIRTY

We had just finished coffee and were enjoying the baseball game on the wide screen TV when the phone rang. I rushed to the kitchen to answer guessing it was a wrong number. Instead I heard the emotional voice of Madison, Sherry Yarmouth's roommate.

"Is this Mary Katz? This is Madison. I talked to you this morning about Sherry."

"Yes, of course, Madison, have you heard from her?"

"No, nothing and I'm so worried. I called Brett, her brother. He's in New York doing an internship. He hadn't heard from her. I thought maybe she went to visit him. He said he'd call their mother. I didn't want to be the one to do that. To tell you the truth, I'm a little scared of Lillian. I met her when I visited Sherry last summer."

"Do you know if Brett talked to her?"

"Yes, he called me back and said Lillian would be up here in the morning. He said she already knew Sherry was missing and had a plane reservation and a hotel booked. I thought maybe you called her."

"No, I haven't talked to her. I really thought Sherry would have surfaced by now."

"Here's the scary part. I told Brett I would call the campus security and the Hanover Police, but he said I was not to do that. I told him you were up here and that you had seen Sherry last Friday. I asked if it was okay to call you and tell you about Lillian. He said it was fine. He should be here soon. He left New York a few hours ago. Why shouldn't I call the police?"

"Lillian must have her reasons. Maybe she knows where Sherry is. Did Sherry ever mention a guy named Conrad that she met at some bar with a funny name?'

"No. Not that I can remember. I'm really scared, Mary."

"Just get some rest. I'll call Lillian and you can give Brett my phone numbers when he gets there. He can call me even if he doesn't get in 'til late."

When I hung up, Dash was standing at the kitchen doorway.

"Is something wrong, Mary? I didn't mean to eavesdrop. I just wanted to make sure nothing was wrong in Miami," Dash said.

"One of my client's children attends college at Dartmouth, and her daughter, Sherry, has gone missing. I had lunch with her up at Dartmouth last week. I may have some important information so I need to call Lillian. She's my client and she's flying up here tomorrow."

"Is there anything I can do? Are the police looking for this girl?"

"Not yet. Lillian told Sherry's roommate not to call them."

"You know Jimmy Parsons, the town sheriff over here, is a friend of mine. Maybe he can help."

"Isn't he the same guy who never solved Carolyn Brousseu's murder? I don't want to do anything until I talk to Lillian. I need to call her right away and then maybe go up to Dartmouth and meet with Sherry's brother."

"I understand. I'm going to get out of your way. Thanks for dinner and let me know if I can help. I'll phone you about the court date for Ken's case."

"Thanks for understanding, Dash. I feel like I'm kicking you out," I said as I walked Dash into the front hall. He shrugged into his rain jacket and turned and before I knew what was happening, he put his arm around my shoulder and kissed me. It was a soft sweet kiss, and I felt—nothing.

# THIRTY-ONE

As soon as Dash drove away, I rushed to the phone and dialed Lillian Yarmouth's home phone number. I remembered all her numbers by heart. I had called her so many times when I represented her in the murder of her husband, the case that made my little law office famous. Well, famous in South Florida anyway. After five rings, Lillian's voice- mail answered. Her cool cultured voice announced that she was unable to take my call but please leave a message and someone would contact me.

It was too late for her to be at the office where she was president of Elite Wine Distributors, a job she got herself elected to after her husband's death. I elected to try her mobile phone. I was surprised when I heard a familiar voice answer which wasn't Lillian.

"This is Mary Katz. Who is this? Is Lillian Yarmouth there?'

"Mary, this is Beverly. You remember me, don't you? I was Gary Yarmouth's assistant."

"I was trying to get Lillian. Where is she?"

"She's right here. I'm her assistant now and I'm helping her to, ah, to get ready to leave for New Hampshire. Just a minute."

"Mary, I don't know what you're doing up there, but I will need your advice as soon as I get there. Madison said you had some information that might help about Sherry," Lillian sounded breathless.

"Lillian, I had lunch with Sherry last Friday. Please, don't be upset. Sherry didn't want you to know that she has a boyfriend. Someone named Conrad, who has a farm somewhere in this area. She was going to his farm for the weekend."

There was a long pause. "This may be very helpful. I can't tell you more on the phone but I'll be there soon. My plane gets in at ten-thirty tomorrow morning. I tried to charter a plane but it was too short notice."

"Lillian, why don't you want the police called?"

""Don't do anything like that, please. I'll explain tomorrow." Lillian clicked off and I was left with a growing guilty feeling for not having told someone about Sherry and the guy named Conrad.

I puttered around the kitchen washing dishes, filling Sam's water dish, anything to keep from speculating about Sherry's disappearance and Lillian's odd request about the police. Maybe Sherry and this Conrad guy eloped and Lillian was rushing up here to get an annulment or to drag Sherry back to Miami.

At ten o'clock the phone rang again. This time it was Brett.

"Mary, I'm back on the campus in my apartment. Is it too late for you to come up here and meet me? I need someone to get my head together. This just isn't like anything Sherry has ever done before."

"Sure, I'll leaver right away. I'm only about fifteen minutes away. Where shall I meet you?"

"How about the Dirt Cowboy? It's right on Main Street, and they should still be open. It's a coffee bar."

I put Sam back in his crate. He gave me a dirty look as if to say, this is turning into another Miami. I thought we were on vacation.


Students were still strolling around the shops on Main Street, and it looked like a movie had just let out. I had no trouble finding the coffee bar. It was crowded, but I spotted Brett near the door. He looked tired and disheveled. He must have left in a hurry and was still wearing the pants and shirt of business attire with the sleeves rolled up.

"Brett, I'm so glad to see you. It's good you'll be here when your mother arrives in the morning."

Brett gave me a hug. He ordered two coffees and we carried them outside to sit on a bench where we could talk. The rain had stopped but the damp cold seeped through my layers of clothes.

"It seems like my family is always calling on you in an emergency," he said. "Madison said you asked her about a boyfriend of Sherry's."

"I had lunch with Sherry last week. She confided in me that she'd been seeing an older guy who owns a dairy farm somewhere around here. She didn't want me to tell anyone about him. She told me she was going to spend the weekend with him at his farm. I tried to get her to let me do a background check on him, but she got angry with me. I could just kick myself for not alerting someone about this or trying to talk her out of going."

"How could you just let her go off like that?" Brett looked furious. I remembered his hot temper.

"I'm not her mother or her sister. She's not a kid. If I hadn't happened to be visiting up here, no one would know about this boyfriend."

"I guess you're right. What's his name? Where is this farm?"

"She only told me his first name which is Conrad and I don't know where this farm is."

"She didn't take her car. It's parked outside her dorm. How did she get there?"

"I don't know. What about your mother? Where is her flight coming in? There isn't any real airport around here, is there?"

"She's arriving in Manchester. It's ninety miles from here. I'm going to pick her up. Beverly booked her a room at the Hanover Inn. She's been up here many times to see us and for parents' weekend, so she knows her way around."

"Why won't she let us call the police?"

"You know Mom. Everything is a secret with her. She said she'd talk to me when she got here. She didn't want to talk on the phone. She said she had a lot of details to take care of. Beverly was sticking close to her, helping her with whatever."

"Okay, Brett, you look like you could use some sleep. Call me when you're on the way from the airport and I'll come over and meet you at the inn. I'll write my phone numbers down for you. Say, hasn't anyone called Sherry's cell phone or texted her?"

"Of course, but all we get is voicemail. What if something awful has happened to her?"

"If she was in an accident, you'd know it. A hospital or police would have called long ago. Let's go get some sleep and wait for Lillian."

Brett walked me out to my car. I glanced at my watch and realized it was well after eleven. Once I left Hanover, the road was completely dark. I remembered Hal's warning about moose and deer. I had also read in the local paper about a moose-car collision. The story reminded readers that the leggy animals were impossible to see until they were on top of your car.

I drove slowly for once in my life, constantly looking to the sides of the roads. The River Road with its snakelike curves was the darkest of all. I vowed not to miss the turnoff to Lucy's house. I was driving at turtle speed when I recognized the road up to the Brousseau house. I was almost even with that road when something big moved from the road into my path. I drew to a stop, my eyes straining to see the shape. It wasn't an animal at all. It was a car with headlights off. As it turned ahead of me, I realized that it was a black SUV Subaru. My curiosity screamed at me to follow it.

Then I remembered the gunshot and decided to get home. But one thing was certain now. Someone definitely was living in the house where Carolyn was murdered.

# THIRTY-TWO

The rain had given way to blustery north winds by morning. A weak sun tried to shine. Many of the leaves had been crushed to the ground by the downpour and now the wind was whipping them into crunchy piles. Sam and I made a brittle sound as we waded through the leaves even though the ground was still slushy. I dutifully walked him down the long drive and back through the backyard.

The view of the village below us now included smoke curls from wood stoves and fireplaces in the valley. As I stopped to admire the view, my cell phone rang. It startled me, since mobile service was so unreliable.

"Mary, it's Dash. Anything new about your missing friend?

"No, I'm waiting for her mother to arrive this morning."

"Well, I just got a call from Judge McCreary's assistant. You're scheduled for a hearing on Ken's case tomorrow at ten, but the hearing is in Barre, about an hour from here. Will you still be able to handle this? Ken really has confidence in you."

"Of course, I'll follow through. I promised and I never let a client down, but with this problem of Sherry's disappearance, I sure wish I could get a brief continuance Do you think you could request a continuance?"

"I already asked, and the answer was a vehement no. I'm really sorry to put you in this situation."

"It's okay. I can't let Ken down. I'm used to juggling at least two matters at once. Anyway, this hearing shouldn't take very long. It should be an easy order to dismiss."

"Don't count on that, Mary. This is New England, not Miami. I explained to the assistant that you're working through my office, so maybe they won't look at you as a complete flat-lander. I talked to Ken and he'll ride with you so you won't get lost."

"What about the judge? Is the judge a man or a woman? What's the judge like?"

"He's very nice, just not always decisive. The thing I 'm not excited about is the side judge. He's an old-timer and Ken is new to the area, so watch out for him. His name is Calvin Crumb."

"I won't even try to make any bad puns about that name. Okay, Dash. I'll give you a full report tomorrow."

I hadn't mentioned to Dash the sighting of the car at the Brousseau's last night. Something picked at my skin like a scratchy wool sweater every time I thought about that car and that Dash drove the exact same model. I decided to take a trip to the mini-mart to see Riley and pick her brain about Dash. It was also a good excuse to get a good cup of coffee. I was beginning to miss having a Starbucks on every corner.

As I loaded Sam into the Explorer, I couldn't help thinking about that kiss Dash planted on me. For all I knew, he was a serial rapist. And that kiss rattled me into dreaming about Carlos. I had tried so hard to put him out of my mind, and other parts of my anatomy.

I couldn't deny the way I felt about Carlos. We hadn't been out of each other's sight since we met in February. Eight months of great sex is not easily forgotten, nor is the entanglement with each other's family and friends. Part of me nagged that I should have at least listened to his explanation about Margarita. Another part of me, probably my brain and not the other parts of my anatomy, shouted directions like 'don't be a fool, and 'better off a lonely heart than a broken heart.'

Now here I was in this cold isolated village working on a case involving a neighborhood feud and fending off Dash Mellman who might only be a simple country lawyer or might be a murderer. This was anything but the restful vacation Lucy sold me on.

The mini-mart had added pumpkin decorations at its front door and store window. It seemed like Halloween themes were sprouting everywhere. These were real pumpkins too, grown nearby, not the plastic things that Miamians utilize for quickie decorations a day or two before Halloween.

The smell of pumpkin flavored coffee filled my nostrils as I entered the market. Riley was busy with customers so I grabbed the Valley News to wile away some time. The front page slapped me across the face like an angry relative.

## NEIGHBORS' FEUD ESCALATES TO COURT ACTION

The tree controversy between newer resident, Ken Upham, and Roland Behr will be thrashed out in court in Barre tomorrow.

Upham states that he will be seeking a dismissal of the lawsuit for damages filed by Roland Behr. Behr alleges that he has suffered due to loss of privacy when Upham cut down trees and brush separating the two properties.

"My new attorney, Mary Magruder Katz., will be in court with me and believes this case should be at an end. It is a frivolous use of the court's time."

Behr refused to speak to the Valley News. We were unable to locate Ms. Katz by deadline. She is associated with local attorney, Dash Mellman.

I was standing with my mouth gaping open when Riley tapped me on the shoulder.

"Hello, Ms. Celebrity. It hasn't taken you much time to become an Upper Valley sensation," she said.

"Good God. I've got to tell Ken not to give interviews like that without talking to me first. I hope the judge doesn't read this paper. What do they mean they couldn't locate me? Where did they look?"

"Who knows? Probably in the phone book. Obviously you're not listed."

"I thought everyone knew everything about locals and visitors," I said.

"We the people do, but the paper has to fact- check everything. That takes all the fun out of gossip. Are you here for some gossip, or just lonely?"

"Both, I guess, or maybe scared. Remember I told you about my young friend at Dartmouth and her secret boyfriend?"

Riley nodded.

"Well, she's disappeared; totally gone missing. Her mother's on her way up here as we speak. Are you sure you don't know of any dairy farmers in the area with the name of Conrad?"

"Not off the top of my head. I'll ask my parents. They know everyone. What else is on your mind?"

I lowered my voice and leaned closer to Riley. "How well do you know Dash Mellman?"

"I've never dated him, if that's what you mean. He has a reputation of being a good solid lawyer, and his people have lived here forever. Why are you asking?"

"I don't know. It's just that Dash represented Tom Brousseau and his family and I am sure someone is camping out in the Brousseau house. Dash seems utterly disinterested in investigating. Strange things happened when I accidentally stayed in that house. There were unexplained noises. There was a car parked in the barn, a black Subaru SUV, just like the one Dash drives. Then it disappeared when Dash was with me at the house and then it reappeared when he was gone. And last night I saw that same car coming out of the Brousseau's road late at night."

"What were you doing there late at night?"

"I wasn't there. I was on my way back to Lucy's house."

Riley stared at me for a minute. "Are you saying that you think Dash is hanging out in that house?"

"I don't know what to think. And there have been other things too. Like I think someone may have taken a gun shot at me. And someone was running away from me in the woods that run between Lucy's house and the Brousseaus."

"Maybe you're projecting the kinds of things that happen in Miami on to life up here in the Upper Valley. Dash probably isn't too worried if someone was using the Brousseau house. We kind of live and let live around here, unless someone's getting hurt."

"I guess you think I'm paranoid or a drama queen," I said. I picked up the newspaper and searched in my pocket for some change.

"Now don't get your feelings hurt," Riley said. Keep the paper. Stop worrying so much. Wait, are you nervous about Dash because you're sleeping with him?"

"I am not having sex with that man. Hey that kind of sounds like a Bill Clinton statement. No really, I told you I'm not looking for a new boyfriend. The truth is, I can't get the old one out of my mind."

"I think Dash is an okay guy and you could do worse," Riley said as she walked back behind the counter.

I noticed then that two people had been standing by the coffee pots, a young man and an older woman. I picked up the paper and waved to Riley. "See you later," I said as I started out the door.

As I left I heard Riley call out. "Hi, Francie, I haven't seen you in ages. Are you okay?"

The woman said, "Yeah, I want to know if I can use the phone and I need a favor."

I got in the car and turned toward the River Road when my cell rang. I pulled back into the parking area and answered.

"Mary, it's Brett. We're about thirty minutes from Hanover. Mom really needs you. Can you leave from wherever and meet us at the Hanover Inn?"

"Of course, Brett, I'll be there. Is there news about Sherry?'

"I can't talk about this on the phone. Just meet us, please." He clicked off.

I headed back to the house to see what Sam was up to and to get him squared away. I also needed to talk to Ken Upham about the hearing.

I opened the front door and heard nothing but complete silence. There was no barking, no excited leaping, no running paw sounds. This could only mean that Sam had torn something up or broken something and was hiding. I ran through the great room, the dining room and the kitchen and saw nothing out of place. I called over and over, but no naughty dog crawled out of a hiding place. Then I looked in the back hall and saw the door hanging open. I rushed to the back yard. Sam was climbing the steep hill at the back of the yard. His tongue was hanging out of his mouth and he was panting as if the temperature were eighty degrees and not forty degrees. He was muddy from last night's rain.

I dragged him back to the house and into the laundry room where I washed down his paws and legs and set his water dish in front of him. Then I returned to the back door. Nothing was broken. I looked at the handle and realized that it was possible that Sam could push the handle down with his paw, if the lock wasn't engaged. Either someone let Sam out or Sam had actually opened the door. What could have caused him to rush outside? Maybe a deer or worse a bear was behind the house.

"From now on, we keep that door locked, you bad boy," I said. Sam collapsed willingly into his crate.

I pulled out Ken Upham's phone number from my file in the front hall. Ken answered on the second ring.

"Mary, I was just talking about you to my wife. I said I had to call you and make connections for the hearing tomorrow."

"Why don't I pick you up early and look at your property before we leave for the hearing? You can be the navigator. I haven't a clue about where Barre is. Two other things; do you have a survey of your property, and can you reach your arborist and have him available to testify if we need him? Will he come to the courthouse?"

""I'll make sure he's there. I'll pay him for his hours and his gas mileage, and he has the survey. He can bring it. He's pissed about the mess Roland is causing, so he'll come to court."

"Now one final thing, Ken, don't give any more interviews unless you talk to me first. Anything you say could be taken out of context. Nothing was wrong with what you told the Valley News, but let's be sure that nothing you say can be misconstrued."

"I'll keep my mouth shut. I don't want to do anything to prolong this ridiculous case. See you tomorrow."

# THIRTY-FOUR

I arrived at the Hanover Inn just as Brett pulled up. I parked at a meter and hurried over to Brett's car as the doorman unloaded a suitcase and a briefcase from Brett's trunk. Lillian jumped out of the passenger seat and grabbed the briefcase out of the startled doorman's hand.

"I'll take care of that bag myself," Lillian said as she handed the man some dollar bills. "Mary, I am so glad to see you."

I hugged Lillian and felt her slim body shaking. "I'm glad I'm here to help. Come on Lillian, whatever this is, it can't be that bad. Imagine, I just parked my car in a vacant parking place. It's like a miracle. When was the last time you saw one of those in Miami?" I waited for a laugh or a smile from Lillian or Brett. They both frowned.

"I need to get checked into a room where we can talk. Please, just follow me in."

Lillian hurried past me and the doorman. She strode over to the front desk and told the desk clerk that she had a reservation and needed to get to her room quickly.

Brett and I stood away from the desk. "What has happened, Brett?"

"Mom will fill you in as soon as we get into her room, but Mary, this is as bad as you can imagine." He leaned close to me and whispered, "We don't know if we'll ever find Sherry." I saw his eyes filled with tears.

In minutes we were in the elevator. Brett grabbed Lillian's suitcase telling the desk clerk he'd take care of it himself. As soon as the elevator doors opened, Lillian ran out of the elevator and down the corridor. She put the key into room 207. We rushed in behind her. Brett shut the door.

Lillian sat down on the edge of the bed and pulled out her cell phone.

I looked around the small room and was stunned at how shabby it appeared. Certainly not to Lillian's upscale usual taste. I realized that she hadn't even bothered to look at the small space.

"Lillian, tell me what's wrong."

She burst into heavy sobs. Through her tears, I heard her say, "Sherry has been kidnapped."

# THIRTY-FIVE

"Kidnapped! Is that why you wouldn't let anyone call the police? We have to get some law enforcement involved."

"No, Mary, you can't. Don't you understand? They said they'd kill her if we got the police involved." Lillian was on her feet almost screaming. "They want money. I had to get as much cash together as possible yesterday. Beverly was helping me when you called last night. I couldn't risk telling you this on the phone. Maybe they have our phones tapped."

"This is totally bizarre. Like a scene out of *Law and Order.* Start from the beginning and tell me exactly what you know," I said.

Brett went to the phone and ordered coffee to be sent up while Lillian sat down again on the bed. I pulled the desk chair over next to her.

"Monday morning I was in my office when my private line rang. I always think it's one of the kids, and something is wrong, but the caller ID said caller unknown. I picked up and said, 'Brett or Sherry, who is it?' A woman spoke in a muffled voice. She said, "Do you know where Sherry is?" I said "Who is this?" She told me never mind who it is, that they had Sherry and if I ever wanted to see her again I'd better get up to Hanover and bring one million dollars in cash. Then she said if I called any police, I would definitely never see my daughter again.

"I asked her if this was a joke. She said 'no way'. She said someone would call me in a few hours with more instructions but I had better be ready to leave for Hanover with the money. I don't know what I should do. They're going to hurt my baby if I bring in the police." Lillian buried her head in her hands. Her body shook as she sobbed.

I patted her shoulder. "I'm here to help you think this through. Have you heard any more from these people?"

"The same voice called on my cell phone last night. She asked when I would be arriving in Hanover and did I have the money. I told her that I'd be there by noon today and that I had most of the money. She sounded angry and said I'd better have it all."

"Do you have all that money with you?"

"No, of course not. You can't carry that much money in a carryon even in one hundred dollar bills. I have some of it, but it takes time to convert assets into cash. Beverly is managing the rest and it will be special handled by Federal Express. It will be delivered to me tomorrow."

"Mom, how do you know they're not lying to you? Maybe they've already, you know, killed Sherry. Maybe they don't really even have her." Brett's temper was beginning to hit the explosion button.

Brett's impatience with his mother brought back memories of his attitude after his father was killed. Brett never got over his family's implosion. He knew about his father's infidelity and was unable to understand how his mother could have been so blind. Now I realized how we can close our eyes to flaws in those we love, but Brett's life experiences left him with nothing but his simmering anger.

"I told you when you picked me up that I had proof and I would show you," Lillian said as she picked up her cell phone. "Look, they sent me a picture."

Brett and I crowded around the little phone. The picture showed a girl tied to a chair. She had something taped to her mouth. The photo was grainy but it looked like Sherry.

"When did you get this?" Brett asked

"Late last night."

"Oh, great. It's now almost one o'clock. How do you know she's still alive?" Brett asked. Mary is right. We must get the local police or the FBI to help us."

"Lillian, these calls you've received could have been traced if the police were involved. Agencies like the FBI are trained to work surreptitiously in kidnapping situations," I said.

"No, no, please. I don't want to lose Sherry." Lillian was close to hysterics.

"What other instructions have you received?" I asked.

"The woman called again after she sent the photo. She said to go to some place called High Pines. I wrote down the directions. She told me to park in the parking lot at a Shell station and go into the mini-mart. I was to ask for a package for Sherry. She said it would be at the counter, and then to go back to the car and open the package."

"High Pines is where I'm staying. Lillian, I have to tell you something. I've already told Brett this. I had lunch with Sherry last Friday. She confided in me that she had a new boyfriend. She would only give me his first name, Conrad. She said he runs a dairy farm somewhere in the area and that she was going to spend the weekend with him at his farm. She wouldn't tell me anything else except that she was in love with him and didn't want anyone to know about this. I tried to get her to give me more information so I could run a background check on him, but she got angry with me."

"My God, Mary, why didn't you call me? You know how naïve Sherry is. How could you let her go off like that?"

"I feel just awful, but I didn't want to betray her confidence. I thought I'd have a chance to talk to her more after she got back to school. Believe me, I thought once she saw some smelly farm, she'd forget this guy super-fast."

"Mom, this is a little break through. We know this guy's first name at least and that she was going to some farm. Maybe if we get some help from an investigator, this will help," Brett said.

"Lillian, I have an idea. I have a new client up here in High Pines. He's retired from the New Haven Police Department where he was the chief of detectives. Please, let me call him. We could meet him somewhere and maybe he can help us. He's not connected to any law enforcement now and he's not real well known around here."

"Call him, Mary," Brett said. We can't just sit here and do nothing. Brett looked at the photo again and buried his head in his hands.

# THIRTY-SIX

At two o'clock, we pulled into the road leading to Lucy's house. Lillian and Brett were in the back seat of the Explorer. Thank God for the heavily tinted windows in Florida cars. They cut the dazzling sunlight and they also cut the chances of spying eyes.

I watched closely to see if we were being followed, but no suspicious cars were behind us. In fact almost no cars were behind us on the whole trip. There was no traffic on the River Road and Lucy's house was well hidden. I certainly had found that out.

Ken Upham's Lexus sedan was already in the circular drive. He got out of the car as soon as he saw us. I told him very little on the phone, except to say that some friends from Miami were here and needed some law enforcement advice.

I hustled everyone into the house and introduced Ken to Lillian and Brett.

We settled in the Great Room. I started a fire in the fireplace. The sun hadn't dissipated the chill from the brisk north wind. Lillian was shivering probably from fear as much as from the change in temperature from Miami. I handed her a plaid throw from the back of the sofa.

"Ken, Lillian is a former client of mine. She is here because her daughter has gone missing from the Dartmouth campus. We are now sure that she has been kidnapped. Lillian and Brett will fill you in on all that we know. I am hoping that you can advise Lillian about how to proceed. Do you mind getting involved? I know you have your own worries. I will be completely focused on your hearing tomorrow, but I really want to try to give Lillian all the help that I can today."

"I'm certainly willing to hear the details and if I can help you formulate a plan, I will. Let me hear the situation. Time is of the essence in a kidnapping."

"Thanks, Ken.. While you fill Ken in, I'm going to feed Sam and make all of us some sandwiches. Lillian hasn't eaten. She just got off a plane in Manchester."

I left the Yarmouths and Ken, and went to the kitchen where Sam was scratching to get out of his crate. Ken looked like he couldn't wait to get all the details. It occurred to me that he missed the adrenalin rush of a tough investigation.

By the time I returned to the conversation, Ken was totally engaged. He was leaning forward in his chair, a small notepad on his knee.

"I understand why you didn't call in law enforcement. These people meant to scare you from such contacts and they succeeded. I'm glad Mary called me. There are some things we can do immediately. Has anyone talked to her roommate?"

"I did briefly on Monday," I said.

"So did I," Brett said.

"Where did she say Sherry told her she was going? Did she know about the alleged boyfriend?" Ken asked.

"She told me that she thought Sherry was taking the Dartmouth Coach into Boston. It's a bus that leaves from the campus several times a day. Sherry's car is still parked in the lot by the dorm. Madison, that's the roommate, didn't know anything about a boyfriend," Brett said.

"When did she leave exactly? Do we know? Ken continued making notes.

"Madison said she left early Saturday morning." I added.

"Brett, does the bus make other stops besides Boston?"

"Yeah, it stops in New London, New Hampshire, right off of interstate 89."

"Now, this is very important. Did Sherry have a cell phone and did she take it with her?"

"She was glued to that phone. I can't imagine that she'd leave without it. Maybe we can ask Madison to look through her things and see if it's there," Lillian said.

"I know it's not in her car. I looked all through it last night," Brett said.

"Can you get me all the information about the phone, Lillian? What's the number, the make and what company has the account?" Ken asked.

"Her number is 305-982-4448, and it's a BlackBerry from Verizon. I went with her to get it and she wanted Verizon because they had more service up here. You know service is spotty. I can call my assistant to look up the ID number from the billings. They're in my office," Lillian said.

"Use the phone in the kitchen," I told Lillian," so you don't tie up your cell phone".

"One more thing. Do we know where she met this Conrad guy?"

"She told me a group of kids went to some bar with a funny name in another village. It was in Hartland," I said. I remember that name because I thought it was cute that she fell in love with someone she met in Hartland. But I can't remember the funny name of the bar," I said.

"Oh, was it Skunk Hollow?" Brett asked.

"Yes, that's it." I couldn't contain a laugh over that funny name, or maybe it was relief laughter that we were finally doing something to find Sherry.

"Okay, now we need to divide the work. Lillian do you have a picture of Sherry?" Ken asked.

"Yes, in my wallet." Lillian picked up her expensive handbag and pulled out a wallet with the Gucci logo. Here's a snapshot from last summer."

I saw Ken eyeing the elegant leather accessory. I guessed he was thinking what I was. If Sherry carried around such high priced gear, even a dimwit would know that this Dartmouth coed had big bucks.

"Here's the plan," Ken said. "Brett you go back to Sherry's dorm and make sure her cell phone wasn't left behind. Talk to the roommate again. See if she was at that bar with Sherry and get a description of anyone she talked to.

"Mary, you go over to the Dartmouth Coach main bus station and find out which driver took the earliest morning bus route to Boston on Saturday.

Show him Sherry's picture. See if anyone remembers her getting on that bus."

"Of course, where is that station?"

"It's on Etna Road. I'm writing out the directions now."

"Mary, you can drop me back to get my car. It's not far from Hanover to the station," Brett said.

"As soon as you finish there, I want you to head down to Hartland and talk to the bartenders at Skunk Hollow. Show them Sherry's picture and see what they remember. I'm writing you directions there as well," Ken said.

Ken handed me a sheet of paper. "I'm going to stick with Lillian .If it's okay, we'll stay here while I make some phone calls. I need to call a contact at the Secret Service. They've got a high tech guy I know who can tell us the general location of a cell phone. If Sherry had her phone with her on Saturday, we may be able to zero in on her location."

"What if she didn't make any calls?" I asked.

It doesn't matter. Cell phones like BlackBerrys that access internet networks leave behind an electronic trail of their whereabouts even when no one is talking on them. When the phone is in range of a cell phone tower, they can pinpoint the location, Ken explained. "We used this analysis to find a murder suspect right before I retired from the department."

"There aren't many towers up here," Brett said. Will that be a problem?"

"Maybe it'll be helpful. If the phone is reaching out to a tower, we can trace her path. We'll know that Sherry passed that way. Maybe we'll know where to search. Lillian, I will drive you to the gas station at five. When will you have the rest of the money?"

"Not until tomorrow morning. If you are with me at the gas station, they'll think you're a policeman."

"Don't worry about that. You'll sit in the back and explain that you hired a car and a driver. Maybe they won't want to risk two meetings. If we can buy a little time, we may be able to find Sherry before any money drop, but we need more than that photo on your phone. I want you to demand to speak to Sherry today. Okay everyone let's get busy," Ken said. Everyone write down your cell phone numbers so we keep in touch."

Sam had sauntered into the room. Everyone was so occupied that they didn't notice him. I grabbed his collar and pulled him out with me to the car. Nothing like having a big German shepherd with you to scare away almost anyone.

# THIRTY-SEVEN

## SHERRY'S STORY

Sherry tossed and turned almost the whole night Friday, turning her bed into something that looked like a crumpled piece of paper. Saturday morning she would follow Conrad's detailed instructions, and they would leave for his farm and the whole weekend together.

She had her carryon bag packed and ready with the new lingerie she had splurged on; black bra and panties and a short black teddy. Of course, she was taking jeans and a sweater and hiking boots for hanging out at the farm.

It felt strange to be going away without telling her roommate or friends or anyone about where she would be. Mary scared her a little saying they should get a background check of Conrad. She really didn't know much about him, but a background check sounded like what her mother would want. Maybe if her dad were alive she would have told him about Conrad. He had been poor once and he wasn't as much into being socially correct.

But he wasn't alive and he had screwed up his own life. Why couldn't she trust her own instincts? She was an adult.

Yesterday she had actually Googled Conrad Peters, Vermont, and gotten back no hits in New England; just some in California and New York, but they were much older. If he was a criminal, there should have been something in his Google file. She felt stupid for even trying to get information on him.

At six she got up and dressed and put her cologne and cosmetics in her backpack along with her wallet and cell phone. She was about to walk out the door when her roommate, Madison, called out.

"What time is it, Sherry? Why are you up?"

"Sorry, I didn't mean to wake you. It's six thirty. Go back to sleep."

"Where are you going/"

"I told you yesterday. I want to catch the first Dartmouth coach this morning."

"Why are you going to Boston?"

"I already told you. You'll remember when you're awake. Go back to sleep. I'll see you Sunday night." She walked out quickly before Madison asked more questions.

After coffee and a roll at the cafeteria at the Hopkins Center, she went out to the coach stop. A large crowd of students and a few visitors were gathered already even though the bus wasn't due for another twenty minutes. There was always a crowd on Saturday morning, students and professors going to Boston for the weekend. Sometimes people doing business with the college during the week left on Saturday. The coach connected to Logan Airport as well as downtown Boston.

She glanced at the crowd hoping not to see anyone she knew. She saw two freshman girls she knew slightly from lacrosse practices, but they didn't notice her.

Conrad and she had planned carefully. She would mingle with the crowd as if she were getting on the bus. Conrad would pull his truck up at the last minute across the street and while everyone was loading on the bus she'd run across to his truck and they'd be on their way. She felt like a character in a mystery novel. It was so secret. She shivered a little.

"Ms. Yarmouth, are we to have your company on the trip to Boston?"

Sherry whirled around. It was Professor Roden, her art history teacher.

"Did I scare you? Sorry," he said. Can I help you with your bag?"

"No, thanks, I can handle it." He was the last person she wanted to see. He was an old fart, who was always coming on to the female students. Just then an older woman came up and took his arm, leading him over to a group of faculty.

Sherry turned her attention to the street. Conrad's truck was nowhere in sight. The air was brisk and she shivered again. Within minutes the bus pulled up and the driver disembarked. He opened the luggage compartment and then began his standard announcements.

"If you have a ticket, I'll take it after you're seated on the bus. If you need to purchase your ticket you must do so when we stop at the main terminal in Lebanon before we start the trip to Boston. Our only other stop will be in New London to take on passengers if there are still seats. We'll start boarding as soon as all baggage is loaded. Please form a line now."

Sherry mingled with the passengers who soon started boarding the bus. Still no sign of Conrad. Maybe he changed his mind and was going to stand her up.. In a few minutes everyone was on board.

"Are you getting on, Miss?" the driver was speaking to her. "We're about to leave. Are you okay, Miss?"

She realized she must have looked close to tears. "I'm waiting for a friend, so go ahead," she said.

"Well, suit yourself. Haven't got all day, you know." The driver hoisted himself up the steps and shut the door.

Just then Sherry saw Conrad's black pickup pull into a space across the street. She grabbed her bag and bolted across to meet him.

"Hi, you're late. I thought maybe you weren't coming," she said as she jumped into the truck, throwing her bag and backpack into the space behind the seat. She leaned over to kiss him. He brushed her lips lightly and stepped on the gas jolting her back against the seat.

"Well, that was some greeting. Aren't you glad to see me?" She looked at Conrad who looked straight ahead.

"Sure, I am. I just need to get back to the farm. Morning chores you know."

He headed on to the freeway. He was driving very fast and Sherry thought she smelled alcohol on his breath.

"Have you been drinking this morning?" she asked.

"What's this? Are you the alcohol police? No, I had a few beers last night. I just need to concentrate on driving. Why don't you listen to your I-Pod or something."

Sherry reached in her backpack and took out her headphones and turned up the volume. Maybe Conrad was just nervous, she thought.

They headed onto Route Four and passed through a village. "Can we stop at that market for some coffee?" Sherry asked.

"No, I told you I need to get back." Conrad barked at her.

They passed through the village and he pulled onto a dirt road. He pulled over on the shoulder. She could see an old house down the road. Conrad honked his horn. She saw two people running towards the truck.

"Get the blindfold on her," a woman's voice yelled.

Conrad pulled her towards him by her shoulders and tried to tie a piece of dark cloth around her eyes. Sherry screamed and began to fight him. She scratched his face and he screamed at her. "You bitch, stop it."

Then she saw an old woman and a young man at the passenger door. They opened the door and the woman came toward her. Sherry saw her white hair and faded blue eyes. The woman pushed something over her nose and mouth.. That face was the last thing she remembered about being in Conrad's truck.


Sherry awoke to a strange feeling. Her head throbbed. She couldn't remember where she was. She tried to turn over, but something held her back. She couldn't move and her wrists hurt. Suddenly she remembered being in Conrad's truck . She could hear voices. She couldn't see anything. Now she realized her hands and feet were tied together and something was covering her eyes. She tried to scream but nothing came out. This must be a bad dream. She strained to hear what the voices were saying.

"You dimwit, all you had to do was get the blindfold on her and you screwed that up. You are the dumbest bastard I ever did see." It was that same gravelly voice of the woman Sherry had seen.

"Oh, shut up, Francie. I got her here, didn't I? I guess I'm not so dumb. Without me, you wouldn't have your prize in sight." Sherry thought she recognized Conrad's voice.

"Stop arguing. We've got to work together here. Let's go through her stuff and plan the phone call. Mom, do you know what to say when you reach Sherry's mother?"

"You're right, Otis, honey. We'll go over it again," the woman said.

"Whew, Pauly, look at that silk underwear. Looks like you missed some hot fucks," the young guy she called Otis was talking. But who was Pauly? In a minute she knew. She heard Conrad answer. He hadn't even given his real name. What an idiot she was. Oh, my God, she had been having sex with a criminal of some kind.

"I fucked her a bunch of times already," Pauly said.

"Hey, there's two hundred bucks in her wallet. That's a start, ain't it?" And here's a real nice cell phone. Can we use it?"

"Quit worrying about this chicken feed. We need to think about how we'll get rid of her." It was the woman's voice.

"What do you mean, get rid of her?" Conrad /Pauly sounded confused.

"You didn't think we was going to just give her back to her folks, did you? She saw us, you moron. She can identify you for sure and now I think she saw me, too."

"But I thought the whole idea was to get the money so we wouldn't have to stay around here anymore. You and Otis are the ones in big trouble, so quit calling me a moron. You said we were just going to steal some stuff," Pauly said, "not kill anybody."

"The plan is to get enough money to get out of here. Don't think you're not in trouble, Paul. You were with us before and you're with us now, so let's do what we gotta do."

Sherry tried to scream again. She felt a prick in her arm. Then she felt herself falling into the black abyss of a drug induced sleep..

# THIRTY-EIGHT

I drove to the Dartmouth Coach terminal following the directions written out by Ken. I found the turn into Etna Road, but then drove past the terminal and had to find a driveway or street to turn around in. "Damn these narrow roads," I yelled to no one in particular. After going a mile out of the way and turning the Explorer back the way I had just come, I finally saw the terminal. A bus had just pulled in under the portico and passengers were piling off carrying shopping bags, small cases, and laptops.

I fought my way through the crowd and into the terminal, and found myself in a compact waiting room. There was a counter with one woman behind it. I pulled out the picture of Sherry from my handbag and approached the woman.

"Good afternoon. I wonder if you can help me with some information. I'm an attorney from Florida and I'm trying to find a family friend who seems to be missing. She may have taken the early coach to Boston on Saturday morning. I'd like to speak to the driver as soon as possible." I handed her my card along with the photo of Sherry. "This is her picture. Did she come in here Saturday?"

"Hard to say," the woman responded. "What's her name? There should be a ticket receipt in our file. Wait, you said Saturday morning early? The driver who just pulled up may be the one you're looking for. Hold on a second." She rummaged through a file box and pulled out a card. "Yes, here it is, Hiram Grady. He's one of our best. Been driving for us almost eleven years. Let me get him before he takes off. Oh, he just drove the bus around to the parking area. I'll walk out there with you."

The woman came around from behind the counter and moved to the side door. I followed her. "This is so nice of you to help me catch up with your driver," I said, as we jogged to the area behind the terminal

"Not at all. Glad to help," she said.

We approached the bus and the woman knocked on the exit door to get the driver's attention. He opened the door immediately, and stepped onto the step. "Something wrong, Ellie?"

"Well, this attorney wants a word with you before you scoot out of here," she said.

"An attorney? Am I in trouble?" Hiram laughed.

"Definitely not, Mr. Grady," I said. "I need to ask you about a passenger on your bus early Saturday morning."

"Please call me Hiram. Everyone does." Hiram stepped out of the bus and stood next to me.

"This is a picture of the young woman I'm trying to locate. She's a Dartmouth student. Do you have any recollection of her getting on the bus early Saturday?"

Hiram looked at the picture for a minute. "Well, I'll be darned. I do remember her all right. She was acting very odd. Waited with the other passengers at the coach stop on the campus, but she never got on the bus. She kept looking around like she was waiting for someone. I asked her was she going to get on the bus or not, and she said she was waiting for a friend. Then just as I was going to pull out, I saw her run across the street to a truck that pulled in. I waited a second because I thought maybe they were going to rush back to the bus, like maybe the friend was late getting there, but she jumped in the truck and they took off real fast."

"Could you see who was in the truck? Can you describe the truck?"

"I saw a man in the driver's seat. Couldn't see if there was anyone else. Didn't really get much of a look at the guy. I think he had kind of long hair. The truck was your regular black pickup, old, kind of dirty, maybe a Dodge or a Chevy."

"Did you see a license number or what state it was from?"

"No, I'm sorry. I didn't look that close. The girl seemed kind of upset."

"Anything else you can remember?"

"No, not really. Well, wait a minute. There were some professors on the bus. They took the seats right behind me. I must have said something about the girl changing her mind, and that I waited for her to get on board and she held up our departure for nothing. I have a great record for being on time unless there's a traffic mess-up."

"So what was it you remembered?" Ellie asked.

"Well, this one professor said something like, 'yeah, that —I think he said-Yarmouth girl. She's been acting strange since her father was murdered.' That's why I remembered because he said something about a murder."

"Thank you, Hiram. You've been very helpful. This girl's family has been through a lot. I may need to come back and see you again. How can I reach you?"

Hiram scribbled his phone number on the back of my card. I rushed back to my car just as my cell phone rang.

"Mary, its Brett. I just finished going through Sherry's desk and dresser."

"Well, I just finished talking to a bus driver who remembers Sherry from Saturday morning. I'll fill you in, but what about Sherry's phone. Was it there?"

"No, and Madison reminded me that if we had been calling Sherry, Madison would have heard Sherry's cell ringing, so she does have it with her."

"That means Ken's Secret Service guy can give us some help."

"I did find something that may help us. I found a photo of Sherry and some guy. I showed it to Madison. She said she didn't know him. Then I asked her about going to Skunk Hollow with Sherry. That helped her remember the guy in the picture. She said she and several others went down there when they finished the summer semester. She said Sherry not only talked to the guy in the picture, she also ended up leaving with him. Madison drove Sherry's car back to campus that night." Brett sounded excited.

"Listen, Brett, let's meet down at Skunk Hollow. Bring the picture. Maybe someone down there can tell us who this guy is and where he lives. I'll meet you there in half an hour, if I don't get lost."

I was studying Ken's directions, while I gave Sam a quick walk outside the bus terminal, when the phone rang again.

"Mary, it's Dash. I thought you might stop at the office this afternoon to get everything you need for court tomorrow."

"Hi, Dash. I think I have everything I need. I'm a little distracted right now. I'm trying to help my friend from Miami. Can I call you later?"

"Sure. I tried to reach Ken, but his wife said he was out helping with some investigation."

"He's actually helping me, Dash. Why don't I call you later, or stop by. I really can't talk right now."

"Sure, Mary. If I can help, please call on me."

I clicked off and started the drive to Hartland . I was hopeful that we wouldn't be too late to get Sherry back. If my mother were here she would tell me to pray. I was more into relying on cell phone technology.

CHAPTER
# THIRTY-NINE

The roads to Skunk Hollow were ablaze in color. Some of the leaves here were still on the trees and the higher elevation seemed to make the colors sharper. I wondered if there were any ugly roads or freeways in this state.

I saw Brett's car as I drove into the parking lot. It was getting close to five o'clock, a little early for happy hour in Miami,, but there were numerous cars and trucks in the lot.

Brett saw my SUV and ran up to meet me. I filled him in on the bus driver's recollections as we made our way to the entrance. Brett pulled out the snapshot of a smiling Sherry and a serious looking handsome man. He looked like a rock star with his hair pulled into a ponytail and an earring in one ear.

"I guess I can see why Sherry was attracted," I said.

"Well I can't. He looks like a dork to me." Brett glared at the photo.

"You have to be female to understand," I said as we entered the half-light of the bar.

The smell of cigarette smoke mingled with the pungent odor of beer. A dozen or so men and a couple of girls were hard at work shaking off the work day. We approached the lone bartender.

"Let me talk to him, Brett. I'm used to getting people to talk with me. I think you're pretty emotional right now," I said.

"Of course, I'm emotional. My sister has gotten herself into a horrible mess. It's possible she may not even be alive. Dammit, I'm sick and tired of picking up the pieces for my family. I never get a chance to just do my own work and be left alone."

I put my arm around Brett and tried to give him an assuring squeeze, but he was as stiff as a cement column. His nerves were stretched to the breaking point, and I sure didn't want him to snap. I remembered again his devastation after his father was murdered. His attitude wasn't going to be much help getting more information.

"Go sit down at the end of the bar," I said. I took the photo from his hand and pushed my way through the growing line of drinkers. "Excuse me, sir. I'm an attorney from Miami. I need some immediate help. I'm trying to find a missing friend. Can you take a minute to look at this photo and tell me if you recognize either of the people?"

The bartender looked at me, then at the photo and then back at me. He looked me up and down.

"Aren't you a little old for this guy?" he asked..

"No, you have the wrong idea. He's not my boyfriend. Do you know him?"

"Sure, I know him. He hangs here a lot. Girls are always latching on to him. That's Paul Conrad. Everyone calls him Pauly."

"How about the girl? Do you recognize her? Have you seen them in here together?"

"The girl looks like one of the Dartmouth rich kids that come in here, but I don't actually remember her."

"How about this Pauly guy? Do you know where he works or where he lives?"

"I don't know, but I think a couple of my customers might know. Hey, Chris, come over here a minute."

A heavy set man wearing a Red Sox cap got up from a nearby table. A short man in jeans and a sweatshirt came with him.

"Chris and Buddy, this gal is an attorney asking some questions about Paul Conrad. Do you know how she can find him?"

"What'd he do now?" Chris asked. "Are you from a collection place?" He turned to me.

"Absolutely not. In fact I may have some money that he's owed. Where does he work?" I asked.

"Hell, no one ever owes Pauly any money. He can't keep a job for more than a week at a time," the one called Buddy said.

"Well, where does he live?"

Chris looked at me for a minute. "I don't want to get him in trouble."

"You won't, I assure you," I lied, looking him right in the eye.

"He lives on an old farm. It's between Woodstock and Bridgewater. I'm not sure exactly how you get there. Only been there once, but I remember it's up a road without a sign that goes up to Cherry Blossom Hill where we used to go sledding."

" Do you know the girl in this picture with Paul?"

"Can't say that I do, but ol' Pauly, he's always picking up some good lookers."

"Thanks for your help," I said. I collected Brett from his seat at the bar where he was gulping a beer.

He followed me out of the place, and opened my car door for me, setting poor Sam barking furiously.

"It's okay Sam. Brett, we made some progress. Conrad is this guy's last name. He gave a false name to Sherry. I've got an approximate location of where he lives. . Let's go back up to High Pines and wait for your mom and Ken. By now they should have made the trip to the gas station. It's not far from the house. I'll follow you up there."


By the time we pulled back into the drive at Lucy's house, Ken's car was there. I looked at my watch. It was just five thirty. I felt like two days had gone by.

Lillian rode in the back seat of Ken's Lexus sedan. She supposed she could pull off the ruse that Ken was her driver. The car looked nicer than the SUV's they passed as they drove toward the meeting at the Shell station.

She wondered what her husband would have done if he had lived to see Sherry in such a mess. He would have been all bluster, ordering everyone around and trying to bull his way into getting Sherry released. Lillian really didn't mean to think about Gary. She tried to concentrate on what she would say when she met the kidnappers. Ken had instructed her to demand to speak to Sherry or the money would not be paid.

"We're almost there, Lillian. Try to stay calm. I'll be sitting in the car watching and listening. You said the instructions were to pick up a package at the mini-mart, unwrap it and then wait in the parking area." Ken turned out of the side road and waited at the stop sign.

Lillian could see the gas station just ahead on the main highway. There wasn't much traffic compared to five o'clock in Miami. Three cars and a pickup truck were parked in the parking area, and one car was at the gas pump.

Lillian got out of the car and walked slowly into the market. Ken rolled down the windows in the Lexus. There were three customers in line at the counter. A pretty young woman greeted each of them and chatted. Lillian shifted her weight, trying to be patient. She felt like she was going to faint or scream. Her ears were ringing. Finally it was her turn at the counter.

"Hi, there, can I help you? I'll bet you're here to see our beautiful fall leaves," the girl said.

"Yes, of course, and I'm supposed to pick up a package a friend left for me, Sherry Yarmouth," Lillian said. She looked around to see who was behind her, but it was just a heavyset woman waiting to pay for a gallon of milk.

"Sure, the package is right here. How do you know Francie?" the clerk asked.

Lillian looked at her blankly.

"Francie, who left the package for you," the clerk asked.

"Oh, she was just doing a favor for someone I know." Lillian grabbed the package and walked swiftly outside. She returned to the car and unwrapped the package.

When she saw the contents she started to cry.

"Lillian what is it?" Ken asked. He swiveled around to see what she was holding.

"It's Sherry's wallet. She liked mine so I got her one just like it. And this is Sherry's sweater. I bought it for her in England." Lillian buried her head in the sweater.

"Is there anything in the wallet?" Ken pulled it out of the box. "There's a note," he said.

Lillian grabbed the note from his hand. The words were letters cut out of a magazine or paper. "Wait by the pay phone. Don't talk to no one." was all it said.

"Damn," Ken said. There's no time to get a trace on that phone. Listen, Lillian, get the number on the phone. Maybe we can get a list of incoming calls when you're through with the call. Get over there now," he ordered, and remember the number. Don't write it down. I'm sure someone is watching you."

I don't think I can concentrate enough to remember the number. Can't we just look at it later?"

"No, not if someone is watching us."

Lillian staggered out of the car and hurried to the pay phone at the end of the parking area. She looked around, but didn't see anyone in the three cars parked nearby.

She opened the door of the booth just as the phone rang. As she picked it up, she saw the number on the base of the phone: 802-295-1154. Fifty-four was her age. She would be able to remember the number. "Hello. Are you calling Lillian?" she asked.

"Who's that guy in the car? I told you to come alone," the same gravelly voice said.

"I had to hire a car and driver to get here. I don't know my way around these backwoods roads," Lillian said just as she had rehearsed with Ken.

"I can see you, so watch it if you want to see Sherry again. Where's the money?"

"I told you I don't have all of it. It'll all be here tomorrow, but I'm not handing it over until I have real proof that Sherry is alive and well."

"I sent you a picture. What more do you want? Me and my friends are not playing here. We're dead serious, if you get my meaning."

"I must speak to Sherry or I won't believe that she's alive. I've followed your instructions and haven't called any police, but if I don't have a conversation with Sherry, I'm not paying any money."

"I'll think about it. Wait for my call on your cell phone."

"When will you call?" Lillian asked, but all she heard was a dial tone. Gravel voice had hung up.

We were gathered back in the Great Room. Lillian finished telling us about the events at the gas station, and Brett and I filled everyone in on the bus depot and Skunk Hollow.

"Okay, we're making progress," Ken said. He was interrupted by Lillian.

"I forgot something that could be important. The clerk in the market said someone named Francie had left the package for me. She acted like I was supposed to know her." Lillian was still holding on to Sherry's sweater twisting it around her hand as she spoke.

"Good girl," Ken said. "Now we've got a lot more information. We know the real name of the guy who Sherry left with. We have a picture of him and a general area where his farm is located, if that's where he took Sherry. We know that the name of the woman who left the package is Francie and that the store clerk knows her. These are not exactly polished criminals."

"What about the phone number on the public phone at the gas station?" Lillian asked.

"Remember, I phoned that into my friend at the Secret Service, when we were on our way back here. He's supposed to get back to me as soon as possible. He's working on the tracing of Sherry's cell phone," Fred said.

"I'm sorry. I guess I was so nervous that I forgot you called from the car" Lillian said.

I looked at Lillian. She was very pale. "Lillian, how about a cup of tea? You need something to calm you a bit. My mother always says chamomile will do the trick."

"Thank you, Mary. You are always so kind. Thank God you were visiting up here, and Ken, you have been so generous with your knowledge and time. I think I need to go back to the inn and lie down for a while. Brett, let's go back to Hanover. I'll wait for the next phone call, and call you with any news immediately."

"And I'll nose around a bit. Everyone knows everyone here, so maybe with some names and this picture, I can find out more," I said.

Lillian and Brett left in Brett's car and I walked Ken out.

"Ken, what do you think? Is there a chance that Sherry is alive?" I hated to ask that question. I was beginning to think that there was so little chance of ever seeing her alive. I wanted to kick myself for not insisting that Sherry forget her plan to go away with a stranger for the weekend.

"I think there's some chance. These people appear to be very inexperienced, but you never know what will spook them."

"I'll see you early tomorrow and we'll go get your nuisance lawsuit out of the way. Call me if you hear more about the trace on Sherry's BlackBerry."

I walked Sam and poured a glass of wine. The adrenaline was pumping and I couldn't seem to sit down for more than a minute. After pacing through the rooms of the house for the third time, I loaded Sam in the Explorer and drove over to Dash's office. He knew everybody in the Upper Valley. I decided to trust him and see if any of the names or faces in Sherry's kidnapping meant anything to him. I missed my support system, my brothers, and Catherine, but most of all, Carlos, who would be so engrossed in Sherry and Lillian's newest mess.

# FORTY-TWO

The front door was locked when I arrived at Dash's office. Daisy's car was gone, but there was a light in the foyer so I tapped on the door. Dash came down the hallway and smiled when he saw me.

"Mary, glad I was still downstairs. I'm happy you came by. How are your friends from Miami?" Dash ushered me in and motioned me back to his office.

I plunked down in one of the chairs across from his desk chair. Dash pulled the other chair close to mine and sat down.

"They're not good. Dash, can I trust you not to breathe a word of what I'm going to tell you? I need to pick your brain, but this is really a life and death matter, and that's not just a figure of speech."

Dash reached over and took my hand. "Mary, you are freezing." He rubbed my hands in his warm grip. "Of course, you can trust me. You look exhausted. Sit here a minute." He went to a cupboard in the bookcase and came back with a bottle of Scotch and two glasses. He filled the glasses and handed me one. "Take some sips of this. What's this about?"

"My client's daughter has been kidnapped. Sherry disappeared over the weekend. She told me that she had a secret boyfriend and was going to his farm to spend the weekend. Then her mother, that's my client, got a call asking for money and she was sent a photo on her cell phone of Sherry tied to a chair with a gag over her mouth."

"That's unbelievable. I don't think I've ever heard of a kidnapping in this area."

"Of course, they told Lillian not to call any law enforcement, and she believed them and refused to let me call. Ken Upham has been helping me. She agreed to let him put some investigative techniques to work. It must be fate that you introduced me to him."

"Tell me what I can do to help," Dash said. I realized that he was holding my hand again.

"Maybe you can tell me who some of these people are who we've managed to uncover. The guy who Sherry thought was her lover lured her away for the weekend. She called him Conrad. She thought he owned a dairy farm. We found a picture in her room at Dartmouth and I found out his name is Paul Conrad. He's some kind of drifter or deadbeat. Here's his picture." I pulled the photo out of my handbag.

"I do know him," Dash said at once. They call him Pauly. He's had an awful life. His dad was a drunk who beat his mom and one day when Pauly was around fourteen, his dad killed his mom. The father was convicted and is serving a long sentence in Kentucky. Vermont contracts with other states for defendants with maximum prison sentences."

"What about Pauly? Does he have a farm?"

"Pauly became a ward of the state and went to a foster home. He stayed with the Wallace family. They had a son around the same age, Otis Wallace."

"What about a farm somewhere between Woodstock and Bridgewater?"

"I think that might be where the Conrads lived, but I don't think it was much of a farm, just an old house and some land."

"Does this Pauly guy still own it? Maybe that's where he took Sherry?" I glanced at my watch and realized it was almost seven-thirty. I stood up getting ready to leave.

"I don't know, but maybe tomorrow I can search the records at the courthouse. Listen, Mary, why don't you stay here for dinner? You haven't seen my upstairs where I hang out. You can chill out and I'll cook dinner for us." He put his arm around my waist and tried to pull me closer.

"Thanks Dash. Maybe I can take a rain check. It's great of you to ask, but right now I just don't need any complications."

"Maybe I'm what you need; an uncomplicated guy," he said. "It can just be dinner. No other *quid pro quo.*"

"I have Sam waiting out in the car, but I appreciate your caring."

I drew away and started for the door. Then I remembered something else.

"I almost forgot. Do you know anyone named Francie? That's another name that surfaced."

"Sure, that's who I was talking about. Francie Wallace is the foster mother of Pauly. I know her. She was Carolyn Brousseau's housekeeper."

# FORTY-THREE

My brain was on speed as I drove home. Carolyn Brousseau's housekeeper was mixed up in Sherry's kidnapping. Francie worked for the victim of an unsolved murder. This news made me totally fearful of ever recovering Sherry.

I made a pot of coffee and sat by the fire. Pauly was the person who lured Sherry away. These kidnappers couldn't turn Sherry over to her mother knowing that she could identify Paul Conrad and perhaps lead the police to Francie and whoever else was a partner in this outrageous crime.

I called Ken, but got his voicemail, so I left a message that I would give him more information in the morning. I am a person who is used to acting, not reacting and this waiting game of taking no action left me feeling like an insect trapped between a fly swatter and an exterminator. Was I killing time until the bad guys killed Lillian's beautiful naïve daughter?

I fell asleep fully clothed on the sofa in front of the fireplace. Hours later, I awoke shivering. The fire was out and cold hung over the house like a dark hand, gripping all the feeling out of my body,

I soaked in a hot bath and snuggled under two down quilts, but sleep evaded me. Sam curled over my feet and gently snored until I got up and began going through the morning rituals by rote.

At eight o'clock, I pulled up in front of Ken Upham's house. I was probably too early, but it seemed like noontime to me after the sleepless night. Sam had protested mightily when I urged him back into his crate after his breakfast and morning walk. Guilt was seeping into my petting of the poor dog who would undoubtedly be ecstatic to return to Miami and our familiar house where he could roam into any room he pleased.

Ken's house was a large chalet style with decks on two levels. I walked down the hill from the road admiring the beds of mums and asters surrounding the front door. Before I could ring the doorbell, an attractive woman opened the door. She was wearing a long terrycloth robe. Her white hair tumbled to her shoulders, .and even with no makeup, she looked interesting Her skin had a natural healthy look with bronze high cheek bones. The white hair against her suntanned skin gave her an ageless look.. She must have been a beauty when she was younger.

`"You must be Mary. Please, come in. Ken is getting dressed and he'll be right down. I've heard so much about you the past few days."

"Sorry I'm here so early."

"No need to be sorry. Come on back to the breakfast room. I've got fresh coffee and some coffee cake ready." She pointed to a chair at a round maple table. Sun was beginning to come through a large bay window behind the table. Somehow, Ken's wife and this room with the smell of coffee and cinnamon reminded me of my mother and mornings growing up. I sat down and felt more at ease than I had in the last twenty-four hours.

"Mary, good morning, I see you've met Rita and she's got you all set with some breakfast." Ken strode into the room smelling of after shave, his hair damp, what was left of it.

"Mary, I have to thank you" Rita said. I know Ken is helping you with some police type problem. Of course, he can't tell me about it. I'm used to that, but I haven't seen him so engaged and animated since he retired. Somehow, gardening and golf just don't turn him on like robberies and murders did." Rita laughed as she looked fondly at Ken.

As soon as I had wolfed down two slices of the delicious coffee cake and gulped a huge mug of coffee, I turned to Fred. "Let's go out and take a look at your land. I don't mean to hurry you, but we don't want to miss your hearing."

We shrugged into our jackets, and Ken led the way down a winding stairway into his back yard. As we walked, I touched Ken's elbow to gain his attention.

"Ken, I got a lot of information from Dash last night. Paul Conrad's father killed his mother when he was a teenager. The father went to prison and Paul became the foster ward of the Wallace family. Francie Wallace was the housekeeper for the Brousseau family. Carolyn Brousseau was the victim of a murder in her own home at night. That murder has never been solved."

"So you're fitting these facts into a pattern?" Ken asked.

I could see that Ken was assuming his cagey police detective persona.

"Can't you see the connection? Francie was the name of the woman who left the package for Lillian at the market and Paul is her foster son."

"My Secret Service contact should have information for us as soon as we leave court in Barre. Let's see what that adds to the picture."

We were walking on the perimeter of Ken and Rita's land, separated by a low picket fence from Roland Behr's property. Ken's newly planted beds, low trees and a trellis with climbing clematis vines were a stark contrast to Roland's yard. It was filled with what looked like trash. There were cardboards nailed to trees and tin cans scattered about. The ground was more weeds than grass.

"What a mess. What is all this stuff?" I asked. You should be reporting him to some zoning board for this eye-sore."

"As best as I can tell, these seem to be some kind of targets.. He and his buddies take target practice out here. We often hear shooting at night. He has concocted some kind of lights that shine on the trees and on that old table over there." Ken pointed out the various areas.

"Isn't this dangerous? What if a bullet ricocheted into your yard?"

"Rita has been worried about that. Let's walk back up to the road. I want you to walk around to the front of Roland's house so you have a complete picture."

Roland's house was well hidden behind a large stand of trees and underbrush. The driveway was unpaved gravel, leading to a detached garage. We took a few steps down the drive. The house was dark brown and melted into the trees. No house number was visible. The place looked deserted. Unless you were looking for it, it would easily be missed altogether.

"When Roland said he valued his privacy, he wasn't exaggerating, was he?" I asked.

"He meant it all right. We better get started." Ken walked swiftly through another neighbor's yard and led me back to the road where my car was parked.

"I'll drive," I said, as I popped the lock on my key fob.

Ken laughed. "No one locks their cars around here. You can leave your purse lying right on the seat and it'll be there when you return."

"Sure, no one steals your purse. They just kidnap innocent young coeds." I said. .

# FORTY-FOUR

The drive took us north past neat villages and farms and into the Green Mountains. More leaves showed their fall hues the further north we drove. Soon we were surrounded by tall walls of granite on both sides of the road. We passed trucks loaded with logs.

As we drove, Ken and I discussed the case that Roland had filed against him.

"I can't believe that this case won't be put out of its misery today, especially after seeing Roland's place. You're the one who should be complaining." I said.

"I've learned not to take anything for granted. Vermont is home to a variety of people. There are true Vermonters who really care about their environment. Then there are the newcomers; the tree-huggers, the 'I care about being green except for my gas guzzling Porsche'. They're the trust fund babies newly arrived from New York."

"Does Roland fit into any of those categories?"

"No, he's a category all to himself. He seems to be just plain ornery."

We had left the highway at the exit marked "Barre, Montpelier."

"The two towns border each other," Ken explained, "but they are nothing alike."

"Isn't Montpelier the state capital?"

"Yes it is, and it's a very charming town with state buildings and well preserved old homes. You'll have to see it while you're visiting. Barre is basically a stone mining town."

Ken directed me through an intersection of roads and we began an ascent up a hilly road of twists and turns. In a few minutes we came upon what appeared to be a main street. The buildings were a jumble of cafes, auto shops, and houses turned into banks or offices.

"We need to make a turn in a minute into the courthouse parking lot, and you're going way too fast. Speed limits are for real here My Google map shows the turn right now"

I suppressed a laugh. Somehow Google and this old brick street didn't seem compatible. I turned sharply into the lot as Ken directed.

"Where's the courthouse?" I asked looking around.

"Right there, that beige building." Ken pointed to the building just ahead of the lot.

We got out of the car. I pulled my file from the back seat and we started up a long walk. I had expected an old courthouse with a feeling of history. Instead I was viewing what was a miniature version of any one of our modern courthouses in Miami.

We walked into a plain vanilla entryway that could have been in any city. The big difference was that no one actually checked our bags or phones. And no one was standing in line to gain entrance. It was just us. A friendly woman at the front desk directed us to a courtroom on the second floor.

The judge was holding a file and conferring with an elderly man seated next to him on the bench. There were the usual courtroom personnel; a young woman court reporter, a bailiff, and a few people seated in the rows of chairs behind the well of the court. A woman attorney was standing as we walked in and identified herself as counsel for a juvenile defendant charged with aggravated battery.

The first thing that I noticed was that both the attorney and the court reporter wore rather long skirts. I glanced down at my pants suit and realized that I must be violating some dress code.

The next thing that I noticed was that the attorney was discussing her juvenile client with the judge but the client was not present. No one else seemed to be present in the case either. The discussion dragged on for what seemed an endless time period. I wondered how the judge could devote so much time to this one case and whispered this to Ken.

"The volume of cases is light here. There's no incentive to make a decision," he whispered back.

I walked over to the bailiff to check in and let him know that Ken and I were here and ready, hoping maybe that would speed things up. The bailiff's name tag said Harry Sinclair.

"Good morning. Mary Magruder Katz representing Kenneth Upham in Behr versus Upham," I said, smiling at the bailiff.

"I'll let you know when the judge is ready," he answered and didn't return my smile.

"Will we have to wait through the arraignment calendar?" I asked.

"It's not an arraignment week. That's next Monday."

Before I could grasp that arraignments don't happen every day in this system, the judge stopped what he was doing and glared in my direction.

"Anything wrong over there, Harry?"

"No, Judge McCreary, just answering a few questions of this here lawyer," the bailiff said. He pointed at me with his chin and grimaced as if he had just tasted something bitter.

The judge went back to conferring with the older man seated with him on the bench.

"Can I just ask you a couple of other questions?" I asked, realizing I was pushing my luck, but curiosity overwhelmed my better instincts. "I'm new here."

"So I've noticed. Go ahead. It beats listening to that gibberish from the lawyer in that juvenile case."

"Why isn't the juvenile defendant in court? Doesn't he have a right to be present at all his hearings?"

"Oh, he's got the right, but he don't want that right," Harry said.

"Why not? Is he scared or sick?"

"I don't know about that, but all the juveniles are kept at a facility that's at the other end of the state. If they want to come to court, it means over an hour ride by van and another hour back. Sometimes the hearing may take only a few minutes, so these kids don't want to go through all that."

"Why are they so far away?"

"Listen, Miss, we can't build a facility for every two or three kids. I don't know where you're from. Did I hear Miami? Well, we've only got 650, 000 people in the whole state. How many have you got?"

"In Miami, about two and a half million. Oh, of course, I see what you're saying."

"You got any more questions or can I get back to my Sudoku puzzle?" Harry waved his folded newspaper.

"Just one, is the plaintiff here with his counsel for my hearing?"

"The lawyer checked in, but his client isn't coming. Christian Berger, that's his name, he went outside for a smoke."

"Okay, thanks. I'll quit pestering you."

"No problem, it's all part of my job, but you sure got a lot of questions."

Harry went back to his paper, and I started back to my seat when I realized I hadn't asked the most important question. I tapped Harry on the shoulder.

"What now?"

"Who's the other man with the judge?"

"That's Calvin Crumb, the side judge. Everyone knows him. He's been reelected seven times. You really are new here."

I retreated to my seat. "Ken, that guy up there with the judge, that's one of those side judges and he seems to be an institution. Do you know him? His name is Calvin Crumb."

"I don't know him, but I've heard of him. He's a real curmudgeon. He was named after Calvin Coolidge who was a native of this part of Vermont."

"Dash told me these side judges aren't even lawyers. Did you have anything like that in New Haven?"

"No, the last of the justices of the peace were phased out about forty years ago."

I looked up and saw that the juvenile matter must have been concluded. The attorney was packing her briefcase.

"I'll give this matter some more thought and issue an order sometime next week," Judge McCreary said, as he left his chair and headed out a side door.

"All rise. Ten minute recess," Harry, the bailiff, bellowed as he followed the judge out of the courtroom.

"I can't believe he's taking a break. This whole hearing shouldn't take ten minutes. I thought we'd be back in High Pines well before noon. I'll go introduce myself to opposing counsel. That must be him," I said, as I watched an older stoop-shouldered man enter the back of the room. He was stashing a pack of cigarettes in his jacket pocket, and since no other logical candidates were present, I decided he must be the guy.

I watched him approach the plaintiff's table. He didn't appear to have a file or papers with him.

"Hi, Mr. Berger, I'm Mary Magruder Katz. I'm representing Ken Upham. It looks like we have a few minutes to talk before the judge calls our case."

"Yeah, I'm Berger, but there isn't anything to talk about in this case. My client's privacy has been invaded. Your client removed living trees. That's downright sinful. We'll let a jury settle this case, or I may be filing for summary judgment." Berger turned his back to me ending any and all future communications.

"Well?" Ken asked.

"Well, Mr. Berger has decided to play hardball. Do you know who he is? The filing notice says he's from Rutland, but he sounds like he's from Germany or Sweden or someplace European."

"I don't know him, but I've only been here less than a year except for ski vacations. I haven't been hanging around the courthouses."

The bailiff caught our attention with another bellowing "all rise." The judge and the side judge returned and took their seats

"The next case is *Behr vs. Upham.* All parties step forward and identify yourselves," Harry motioned us to step in front of the bench.

I placed my card on the court reporter's desk. I saw the side judge eyeing me, looking at my pants suit.

"Your Honor, good morning, Mary Katz. Thank you for allowing me to appear *pro hoc vice* through the office of local counsel, Dash Mellman. I am representing Major Kenneth Upham, recently retired from the New Haven, Connecticut Police Department and now a resident of High Pines, Vermont. He is the defendant in this case. I requested this hearing on my Motion to Dismiss this case." I gestured toward Ken who was standing at our defense table.

"My file indicates that you're from Florida. And we have the defendant from Connecticut. Mr. Berger, where are you from?" The judge frowned as he glanced at the file.

"I'm from Rutland, Your Honor. At least, that's in Vermont." Berger feigned a small laugh. "My client is unavailable this morning and I am waiving his appearance. He has brought this case against Mr. Upham due to Upham's brazen mutilation of the landscape. This has violated my client's right to the peaceful enjoyment of his private property. Mr. Upham has also violated a law against tree removal without government permission which could result in criminal charges. I am requesting a jury trial."

"Well, Judge, I had no idea that Vermont had a criminal code for tree murder," I said.

"Sarcasm will not get you very far in this court, Ms. Katz. Do you wish to present some evidence in defense of your motion?"

"Yes, your honor if I may have just a moment to see if our witness has arrived."

"Witness? She's calling a witness?" The side judge rose half out of his chair.

"Go ahead and check, counsel. Calvin, she's entitled to call a witness," Judge McCreary said.

I hurried over to Ken who nodded his head. "Arthur Woodhouse is here. I just saw him stick his head in the door"

I hurried into the hallway and saw a man who had an outdoorsy look. He was wearing jeans and a corduroy jacket. His face was bronzed and lined from years in the sun. He was carrying some rolled up papers.

After less than two minutes of briefing Mr. Woodhouse, whose name couldn't have been more appropriate, and a quick glance at the survey and pictures of Ken's property, we headed into the courtroom. "Sorry to put you on the stand with so little preparation," I said.

"It's okay. I've been doing work with trees and gardens for thirty years. I guess I can answer a few questions," Arthur said.

The clerk stood as we entered the courtroom. She swore Woodhouse in and pointed to the witness chair.

"Morning, Judge. Morning Calvin," Arthur said.

"Good to see you, Arthur," Judge McCreary said.

I relaxed a little. They all knew each other. That ought to help.

"State your name and occupation for the record please," I began.

"I'm Arthur Woodhouse. I'm an arborist. My company, Woodhouse Landscapes, advises homes and businesses on beautifying their properties. I design gardens and other outdoor amenities. I also care for trees seeing that they are preserved where possible or removed if necessary."

"Now do you know Ken Upham?"

"Sure do. He's sitting right over there at that table."

"When did you meet him?"

"It was this past spring. He called me to come over and give him an estimate on fixing up his place."

"What did you see when you went over to Mr. Upham's property?"

"Well, it was a good looking new house, and the setting was nice with the hills and all, but the front had no plantings and the back was a real mess."

"Can you describe what you mean when you say it was a mess?"

"There were some scrub trees, mostly white pines. They're like weeds. They just grow wherever over the years. There were no flower beds which the Mrs. wanted. There wasn't any grass, just a lot of underbrush, and the builder had left a pile of building scraps."

"Sounds pretty ugly."

"Objection, Judge." Berger was on his feet. "We're not interested in Ms. Katz's opinions. She's not the witness."

"He's right, Ms. Katz., sustained. Ask a question. Don't give your opinion."

"I don't need to. Your honor can see for himself. Mr. Woodhouse, have you brought some pictures with you today?"

"Sure have. Ken said you asked me to, right?" Arthur began to unroll his sheaf of papers.

"Did you take these photos?'

"Yup, first time I went out to the house. It helps me work on a landscape plan."

"Will the clerk please mark these as defendant's exhibits?'

The clerk hunted for her ink pad and labels. "Can I mark them later, Judge? I didn't know we were having witnesses and exhibits and all."

"Okay, Lucinda. Let me have a look. We'll just call them defense one through four." Judge McCreary handed the photos back to me.

I walked over to Berger and spread the photos out on his table.

"Any objection, Mr. Berger?" I asked.

"No, I'm glad the pictures are here. They show what a nice cover there was for my client's privacy," Berger said.

"Mr. Woodhouse, will you explain to the court when and where you took each of these pictures."

"Sure. This first one shows the condition of the backyard such as it was when I first saw it last spring. You can see the jungle of weeds and underbrush covering a good quarter of the yard. Over here, in this photo, you see this stand of white pines. As you can see one of them is partially dead, and the others are choking this pretty maple tree. This is what happens when trees are allowed to grow without any plan. In order to keep the good trees healthy, it's necessary to take out the weeds and worthless trees. That's just healthy foresting."

"What is in this third photo and when was it taken?"

"This is after the clearance of the undesirable growth, and just after I put in the garden beds and the low fence and trellis. I built up the soil with nutrients, fertilizer from my own mixture, and topped the beds with mulch. You can see some of the new plants and the two new trees on the corners."

"When was this taken?"

"Early June. This last photo shows the whole back yard as it looked a month ago. You can see the perennial flowering plants, and the blossoms on the pear tree."

"What is behind the fence on Mr. Upham's property?"

"Looking at this last photo, you can see the back of Mr. Behr's property. You can see a little bit of the condition of that property. Frankly, Judge, it's a mess."

"Objection," shouted Mr. Berger. His answer goes beyond the scope of the question."

"He's allowed to explain his answer," I countered.

"Okay, folks. Let's move along here. Any more questions, Ms. Katz?" The judge was clearly becoming bored.

"No, Judge, thank you. Your witness, Mr. Berger," I said.

Berger got to his feet slowly and shuffled over to Woodhouse.

"Mr. Woodhouse, what's that other rolled up paper you've got there?" Berger asked.

"That's the survey of Upham's land. I always get a survey before I start to work, so that I am sure not to go onto anyone else's property," Woodhouse unrolled the survey and laid it out in front of him.

Berger walked to the side of the witness chair and looked at the survey.

"This line here, is that on Upham's property?"

"No, that's the easement between the two properties."

"Well, when I look at the photos after you clear cut, it looks to me like you cut all the vegetation in the easement?

"I didn't clear cut anything. That term implies that I took out a whole forest of trees. Yes, I cut the weeds in the easement. It looked like it hadn't been cleaned up for years. There was a nest of rats back there. I called the county and asked if they intended to clean out the easement. They said they didn't do work like that, couldn't afford to, so if I wanted to I could go right ahead."

"Now, Mr. Woodhouse, did you go over to Mr. Behr's house and ask him if he minded if you cut out the trees and plants behind him?"

"No, I didn't have to. None of this was on his property."

"Even so, wouldn't it have been the neighborly thing to do?"

"I was hired by Mr. Upham to fix up his place. He's the only one whose permission I needed."

"Sir, are you aware that there is a state statute that mandates there be no cutting down of trees without government permission?"

Listen, maybe that's how they proceed over there in Rutland where you come from, but I've been in business here for twenty-five years and I've never heard of such a statute. No one's ever complained about my work. I received an award from the High Pines Select Board for beautifying the village. I donate my time to planting and caring for the flower beds in front of the covered bridge."

"You needn't lose your temper, Mr. Woodhouse," Berger said. He smiled at the judge. "That's all my questions."

I could see the judge was squirming in his seat.

"Your Honor, I won't call my client. I'll just take a couple of minutes for a summary of my motion," I said.

"Thank you, Ms. Katz." Relief was evident in the judge's words.

"It's clear that Mr. Upham beautified his property. If Mr. Behr is worried about his privacy, no one is stopping him from planting whatever he wants on his own property. It's not up to a neighbor to provide cover for someone else's property. As long as Mr. Upham has not placed an eyesore or a danger on his property, Mr. Behr has no reason to complain, let alone to sue my client. Mr. Behr has failed to state a cause of action and his complaint should be dismissed."

I took my seat and immediately saw that Calvin Crumb, the side judge was whispering to the judge. Minutes passed while the judge listened to Calvin's lengthy and heated discussion.

Finally the judge leaned back in his chair. "My assistant judge has raised some points and I've given him permission to respond to your summation, counsel."

I glanced over at Ken who was frowning.

Calvin smiled at Berger as he began to speak. He looked like he had just won an important battle. "Mr. Berger raised the state statute in his complaint, so I did some research. There is a statute that is still viable today, since it has never been removed by any legislative body, and it says that in order to remove a tree, there must be written permission sought and written permission given by the state government. It was passed in 1817 and still stands today. Mr. Woodhouse or Mr. Upham, did either of you get that permission?"

Woodhouse stood up and glared at Crumb. "I'm a native here, too, Calvin. That law had to do with what went on back then. Farmers stripped all the trees out of this state. That's why the law was passed. But look around you. The whole state is filled with forests. The timber industry is alive and well."

I saw that the arborist was losing his temper. His face was the color of the apples in the farmers market. I stood up and signaled him to sit down.

"Judge, there are thousands of old laws on the books in every state, but common practice allows them to die if never used. If a law has been dormant for vast periods of time, it is considered discriminatory to use it against just one person decades later."

"Well, maybe where you come from, lady, but here in Vermont we value our history. Now I'll give you an example. The Ancient Roads Act. It was found in 2006 that there were maps of ancient roads all over the state, roads that weren't in use anymore, but they still existed on old maps. Municipalities were given a body of time to look into these roads and file certificates reviving these roads, even if it meant that they ran right through someone's house or barn, or corn field. In fact the towns were asked to include all class four roads and trails in their certified maps. It just shows laws don't die unless they are removed with proper procedure." Calvin finished with a flourish.

"Judge that defies common sense. But even if someone wants to run a road through the middle of someone's living room, that doesn't prove that the tree statute can be called out of its grave," I said.

"Well, I was about ready to rule in this matter, but I think I'll need some time to research this matter, so I'll take it under advisement for a while. You'll be notified when I issue my order." Judge McCreary walked swiftly to the side door. Calvin Crumb strode beside him still talking.

"The town of Barnard added fifty miles of ancient roads this year." We heard Calvin saying as the two left the courtroom.

CHAPTER
# FORTY-FIVE

Ken and I were silent as we began the drive back to High Pines. He looked angry and I felt crushed. I couldn't believe that such a simple case was turning into a crusade for trees. The silence was so thick that it felt like we were enveloped in fog even though the sun was slanting off the windshield.

"Ken, I am so sorry this didn't go as I had anticipated, but we're not through yet. Common sense is still on our side. Perhaps you would have been better off if Dash had continued to handle your case. You were hampered by being represented by someone 'from away' as they say here."

"I'm not upset with you, Mary. This side judge, Crumb, is a crumb or worse. He's the problem. I think the judge was ready to rule in my favor when he butted in. There's something very funny about Roland Behr and his super privacy paranoia. The cop in me tells me there's a lot more to this."

"Maybe Roland and his lawyer and the side judge are just some old coots who don't have anything else to think about."

"Maybe, but I think there's more to this. What's our next move?"

"We need to wait for the judge's ruling. When he has time to think about this, he still may rule in our favor. If not, we can begin the discovery process; take depositions, round up other witnesses who have removed trees and never had anyone bring up this ancient statute; maybe find some state officials who can testify to the disuse of the statute and the amount of bureaucracy that would be necessary to process each and every request, statewide. I'll go to see Dash this afternoon and give him a report on all of this."

We reached Ken's house in record time, mainly because my lead foot pushed the speedometer into the stratosphere. Funny how anger and speed seem to go together. In spite of this being high leaf peeper season, we passed no tour buses and traffic was not only minimal it was nonexistent.

"Come on in, Mary. I want to try to get my Washington connection and find out if there's any information on the location of Sherry's cell phone. There weren't any messages on my cell phone when we left the courthouse, but that doesn't mean I didn't get any calls. You know the routine by now. Cell phones work when they feel like it."

As we walked down the long path to the house, Rita opened the door and waved us in.

"Ken, you're just in time. Randy Patterson is on the phone. I just answered. He's been trying to get through to you," Rita called to us.

Ken motioned to me to follow him into his den. He shut the door. "I'll put him on speaker so you can hear. Randy, thanks for getting back to me. I have Mary Katz with me. She's the attorney I mentioned to you. The mother of the girl who we're trying to find is Mary's client."

"Okay, Ken, but please don't get my name around as the go- to guy for tracing cell phones. You understand?" Randy sounded annoyed.

"Of course, I won't give your name to anyone, and I really appreciate any help you can give us," I said.

"So what can you tell us?" Ken interrupted me and held up his hand to keep me quiet, usually not an easy task. After all I am a lawyer.

"I was able to track the cell phone to a tower in Ascutney, Vermont, on the day that you phoned me shortly after I started my work on this. There aren't too many towers in the area and my technical people tell me this one covers a pretty wide area. I'm going to send you a map of the area on your e-mail in a few minutes, but here's the interesting thing. After you called again with the phone number of that pay phone, and the time of the call, I found that the call was made from that same cell phone number."

"What do you mean?" Fred asked. "What same cell phone number?"

"The smart phone that I was tracking. Whoever called the pay phone was using that same cell phone. We tracked it later that evening and it was again at that Ascutney location. It looks like your bad guys are using the girl's phone."

"Randy, thanks. I owe you a big one," Ken said as he clicked off.

"Let's go look for the e-mail map," I said.

We moved over to Ken's computer desk. "You know, Mary, that's not such a stupid move, the kidnappers using their victim's phone. It keeps us from identifying them by any phone traced back to them."

The bell chimed telling us a new e-mail had arrived. Ken opened it and we saw a map of an area stretching from High Pines through a number of villages south and west. Ascutney Mountain had a large star, pointing to the area of the cell tower.

"How far is that from here?" I asked.

"About forty miles," Ken said.

"No wonder our cell service is spotty. This is a huge area." I examined the map.

"Look, remember those two guys at Skunk Hollow told me that Paul's farm was somewhere between Woodstock and Bridgewater. Here are those two villages." I pointed them out. "And here is the tower. It looks like we can draw a triangular area. Doesn't this mean that Sherry must be somewhere in this area?"

Ken hit the print icon and in a second the map came rolling out of the printer. He pulled out a ruler and drew lines around the area. "It's still a big area with lots of back roads and steep hills. Rita and I have skied that area," Fred said. "We're going to need more resources fast if we're going to search for Sherry."

"I need to go over to Dash's office this afternoon. I confided in him about the kidnapping. He knows so many people. I thought maybe he could help us. Time is not on our side. Do you think that I shouldn't have talked about the kidnapping with him?"

Ken was quiet for a minute. I could see his investigator brain weighing our options. When he finally spoke, it was with the authority he must have used when he was directing his detectives.

"Dash seems like a good guy to me. He's well respected and he does know everyone in the valley. We won't tell Lillian that you spoke to Dash."

"I'm glad to hear what you think of Dash. I guess I'm skeptical of every new person; my lawyer's psyche, you know. I feel better hearing your opinion. I'll share what else we've learned in strictest confidence."

"And I'll head over to the inn and show Lillian and Brett the map and what we've found out."

"Please, call Lillian right now. She likes to charge ahead. I'm afraid that once she has all the money in hand, she may do something rash. She should have received another call by now."

I headed for the front door and Ken headed to the phone. What a morning this had been. I realized that it was now afternoon. I was hungry and exhausted. This was not very different from my life in Miami except that there was no Carlos to look forward to, no passionate night ahead.

Every day and especially every night I missed him more.

If I was honest with myself, I also missed his tribe of relatives. There was always a cousin who knew how to fix whatever needed fixing. I sure could use some fixers to get Sherry back.

# FORTY-SIX

I decided to make a quick stop back at the house to shed my courtroom garb, change to jeans, and walk Sam who raced in circles around the hilly backyard. I realized I hadn't checked my e-mails lately. I hadn't been keeping up with Catherine and Joe's day to day messages about clients in Miami. Sometimes I didn't answer until late evening and days after receiving them.

Catherine's latest message was a basket of worries. The clients were getting disgusted with my absence. Some of them wanted to switch to Joe permanently. Was I going to let all my hard work building the office disappear because of my own personal problems? When would I stop being so selfish and get back to Miami and back to work, and by the way, everyone sympathized with Carlos including my mother and even Lucy.

I couldn't possibly answer all of that rant in an e-mail, so I picked up the phone. Catherine answered on the second ring, meaning the office indeed was not busy.

"Catherine, it's me, the long lost Miami attorney."

"Oh, really. I thought by now you'd be printing cards saying you are a Vermont attorney."

"I'm sorry I've neglected you. I've gotten myself super involved here. I told you about the tree case. Well, it's not going well, so I can't leave right now."

"The tree case? You mean the neighborhood mish-mash over someone's trees? You can't resolve that? The great Mary Katz who wins murder cases, and federal terrorism cases? Come on, Mary. You just don't want to be here anymore."

"That's not true. You don't understand how crazy this place is over trees. Anyway, Dash, the lawyer I'm doing the work for –I can't just leave him in the lurch."

"I take it this Dash guy is young and cute."

"Sort of. There's another problem. But I must swear you to total secrecy. I mean it."

"Since when have I ever divulged any private matter, client or personal?"

"You're right. Lillian Yarmouth is here. Sherry's been kidnapped and the bad guys want a lot of money. I am totally freaked out that we'll ever get her back. Lillian won't let anyone call the FBI. I'm helping all I can, so you can see I'm not just sitting up here feeling sorry for myself. I can't leave Brett and Lillian now."

"I thought you said you had lunch with Sherry and she had a new boy-friend. That was in your e-mail a few days ago."

"Yeah, I did and she did. That's who kidnapped her. At least he's one of the people. God knows how many are involved."

"I can't believe it. The Yarmouths walk around with a black cloud hanging over them. Okay, I'm not so mad at you, but I hope you can get out of there soon. I miss you, your parents and brothers miss you, and I think Carlos has given up on you. He's stopped calling here every other minute. Marco says he's resigning himself to moving on. He's very disappointed that you wouldn't even give him a chance to explain anything to you."

"Catherine, this is also very confidential. I miss Carlos a lot, but I just can't think about him now. I've got to concentrate on Sherry and, of course, my tree case. Don't abandon me."

"Never, Mary. Just come home soon."

I sat down in the kitchen. Sam put his head in my lap. I was homesick or lovesick. Either way I felt so down. I kept seeing Carlos and Margarita in that cozy booth at the restaurant. I felt tears running down my cheeks and a lump forming in my throat. Sam nuzzled against me, and then he went over and picked up his food dish in his mouth and deposited it at my feet.

"Sam, you're right. We're probably both hungry. I filled his dish even though it wasn't time for his dinner. While he ate, I checked the fridge, but there wasn't much that looked appetizing. As soon as Sam finished which is only a matter of seconds, I packed him in the Explorer and took off for the general store. A mood this bad called for one of Hal's super sandwiches.

The store was quiet. There were few cars parked outside, so I took Sam in with me. Hal was nowhere in sight so I rang the little bell on the counter. He came from a back room, wiping his hands on his apron. I had to laugh as I looked at his tall imposing figure. He was never without his Boston Red Sox cap. I wondered if he slept in it.

"Well, you're in a jolly mood. Does that mean your hearing went well over at Barre this morning?" Hal asked.

"Just the contrary. Things were looking good until the side judge, Crumb, decided to give me a history lesson about an ancient tree statute which he compared to the ancient road controversy."

"Ah, yes, Mr. Crumb. What a character. I suppose you know about his adventure with a large pine tree on the River Road last year," Hal smiled.

"I have no idea what you're referring to." I shook my head.

"Well, it seems Crumb was coming home from somewhere around midnight in his old Cadillac. It was a dry night, no snow, no rain, when he slammed his car into a huge old pine tree. Half of it broke off and took out the electric wires causing a power outage to at least 100 homes. They were without power for a day or so. When the sheriff came out to see what was wrong, he found Crumb passed out behind the wheel. Lucky for him, he was in that heavy tank of a car."

"Did he get charged with DUI?"

"Sure. They took him to the hospital and checked his blood alcohol level which was about as high as Mt. Ascutney. He also had a broken arm."

"So what happened? Did he go to court? Don't leave me in suspense."

"He went to court but amazingly, the sheriff didn't show. Seems he was away in a training program, and Crumb argued that he was pre-diabetic, whatever that is, and the blood test was wrong. The judge found him not guilty. Of course, the next time he ran for his position, his challenger brought the whole thing up, but a lot of folks around here do some fancy drinking themselves so they voted him in again."

"I appreciate the entertainment, Hal. I'm feeling a little off balance today. How about fixing a couple of your super special turkey sandwiches to go?"

"You must be pretty hungry."

"I thought I'd bring one over to Dash. I have to stop in the office."

Hal started carving bread and turkey. "You and Dash are getting pretty friendly, so Daisy tells me."

"Don't start match-making, Hal. We're just lawyer buddies."

Sam tugged at his leash, trying to get to the cheese display. Hal looked up and threw him a piece of the savory turkey. That kept him happy for ten seconds.

While Hal finished the sandwiches, I thought about the rumors that must be circulating that Dash and I were a new romance. Maybe if there had never been Carlos in my life, I would appreciate Dash more, but if there had been no Carlos, I never would be here in High Pines. I never would have met Dash. How much in our lives is destiny and how much is nothing more than accidental happenings.

# FORTY-SEVEN

I moved the car up the road and parked in the drive in front of the barn at Dash's office. Daisy's car was usually parked there. My first piece of good luck of the day was that Daisy's car was nowhere in sight. I wouldn't have to field her twenty questions like: didn't I love working with Dash and wasn't it great being in the beautiful Upper Valley, just the right place to settle and raise kids.

Dash was seated at Daisy's reception desk, looking through a file drawer. He looked up and grinned as I came in.

"Mary, come on in. I just got off the phone with Ken."

"Well, then you know how the hearing went. But I have brought a peace offering for how I bungled things." I held out the bag with the sandwiches.

"You didn't bungle anything. From Ken's description, I think Crumb just wanted to yank your chain and show you that native status triumphs over good lawyering from out of town. There'll be other hearings. This case will be around awhile."

We took the sandwiches into the library and unpacked them on the round table. Dash poured two cups of coffee from the pot in his office and returned with the coffee and two slices of some kind of pie.

"George Cohen's wife baked me a pie. I took care of a little matter for them last week. It only required a couple of phone calls, so I didn't want to charge him. He dropped off this rhubarb pie this morning."

We were quiet while we wolfed down the late lunch,

"Did you say George Cohen?" I asked after sitting back comfortably full.

"Yes, do you know him?"

"No, but the name Cohen surprised me. I didn't think there were any Jewish people in this village. I thought Jewish people usually live where there is a synagogue with a congregation."

"Sure there are. What kind of name do you think Mellman is?" Dash asked.

"I didn't give it much thought," I said.

"You think Miami is the only place with mixed marriages? My family is a conglomerate, too. Dad was Jewish. Mother wasn't when they married but she converted. We even have a synagogue not far from here. Want to see it sometime?"

I tried not to look surprised. I had a mental picture of Daisy with her beehive hairdo draped in a prayer shawl. "Sure I'd like to see it. Are there a lot of members?"

"Quite a few. Lots of kids in Sunday School and older folks who retired in the area, and other mixed couples. We even have a holocaust survivor, Franz Goldstein. He's eighty or more now. He taught us a lot about Germany and how Hitler came to power. His point was that if you do nothing and ignore threats to democracy, a despot can take power. Franz lost his whole family. He was only sixteen when he got to the U.S.

"I'd love to meet him and talk to him .while I'm here."

"He's not too rational these days. His grandchildren live up here and look out for him."

"This is an amazing area. Every day I learn something new about life here; like I learned today when I got my head banged in court."

"Mary, I don't want to pry. Is there any news about Sherry that you feel you can discuss with me? Can I be of some help? Don't think I'm prying into your business,"

I looked at Dash who looked so open and actually appealing. I must have been super paranoid to think that he was hanging out in the murder house and was involved. He had been nothing but nice to me. What is it with me, I thought. Can't I take anyone at face value?

"That's okay," Dash said. "I understand if you don't feel comfortable confiding in me. Just know that I'm here to help if you want help."

"I do want to talk about this with you," I said. "Lillian has a million dollars ready to turn over to the kidnappers, but I'm so scared that they'll kill Sherry anyway. After all, she can identify Paul Conrad. She's been having sex with him."

"That's why you need professional law enforcement working with you, regardless of the threats of the kidnappers."

"We have a professional, Ken Upham. He's been wonderful. He even had some 'techie' that he knows trace her route through her cell phone. So now we know that she's within a certain area. The only problem is the area is huge and mountainous."

"Now I understand why you wanted to find out if Paul still owned the Conrads' land. I didn't know how important that information was. I'll go to the courthouse in Woodstock first thing in the morning and research the records. No wonder you've been so nervous. Where is Lillian now?"

"At the Hanover Inn, I guess. I believe Ken was going to go up there this evening. Ken is posing as Lillian's driver. There's already been one meeting at a gas station where she received a call from the bad guys. Ken won't let Lillian give over any money until she hears Sherry's voice on the phone. So far they've sent a photo to Lillian's phone showing Sherry tied to a chair. This is so bizarre. I feel like I'm part of a bad movie."

"Let's call Ken's cell. If he's up at the inn, I'll go up there with you."

"Oh, Dash, I can't expect you to drop everything and –"

"Don't give it a thought. I'm happy to lend another brain to help resolve this awful event. I can't believe something like this has happened in the Upper Valley. I can't believe Pauly would be involved in something like this. He's never been the brightest kid, but when Francie took him in, everyone thought he'd be okay."

"Good God, I came up here for R and R, and now I'll need to get back to Miami for some peace. Car theft defendants are looking better and better."

Ken didn't answer his cell phone, so I tried Brett. No answer there and also no answer from Lillian. Now I was consumed with worry.

"None of them are answering. I'm going to walk Sam and then go up to Hanover and see if they're at the inn," I told Dash.

"Just let me lock up here and I'll ride up there with you." Dash began turning off the lights and forwarding his office phone to his cell phone.

I made record time to Hanover, driving eighty all the way. But when we pulled off the freeway, there was bumper to bumper traffic up the hill into the town.

"What's this about? I've never seen traffic like this up here," I slammed my hand on the steering wheel.

"Better take it down a notch or two, Mary. Impatience is not much tolerated here. I think this might be the start of parents' weekend at Dartmouth. They have four days of activities. I guess the college needs to give the parents some reason to be paying all that tuition."

"The weekend is days away. Where can I park? I can't leave Sam in a parking garage."

Pull around the corner and park near the library. It will be closing soon for the evening. We'll take Sam in with us."

"Will they let him in the hotel?"

"Leave that to me," Dash said.

We walked through the throngs of students and parents. The parents were wearing name tags and were headed for the Hopkins Center next door to the inn. We entered the lobby where more parents were milling about. We headed directly to the elevator, and were about to enter when a man in a suit pulled on my arm. I whirled around.

"Hotel security, ma'am. Sorry, you can't bring that dog in here."

Dash squeezed my other arm. "It's okay Graham. This is Ms. Katz's therapy dog. She has to have him with her at all times. She has a little-uh-problem. He pointed to his own head."

"Oh, sorry, Dash, I didn't see who was with her. Too busy looking at the dog." The security guy stepped away and we boarded the elevator.

"Thanks a lot, Dash. Now everyone in the Upper Valley will be buzzing about the nut case from Miami," I said.

"We got the dog in, didn't we?"

The elevator stopped and we raced down the hall and knocked on Lillian's door. Brett looked through the small opening with the chain lock in place. I waved and he opened the door.

"Come in quick. Did anyone see you?"

"Not on this floor. What's happening?" Why didn't you or Lillian or Ken answer the phone?" I asked.

"Ken was here for a while, but he left to go home. I don't know why he didn't answer. Mother and I are staying off the cell phones waiting for a call from the people holding Sherry," Brett explained. "Caller ID showed your name."

Lillian came out of the bathroom. Her eyes were red and she looked as if her age had finally caught up with her. Dark circles outlined her hazel eyes and fine lines creased her cheeks and chin.

"Who is this?" she looked at Dash as if he were a home invader. "You better not have brought the FBI here."

"This is Dash Mellman, the attorney I've been working with. He knows everyone in the valley and he's here to help. He knew Paul Conrad as a kid and his family." I gave Lillian a hug, and she held on to me as if she were drowning. She didn't let go of me and whispered in my ear.

"It's my punishment, isn't it, for being a bad person."

"Lillian, don't be silly." I whispered back. I led her over to the bed and almost pushed her into a sitting position. "Why don't you put your feet up for a few minutes? Can you tell us what news you have?"

"I'll tell you," Brett said. "Mother, you try to rest. Dash, I hope Mary has explained to you how sensitive this is,"

"Of course, I only want to help you get your sister back, Brett. If you aren't comfortable, I will leave," Dash said.

"No, it's okay. We need all the help we can get. We got a call at noon from the same woman, asking if we had the money. Mother has the rest of the money, but she stalled them, like Ken told us to do. She said she was still waiting for Federal Express, and that she would need to talk to Sherry before she'd give them the money."

"Did they let her talk?" I asked.

No, they said they'd think about it and hung up. Ken got here shortly after that and told us everything about the cell phone trace and we looked at the map of the area where Sherry might be. He wanted us to get the FBI involved to begin a search of the area. I don't know how we can do it alone."

"No police!" Lillian shouted.

"I may be able to narrow the area more," Dash said. "I will look at the property deeds at the courthouse. Paul's family owned land in that quadrant. If he still owns it that may be where they're hiding her. It's all dirt roads up there. It's pretty secluded."

"While Ken was still here another call came. The same woman said that they might let mother speak to Sherry tonight, and that they'd give her directions for dropping the money. Then the phone went dead," Brett said.

"Ken put a trace on the phone as soon as it rang. About a half hour later, his contact called and said the call was made from Sherry's cell phone again. Of course, we knew that much from the caller ID. Ken thought the battery probably went dead and that's why it cut off, or maybe they were out of range of the tower again. But the call came through that tower at Ascutney Mountain again, too."

"These have to be the dumbest criminals. They probably don't have the charger for the phone or they don't know how to charge it." I said.

"We've been here waiting for another call. If it comes, I need to get Ken on the phone to trace the call again," Brett said.

"Ken didn't answer when I tried to get him. I'll try again," I said. "Brett, you need to order some dinner for your mother."

"I can't eat, please, Mary, don't even suggest it." Lillian had her phone in her hand and stared at it constantly.

I dialed Ken's cell but still got no answer. The little room was claustrophobic with four adults and one large dog. Sam was lying on the floor next to Lillian and the bed. Every few minutes he eyed the bed. I prayed that he wouldn't decide to leap up there next to Lillian. She would have a heart attack for sure if he did.

Brett turned on the television and we sat in silence watching the evening news. It was followed by a Hollywood gossip show. Brett switched to a baseball playoff game. I had forgotten that it was almost World Series time. Dash and Brett talked Red Sox baseball for a while reliving the past season. Lillian stared into space and I pulled Sam over and petted him to keep him from any sudden leaps.

It was after seven-thirty when Lillian's phone rang. Brett jumped to his cell and dialed Ken to try to pick up the trace again.

Lillian answered after four rings. Brett shook his head. Ken still wasn't answering.

"Put it on speaker." Dash whispered.

"This is Lillian"

"I know who you are," a husky woman's voice said. "Do you have this on a speaker phone? Who's there with you?"

"Just my son, Sherry's brother.. He wants to hear you, too, please."

"I'm gonna let you talk to your daughter for about ten seconds. This is the one and only time, so listen. Then we'll talk about that money."

There was a long pause. Then we heard Sherry. "Don't push me." She spoke as if she was in a stupor.

"Sherry, darling," Lillian let out a small sob. "Are you all right?"

"Mommy, do what they ask. Just get me out of here. I'm sorry to cause you so much trouble. I was so stupid."

"That's enough. Shut up." The woman's voice came on again.

"If you hurt her, I'll find you," Lillian screamed.

"Listen, bitch, I want that money. At nine o'clock tomorrow morning, be back at the Shell station. Wait by the phone. Bring the money. I'll tell you where and when. No more stalling." The phone went dead.

"I couldn't get Ken," Brett said.

"Lillian, I know for sure who that is," Dash said. That's Francie Wallace. She was Carolyn Brousseau's housekeeper. I must have spoken to her a thousand times, and she's the person who was the foster mother of Paul Conrad."

"Who is Carolyn Brousseau?" Lillian asked.

I frowned at Dash, hoping he wouldn't mention that Carolyn was quite dead. "The Brousseaus are clients of Dash. Maybe Dash knows where this Francie lives. That might be another area to look for Sherry," I said.

"I think she lived off of Route Four on the way to White River Junction, but the calls are all coming from an area west of there. I can make some calls and find out if she moved," Dash said.

"Lillian, do you think there's anything else we can do this evening?" I asked. Lillian gazed at the floor. She appeared not to hear. Sherry's strained voice took the last bit of resilience out of her.

"We need to reach Ken and plan for tomorrow morning," Brett said.

"The courthouse opens at eight, and I'll be there to get an exact location of the Conrad place and see if it's still owned by Paul," Dash said.

"I'll go with you. Maybe we can drive out there immediately and Lillian you can go to the Shell station and get the phone call. If she's on that farm, hopefully we can find her while these jerks are meeting you to get the money," I said.

"Mary, you can't go barging into a place out in the boondocks without any protection," Brett said.

"Well, what are our options? Lillian won't let me call any law enforcement. Besides, Dash will be with me."

"I will?" Dash asked.

"Let's all keep trying to get Ken." I gathered Sam's leash and headed for the door.

The lobby had cleared out by the time we left the elevator. We walked back toward my car through streets that were quieter now.

"Dash, I'm sorry to involve you like this. I didn't want you to tell Lillian about Carolyn Brousseau's murder. That's the last thing she needed to hear."

"I got your thought wave on that. Are you honestly suggesting that you and I storm the Conrad farm in the morning?"

"Yes, but not alone. I think we need to get your friend, Sheriff Parsons, involved. We're going to need trained law enforcement. If we can get to Sherry early enough, we may save her life. Once they have the money, they'll surely kill her, if they haven't done it already. At least we know she was alive a little while ago."

"Thank God you want me to call Jimmy Parsons."

We reached the car. I looked up and saw a huge orange moon and smelled the chilly fall air heavy with the odor of fallen leaves and wood smoke.

"It's a beautiful night," I said as I looked up at the light of the strange moon."

"That's what we call a harvest moon," Dash said.

He put his arm around me, and I didn't move away until he finally opened my car door. "Let's go back to the office and start making some phone calls," he said.

# FORTY-NINE

Dash unlocked the office and went immediately to his desk where he started looking through files.

"Here's what I want to do," he said. "I'm going to call the clerk of the court and get him to come over and let me in to look at the property reports tonight. I'm also going to call Jimmy Parsons to meet me over there. You better come with me to brief him on this whole kidnapping. He'll need to get some deputies lined up for the morning."

"Dash, this is great. This means we can be organized to look for Sherry as soon as it's light out in the morning. I can't thank you enough."

"Don't thank me yet. Right now, it's just a plan, not a success story." He picked up the phone and began the first call.

Thirty minutes later we were on our way over to Woodstock to meet the court clerk and the sheriff.

"Do you mind if I stop at the house and get Sam settled in? He's been dragged along enough."

"It's on the way. It's no problem, but don't you want him around for protection?"

"Protection? From what?"

"From me. You always seem to have him by your side whenever we're together," Dash said.

"That's not true," I said. "Sam is actually my best friend, so of course, he hangs out with me."

I thought about Dash's statement for a minute. Maybe subconsciously I had been keeping Sam on a short leash when Dash was around. But now that Dash had jumped in to help me find Sherry, I felt ridiculous being skeptical about him. This lawyer paranoia of mine was getting out of control.

I walked Sam and settled him in his crate. In a few minutes we pulled up in front of the courthouse in Woodstock. This one was an historic look-ing building of dark red brick. It looked like something in a scary movie. Not charming, just forbidding. We sat down on the bench in front of the building waiting for Dash's friends.

The sheriff and the clerk pulled up at the same time, coming from opposite directions. We all entered the building that smelled of musty papers and dusty books. While Dash researched the property files, I fol-lowed Sheriff Parsons into the library. He turned on a few lights and we settled at a long table where I told him as completely as possible every detail of Sherry's kidnapping starting with her affair with Paul and ending with the phone call to Lillian tonight.

Jimmy Parsons was a large, solidly built guy. He was quiet as I spoke. He seemed almost shy from the minute Dash introduced us. When I fin-ished my description of the events, he stared at me for a minute. Then he stood up and walked around the table before sitting down and staring at me again.

"All this has been going on and just now you decide to call me in on it? This county is my jurisdiction. Maybe you could have gotten this girl back sooner and alive if you'd left this in the hands of the police."

"I wanted to but Sherry's mother was adamant. She still doesn't know that I'm meeting you now. Will you help us as soon as it's light enough to go out to wherever Dash finds out this property is located?."

"If you'd called me earlier, I'd have saved you a lot of time. I know where the Conrad place is. Francie Wallace moved out there in June. She couldn't hold on to her house anymore. The taxes hadn't been paid in a few years. Her husband hanged himself after the mill closed and he couldn't get any work. Francie's been taking care of Pauly for quite a few years. It's just hard for me to believe that she would do something like this; kidnap someone for money"

"Let's go tell Dash to stop looking through the property records. You can lead us to the Conrad place in the morning. Can you get some deputies to go with us?"

"I only have two that I can get for sure, but we have volunteers when someone is lost on a hike. I'll get people lined up, but I sure wish you'd called me early on. I don't know why people don't trust me to do my job. Maybe I won't run for this job again."

Jimmy left me in the library. He called to Dash as he left the room, turning out the lights as he went. Something told me he didn't like me. I remembered the conversation at the mini mart about firing Parsons. He probably knew the talk around town. Now I had removed an opportunity for him to find Sherry and redeem himself in the eyes of the village.

Dash and Jimmy poured over the county map hanging in the clerk's office. They pinpointed the Conrad property and Dash wrote down the directions.

"I'll get some boys together tonight. Let's meet at six at the diner by the Gorge. I can give everyone directions there. We won't want to approach together. It'll be better if we can surround the property. We don't know how many people are involved or whether that is the place they have the girl."

We all shook hands and I thanked everyone for coming out.

"Dash got back in my SUV and put his head back against the head rest. I noticed how exhausted he looked.

"I'll get you right back to your place. I'm sorry for uprooting your whole schedule," I said.

"It's fine. I think we never stopped for any dinner. I'm starved. Come on in and I'll fix us something," Dash said

"I guess I am hungry. We haven't eaten since Hal's sandwiches and that seems like days ago," I said.

# FIFTY

I followed Dash up the stairway in the office reception area leading up to his second floor living area. The stairway had a landing with a high stained glass window. The moonlight filtered through the colored shapes making dancing shadows on the dark wood floor. Dash opened a leaded glass door at the top of the steps. We stepped into what I guessed was the living room.

Crown moldings lined the high ceiling. A fireplace was framed in marble. The mantle held small framed photos of outdoor scenes of the Vermont countryside. One photo showed Dash holding up a large fish of some kind. Hanging over the fireplace was the head of a moose complete with antlers.

The bachelor coldness of the room was broken by floor to ceiling book shelves on either side of the fireplace. One corner of the room held a round maple table and chairs which I guessed was a dining area.

"All of this furniture was made in Vermont," Dash said, sweeping his arm over the area. "Come on in the kitchen and I'll whip up one of my special omelets."

I followed him into a galley kitchen with oak floors and cabinets. In the center was a long counter with two bar stools. Dash began assembling bowls and plates and various ingredients from the refrigerator.

"Make yourself comfortable. This won't take long. How about some wine while you're waiting?" Dash moved easily around the kitchen, looking like an experienced cook.

"Something to drink would be great. I'm feeling awfully cold," I said. Actually I was a step away from teeth chattering and shivering from the brisk night air or from the fear of what might be happening to Sherry.

"It might not go with the omelet, but I think a shot of brandy might be better than wine," Dash said. He reached into a cabinet and brought out a bottle of cognac and two small glasses. He poured two shots and passed one over to me.

The amber liquid slid down smoothly and I felt a warm burn in my chest. Dash pulled my glass back and poured another shot.

In a matter of minutes, Dash expertly flipped the omelet. He filled two plates with the omelet filled with sharp Vermont cheddar cheese. Buttered cinnamon toast completed the impromptu entree.

Dash sat down next to me on the other bar stool, and we dug into the welcome late supper .We cleaned our plates like two starving refugees who hadn't seen food in weeks.

I got up to rinse my empty plate.

"Hey, you don't have to clean up," Dash said, as he moved over next to me.

He took the plate out of my hand and looked at me. I looked up at him and the next thing I knew he was kissing me. The warmth of his body felt good pressed against me; or maybe it was the warmth from the brandy. Either way, I was thawing out.

"Come with me," he said as he finally released me. He took my hand and led me back through the living room and down a short hall into the bedroom.

I glanced around for a minute. There was old-fashioned patterned wallpaper. A huge bed with a maple headboard took up most of the room. Wooden shutters at the window were open and there was a view of the town green.

My thoughts were jumbled from the cognac, the long day, and the lack of a regular sex life these last weeks. For some reason, I hadn't stopped taking my birth control pills during this whole trip. I guess they were a part of my routine, like taking a shower and brushing my teeth, so one of my jumbled thoughts was thank God I'm still on the pill.

Dash pulled me to him and kissed me again. Then he lifted me up and placed me on the bed. He pulled off his sweater and shirt and began removing my sweater. I looked at his thin runner's frame and hard muscles in his arms. He looked like someone who worked at outdoor physical jobs. My next thought contained a picture of Carlos and his sturdy large boned body; the picture of a gym rat. I felt a huge wave of sadness. I closed my eyes and put my arms around Dash.

A few minutes later when he rolled off of me and lay quietly next to me, his eyes closed his breathing heavy, I felt terrible. I also felt nothing except regret that I allowed this to happen. I longed for sex with Carlos and now I had rushed into sex with Dash who was a perfectly nice guy. A guy I liked as a friend, but not one that I wanted to have daily sex with. How could I have allowed myself to get to this point? I knew that Dash wouldn't look at this as just sex with a friend on a cold night. He was looking for a steady partner. Now I had probably lost his friendship. .

I lay very still until I realized that Dash was asleep. Carefully I retrieved my clothes and snuck out of the bedroom and down the hall to the living room. I was searching for my purse when I heard a noise behind me. Dash was standing in the doorway.

"Mary, where are you going? Are you all right?"

"Yes, I'm okay. I just need to get home."

"Are you upset? Please, you can stay here tonight. We have to be out early in the morning anyway."

"I really can't stay. Sam is home alone and I have to take him out."

"I feel like you're running away from me."

"Can we talk about this after we get through tomorrow?"

"Sure. Okay. Just drive carefully. It's late and dark out on the River Road. Wait, at least let me walk out to your car with you."

Dash followed me down the stairs. He unlocked the door to the office and we walked silently out to my car.

"Shall I come and pick you up in the morning? You probably don't know where the diner is where we're meeting," Dash said.

"No, I'll meet you there. Don't worry, I'll find it," I called as I started the car and quickly made my escape.

I glanced at the clock as I hurried into the kitchen to release Sam from his crate. It was eleven-thirty. I gave him one of his favorite liver treats and grabbed my flashlight to take him out.

We went out the front door and as I walked down the long driveway, I heard a car motor. Then I saw it; a black Subaru SUV with its lights off at the end of the driveway. I flashed the flashlight in its direction hoping to see the occupant. I could only make out one shape. The driver must have seen the light because the car took off quickly and turned left down the road toward Carolyn's house. Could it be Dash? He could have followed me home, but why would he take off like that, unless he is the person who is hiding out in the house where the cold blooded murder took place.

Sam yanked me back to the house, and I retreated willingly. I slammed the door and double locked it, even though everyone says the beauty of living in this rural Valhalla is never having to lock your door. Just the same, I felt better when I heard the locks click.

As exhausted as I was, sleep wouldn't come. My discomfort for having led Dash on, my fear of the black Subaru that turned up at night, and most of all my picture of Sherry being tortured and murdered kept me staring into the dark. I must have slept at some point because I woke with a start. The phone in the kitchen was ringing.

By the time I picked it up, all I got was a dial tone. I hung up and it rang again.

"Yes?" I said, showing my annoyance.

"Mary, it's Rita Upham, Ken's wife."

"Rita, we tried to get you and Ken last night but never got an answer. Is everything okay?"

"Not really. Ken spoke to Brett last night and heard about your plan. I knew you'd be up very early."

"What time is it?"

"It's five-thirty. Mary, Ken had a scare last night and I took him to the Dartmouth-Hitchcock emergency center. I thought he was having a stroke. His hand and arm were numb and his vision blurred. They ran some tests, mainly a cat-scan of his brain."

"Oh, my god, how is he now? I'm so sorry for getting him involved in this problem."

"They couldn't find anything and the symptoms subsided in a few hours so I brought him home. We'll have to wait for the results of the blood tests, but the hospital is part of the Dartmouth Medical School so I guess they know what they're doing."

"Just tell him we'll handle everything with Lillian and he should rest."

"He is insisting that he accompany Mrs. Yarmouth to her meeting as planned. I just wanted to alert you in case he becomes ill again."

"He shouldn't go. I can make some other arrangements."

"He won't be dissuaded. He gets so upset when I try to make him stay home, and now he's worried about you."

"No need to worry about me. Dash has friends to help and we're under control."

"I'll tell him, but he said to tell you to call him and he'll get to you if he's needed."

I realized that I only had a few minutes to get to the meeting place by six. How could I have overslept? I threw Sam's food out on the back steps while I donned jeans, boots and the ever-present leather jacket. I threw Sam back in his crate with the door open so he could roam the kitchen. "I'm sorry you good old dog for all the neglect I've been heaping on you. I'll make it up to you, I promise."

Sam wagged his tale and licked my hand as I flew by on my way out.

CHAPTER
# FIFTY-TWO

## Sherry's Nightmare

Sherry had lost count of the days. She was in the dark or blindfolded all of the time, so there was no way to tell day from night. She was moved from what she thought was a basement to another building. It smelled of hay or grass and manure so she guessed it was a barn.

Once when the old lady took her to an outhouse and removed her blindfold, she tried to see her watch, but it was no longer on her arm. This made tears well up in her eyes and trickle down her cheeks. The watch had been a gift from her father when she graduated from high school. It was a Rolex, water-proof and shock-proof so she wore it all the time. She guessed one of these people had taken it while she was in a stupor from the knockout meds they were feeding her.

The tears burned her cheeks. They must be chapped from the cold in the barn. She couldn't rub them away because her hands were tied all of the time. She was always cold now. She almost laughed, thinking how mother was always instructing her to moisturize her face twice a day and "for heaven's sake, Sherry, put on more sunscreen before you go out to the pool."

When she tried hard, she could picture the pool and the patio in Miami. She tried to remember the feel of the hot tropical sun on a lazy Miami morning. But the cold in the barn transcended her image.

Of course, it really didn't matter what her skin looked like or any other part of her. She was sure that death awaited her as soon as Paul and his friends collected their money. The old lady wasn't his mother she guessed because he always called her Francie. And the other guy, Otis, she had only glimpsed a couple of times; when they first grabbed her in Paul's truck, and once when they were moving her and the blindfold slipped. But she heard him yelling at Francie and Paul. He looked and sounded disgusting.

She wasn't actually hungry anymore. They fed her once in a while and Paul came out to the barn with hot tea and some bread twice, or was it three times? How could she have fallen for Conrad/ Paul. She was a total idiot. It would all be over soon and she'd never have to face her family or friends and try to make them understand how she could have been so misled.

She heard something like the squeak of the door opening. A gust of wind blew against her body. She listened for footsteps but only heard the rustle of leaves somewhere nearby. Then she heard a voice, just a whisper saying her name.

"Who is it?"

"Shh. Don't speak. Just listen to me. I'm going to put something over your mouth. Don't make a sound. It's me, Paul."

Sherry's first thought was that this was the end. Paul was the one who was here to kill her. How ironic, that he would be the one to finish this.

Something was shoved inside her mouth. She gagged for a second. Then she felt tape stuck to her lips and chin.

"Sherry, just listen. Try not to make any noise. I'm going to get you out of here before it's light out. I'm going to untie you. Don't try to run or struggle with me. You can't make it out of here in the dark alone. Do you understand me? If you do, just nod."

Sherry couldn't process this for a minute. Was this a trick to get her to move somewhere to be shot or something? Paul's voice came again.

"I know you don't want to trust me. I don't blame you. This is your only chance so please do what I ask. If you don't, Francie will kill you. Do you understand what I'm saying?" Paul was whispering directly into her ear.

This time she nodded.

Sherry felt the ties on her hands loosen and then release. She moved her arms free. They tingled as if a thousand thorns were attacking her. Then she felt the ropes on her legs that tied her to her chair loosen. She wasn't sure whether they were gone. She had no feeling in her legs. She felt a heavy jacket being put on her. She shivered.

"Can you stand?" Paul whispered.

She tried to get up but sank to the ground. Paul scooped her up and began carrying her. She tried to break free but her arms and legs felt like they belonged to someone else.

"Don't struggle; any noise will wake them. Stay still," Paul whispered.

They were outside now. Sherry could feel the wind against her. Paul was running. He was breathing hard and she could feel sweat from his body against her.

It seemed like hours that he ran carrying her through bushes or branches that scratched her and caught on her hair. Finally he laid her on the ground.

"I'm going to take off the blindfold now, but you still can't talk or scream," he said.

Paul was beside her on the ground when the blindfold came off. It was totally dark, but she could see the outline of trees. They must be in some woods.

"I don't think anyone can see us here. Let me help you try to stand," Paul said.

He pulled her up, his hands under her arms, until she was upright.

"See if you can take some steps." He held her arms as she began to move in small shuffling steps.

"I couldn't start the truck or they would've heard us. While it's still dark, we've got to get out to the dirt road and then down to the highway. It's your only chance. Do you think you can walk?"

She nodded even though she wasn't sure that she could.

"I'll help you but we have to move. It won't be light for at least an hour. When we come out of the woods, we'll be far enough away from the house and they won't be looking for us yet."

Sherry pointed to the gag in her mouth and made a slight noise.

"Can you promise not to scream?"

Sherry nodded again, and Paul slowly removed the tape. It made a scratching noise. Then he pulled the rag from her mouth.. She tried not to cough.

They began to move together. Paul was leading her through the thick stand of trees and brush. He began to move faster dragging her behind him. Something flew across her face. She almost screamed but stopped herself. She tripped and fell to one knee. Paul pulled her up and kept moving.

Sherry tried to say something but her voice was a croak. It had been so long since she had spoken. She wondered how many days she had been there. As they moved, more feeling was returning to her feet and legs. She felt a sudden surge of energy. Adrenalin forced her to move faster. She could see they were now on some kind of a path and the trees were not as thick,

"I know these woods real good. I played and hunted here when I was a kid. This land used to be my family's farm." Paul looked at her for a second and then continued pulling and leading her away from this terrible place.

"When we get to the main highway, we'll stay over on the edges in the trees. Hopefully, a car will stop for us, or we'll walk to where there are some houses. I'll get you out of here. Just keep moving." Paul pulled her along again. Sherry felt a lightness that made the ground whirl. She was dizzy with hope.

# FIFTY-THREE

I was the last one to pull up in front of the diner. Dash was looking down the road as I pulled in.

"I thought you were lost," he said. He was holding a tray of cardboard coffee cups, and I grabbed one gratefully downing several swallows.

It was cold and still dark. The wind had kicked up again and the leaves swirled around in small piles covering part of my boots.

Sheriff Parsons was standing next to two huge guys. One looked like a Suma Wrestler and the other looked like a full back on the University of Miami football team.

Dash took my arm and led me over to the group.

Parsons had a map open and was giving each of us directions. "Our best bet is to surround this place as close as we can get. A dirt road leads up to the house and they would sure hear our trucks coming down there. But there is a meadow behind the place. We can get there through this back road. We'll have to drive off road for a bit. Dash is your vehicle four wheel drive?"

"Of course, how else do I get around in the winter?"

"Okay, Mary you leave your car here and go with Dash. I'll be in the truck and Lonnie and Sean, you guys take Lonnie's SUV. We'll move into the meadow and walk up the hill to the house. There's an old barn, too. We'll stop about 200 yards from the house and approach from the left and the right. I'll show you when we get out of the cars." Parsons looked at each of us. "Any questions?"

One of the giants spoke. "You want us to take our rifles, right?"

"Sure you all take your guns. Lonnie, that's a dumb questions. Anyone else?"

"Jim, how far is it before we turn left to get to the back road?" Dash asked.

"It's ten miles from here on Route Four, before we get to the turnoff. Then we've got another two miles and another turn. Just follow me. We'll get there before it's completely light."

We broke from our huddle and headed to our trucks. My heart was beating hard. A murder trial paled in comparison to my level of nerves this morning. This time we had to prevent a murder.

I locked my car by force of habit even though everyone here laughed at me each time I locked up. "Don't you know it's perfectly safe here?" I was repeatedly asked. Sure, I thought. The car is safe, but coeds are not! Dash was holding the passenger door of his Subaru open for me. I climbed in and he took off quickly to keep up with the others. We pulled out onto Route Four, the sheriff in the lead followed by the big guys in the tall SUV. We brought up the rear.

I shivered a little, more from nerves than cold. Dash noticed and turned on the car heater. "This whole event must have you feeling like you're in a foreign place," Dash said.

"The temperature is not what we encounter in Miami. It's probably still ninety there. As far as kidnappings go, they do happen. It's just that I've never been on a rescue mission, and I've never had a friend become the victim of a snatch like this. You know Lucy sent me up here for some peaceful head-clearing time. What a laugh."

Dash looked over at me, taking his eyes off the road for a minute. "Listen, Mary, I guess things feel a little awkward between us, and I don't want that. I care about you. That wasn't a one-night-stand for me."

"That's exactly why I feel uneasy around you now. I think this has spoiled our friendship. I need to be honest with you. I'm not over my relationship with Carlos, the boyfriend I came up here to forget, so becoming more entangled with anyone now just isn't right."

"I get what you're saying. I don't want to lose our friendship. Maybe with some more time here, you'll feel more than just being my friend."

"That's another thing. I can't go on hanging out here. I have my career in Miami; my office and clients, if I have any left. And my brothers and their wives and kids, and my parents are all in south Florida. I need to make plans to get back to Miami."

Dash didn't answer. He kept his eyes on the road and the cars ahead of us. I could see that I had disappointed him. He clenched his jaw as if he had encountered a difficult legal problem.

We rode in silence heading west. The sky was still dark ahead of us. I looked back behind us. The first streaks of purple outlined the morning sky where the stars still formed a polka dot pattern. Soon the hills ahead of us took on the same purple glow. It looked so serene, presenting a contrast to what might await us on the Conrad farm.

Our caravan began to slow slightly as we passed through the village of Woodstock. There was no traffic on the main street that generally abounded in leaf peepers, walkers, joggers and shoppers.

"Why are we slowing down? Don't we need to get out there before it's any lighter?" I asked.

"Remember, I told you before when Woodstock posts a twenty-five mile zone, they really mean it," Dash said.

"Even at this hour?"

"Absolutely. Look over there." Dash pointed to the old deserted railroad station. At the side of the crumbling wooden structure sat a police cruiser, its lights off but engine running, waiting to pounce. We both laughed breaking the tense jitters that filled the air in the Subaru.

Soon we were speeding past the high school still completely dark, a produce market and a large post and beam structure outside the village boundaries.

"That's the synagogue I told you about," Dash said pointing to the building.

We were in the countryside again, passing the remnants of corn already harvested, bales of hay ready to be brought in. A sign advertised firewood for sale.

"I guess all these are signs of winter approaching," I said.

"Yup, the almanac says it'll be a cold one with plenty of snow."

I realized that Dash and I were making small talk to cover the uneasy feeling we had about Sherry and the unease with trying to put our relationship back to just plain friendship.

We slowed again near a sign that told us we were two miles from Bridgewater.

"Jimmy must be looking for the road where we're going to turn. It's sure hard to see with all these trees lining the road and no real light yet." Dash said.

I peered out trying to look for anything that resembled a road. I rolled down my window and stuck my head out hoping to watch for a turn. The truck and SUV ahead of us were slowed to a crawl too. Something caught my attention coming out of the trees, moving into the road.

"Dash, look out. Maybe that's a deer or some animal moving into the road," I yelled.

The car lights outlined two figures. A tall male stepped almost in front of the car. He was waving his arms and yelling something. The other figure was half bent over and stood on the shoulder of the road.

"My God, what is that?" Dash said as he hit his brakes.

With my head out of the open window, I heard the male yelling 'help' and then a female voice screaming. Dash jumped out of the car and I followed him. As I ran around the front of the car, the headlights blinded me for a minute and then the female was running toward me.

"Mary, is it really you? Help me, oh please. The figure fell over a tree stump and held out her arm. The headlights hit her face.

"Sherry, Sherry, oh my God." I reached her and pulled her up. "Dash, it's Sherry."

Dash ran back to his open car door and blared the horn. The truck and the SUV stopped. I watched the SUV back down the road until it stopped in front of Dash's car. Jimmy's truck was turning around and moving back to our location. The male stood between the two vehicles, hesitating before he suddenly bolted into the trees.

"Stop him," Dash screamed. "That's Pauly Conrad, one of the kidnappers."

Sean and Lonnie began to run in the direction of the fleeing Pauly, but these enormous guys couldn't move very fast. Then I saw Dash streak by me. In seconds he had disappeared into the woods. At that moment I remembered why his nickname was Dash.

# FIFTY-FOUR

Sheriff Parsons was out of the truck. As soon as he was in earshot, I told him that I had spotted Sherry and a male coming out of the trees onto the road.

"Dash and your deputies are chasing down the male now and Dash said it was Paul Conrad."

The sheriff looked at Sherry's pathetic figure. "Are you Sherry Yarmouth?" he asked.

Sherry nodded.

"Who is the man who was with you?"

"Paul. His name is Paul."

"Sherry, we're going to get you to a safe place in a few minutes. How did you get here to this road?"

"Sheriff Parsons, Sherry needs medical help. Can't this wait?" I asked.

"I just need to know a few things now. It's important." The Sheriff stared at me as if I was an idiot. "How did you get here?"

"Paul untied me and carried me most of the way from the place they were keeping me. He said they were going to kill me today and this was the only way out." Sherry began to cry.

"How many other people were holding you? Do you know who they are?" the sheriff asked.

Sherry tried to control her sobs and spoke softly through the tears. "There are two others. One's called Francie and a man called Otis.

"What kind of weapons do they have?"

"I don't know," Sherry leaned heavily against me. "They must have guns. Paul said they were going to shoot me, I think."

Just then Lonnie and Sean appeared each holding one of Paul's arms. Dash was just behind them. All of them were out of breath.

"Paul Conrad, you are under arrest for the kidnapping of Sherry Yarmouth." Parsons moved quickly to handcuff Paul who put up no fight. "Do you understand that if you talk to me, what you say can be used against you in court? You're entitled to have an attorney present, but I really need to ask you some questions right now so I can go onto your farm and grab the rest of the people who held Sherry. Do you understand?"

"Yes, Sir," Paul answered.

I winced, the defense attorney in me figuring how good counsel would get any confession suppressed after that abbreviated Miranda warning coupled with the threat of arrest of his cohorts.

"Now, Paul, if you help me here, I may be able to help you down the road," Parsons continued. "Who else is at the house and what kind of weapons do they have in there?"

"Just Francie and Otis Wallace. Otis has a revolver and Francie has a hunting rifle."

"Paul don't have no weapons on him. I made sure of that." Lonnie said.

"Okay, Paul. I'm going to put you in the back of Lonnie's car and lock you in there, while we go over to the farm and get Francie and Otis," Parsons said.

"I'd just as soon you'd take me to the jail right now. Francie's gonna kill me for ruining her shot at the money," Paul said.

"What did she want with all that money, anyway?" Jimmy Parsons asked.

"She wanted us to get far away from here before you came after her," Paul said

"Why would I come after her?"

"For shooting Carolyn Brousseau. She said sooner or later someone would figure it out. She said we was only going to get the money that time too and then she shot Carolyn, and now she was going to kill Sherry so I had to get her out of there." Paul looked at Sherry. "I know you don't believe me, but I really did care about you, Sherry. It's just that Francie took me in, you know. I was just a kid."

"Okay, Paul. We'll talk some more later. Lonnie and Sean, let's go get the bastards. Dash, you take Mary and Sherry back to town," Jim said.

"I can come with you. Mary can drive my car back with Sherry," Dash said.

"No, Dash, this isn't a deer hunt. You're not deputized. Just get Sherry back to her family." Jimmy and the big guys piled into their vehicles and took off with Paul handcuffed in the back of the SUV, and Sean pointing a deer rifle directly at him.

I helped Sherry into the back seat of Dash's car, and got in next to her.

Dash opened the back of the little SUV and removed an army blanket. He handed it to me and I draped it over Sherry. I saw bruises on her arms and face, Her hair hung in limp, dirty clumps around her face.

"What day is it, Mary?" Sherry asked.

"It's Thursday, honey. We're taking you to your mom and Brett. They're at the Hanover Inn." As I spoke, Sherry closed her eyes and fell asleep.

"Dash, can you call Lillian or Brett on your satellite phone?" I told him the numbers but neither one answered.

"Let me try to get Ken Upham. He was going with Lillian to the gas station for the money exchange." I pulled my phone out of my bag and dialed Ken. It was a miracle. I actually got a connection and Ken answered.

"Ken. It's Mary. Are you with Lillian?"

"Yes, we're getting ready to go over to the gas station, just going over what Lillian is going to say."

Never mind the gas station or the money. I have Sherry with me. She's okay, Dash and I are bringing her to the inn right now."

Ken turned and repeated what I told him. I heard Lillian scream and then Brett took the phone.

"Mary, you're the best," he said.

"No, I'm just the luckiest. See if Ken can get a doctor to come over to the inn to check Sherry out. She's asleep. You'll see her for yourself in a few minutes. We're halfway there."


Lillian and Brett were in the lobby when I helped Sherry in. Lillian grabbed her and held her so tightly I thought she'd squeeze the breath out of her. Lillian and Brett helped her over to the elevator. Ken stood a little apart from the Yarmouths watching the reunion and smiling broadly

"I have a nice hot bath ready for you, baby," Lillian said.

"Mom, I'm so embarrassed. How could I have been such a dolt?"

The elevator door closed. Ken and I waited in the lobby for Dash who was parking the car. As soon as Dash appeared, I suggested we leave the family alone for a little while.

"Anyway, I'm starved. Come on, let's go get a big well-earned breakfast," I said. I linked an arm with each of them and we marched over to the inn dining room where I gorged on pancakes with Vermont maple syrup, bacon, and a bucket of coffee.

By noon time we were all in Lillian's room. Sherry was dressed in jeans, a sweater and a sweat shirt retrieved by Brett from her dorm room. An intern had been sent over from Dartmouth Medical School courtesy of the administration office after Lillian called to inform the school that her daughter had been abducted from right under their noses and what were they going to do about it or should Lillian just go ahead and sue them for lack of campus safety.

The intern found nothing permanently wrong with Sherry that time, sleep and food wouldn't cure physically. He did recommend that Sherry might benefit from talking to a psychologist, and warned Lillian about Post Traumatic Stress Syndrome.

Brett thanked Ken over and over for his police expertise. It was a totally happy scene although Sherry was still subdued from the knockout stuff that was forced into her over the past days.

Dash, Ken and I were just about to leave when there was a knock on the door. Brett opened it and Jim Parsons identified himself, showing Brett his ID and badge.

"Come in, please," Lillian said. "I wanted an opportunity to thank you."

"It's not necessary," Mrs. Yarmouth. I'm really here about something else," Jim said.

"Did you get the others? Are they under arrest?" I asked.

"We can discuss this later. I was summoned an hour ago to Roland Behr's front yard. Mr. Behr has been murdered. Mr. Upham, you'll have to come down to my office. I need to ask you some questions. I hope you'll come voluntarily." Parsons had a pair of handcuffs dangling from his front pocket.

"I'm coming with him, as his lawyer," I said, immediately switching into lawyer high gear.

"Me too," Dash said

# FIFTY-FIVE

"What kind of a place is this?" Lillian asked. "Kidnappings, murders. I thought this was a bucolic safe environment. Sherry, I'm taking you back to Miami."

"It's okay, Mom. I don't want to go back to school here. Can I transfer to the University of Miami?" Sherry closed her eyes again. The effort to talk exhausted her.

"Sheriff Parsons, Dash and I will drive Ken to your office. But I want to know now whether the kidnappers are locked up. They aren't still out there somewhere, are they?" I asked.

"We got them just as they came out to get into a car in front of the farmhouse. They'll be appearing before a judge tomorrow morning and then they'll be transferred to holding facilities. I alerted the prosecutor and they'll seek a 'no bond' status. Francie has already confessed to Carolyn Brousseau's murder. I also have a statement from Paul Conrad about that murder. He told us that Carolyn got him and Otis to go with her to burglarize the Brousseau house. Paul waited outside as a lookout. Francie thought Carolyn was out of town. Too bad she wasn't."

"So you were completely wrong thinking Carolyn was killed by her son," Dash said.

"I know I wasted a lot of time looking at Tom. Well, with this Roland Behr murder, things are going to be different. I'll follow your car, Dash, but I want your word that you'll bring Ken directly in."

"Are you charging Ken with this murder?" I asked.

"Let's just say for now he's a person of interest," Parsons said.

I grabbed my purse and jacket, gave Lillian and Sherry hugs and headed out to the elevator. Ken looked as if he were in shock. I wondered if I was ever going to get back to Miami. My vacation had turned into a major crime spree.

# FIFTY-SIX

The police department was housed in the back of a converted school. The sign over the building read 1898. The building smelled of mildew mixed with the smell of coffee coming from a pot in the front office.

We walked through a series of rooms arriving at what must serve as the interrogation room. It contained a square table surrounded by four mismatched chairs, two wooden and two folding. Long windows faced the lawn in back of the building. The sun was shining on two maple trees whose red and yellow leaves fell into hills of brown dry leaves.

Sheriff Parsons sat at one end of the table. Ken sat across from him while Dash and I each pulled our chairs on either side of Ken.

"I need to read you your rights before we begin." Parsons pulled a worn card from his pocket and began reading, "You have the right to remain silent—"

"It's not necessary, Jim. You seem to have forgotten that I spent almost thirty years in law enforcement. I understand all of my rights. Let's get to your questions." Ken's annoyance was evident.

"Why are you even bothering to question Ken? This is silly. Shouldn't you be out at the murder scene, looking for evidence?" I used my most assertive voice.

"Listen, Ms. Katz, I didn't invite you to my office or to High Pines. This is my investigation. I don't need some flatlander woman telling me how to run things,"

"Now, hold it, Jim. Mary is here as an attorney,. She isn't to be insulted. You're making this personal. We're all professionals here. Do you understand?" Dash was half out of his chair.

"Okay, everyone, let's just let Jim ask me whatever and get on with this." Ken had his hand on Dash's arm.

"That's what I'm trying to do," Parsons said. Now Ken, Roland Behr was found by his attorney at eight this morning. The lawyer stopped there before going back to Rutland. He got no answer when he knocked on the door. Lights were on inside the house. Then he saw Roland's body lying in some bushes. The body was cold and stiff as if it had been there for some hours. We'll get a more definitive answer from the coroner later, maybe tomorrow. Where were you last night, Ken? Can you account for your whereabouts?"

Sure, I spent most of the night at the Dartmouth-Hitchcock emergency room. My wife was there with me. Then we went home and we got a few hours' sleep. Then I went to help Lillian Yarmouth get ready to go meet her daughter's kidnappers."

"Do you have the hospital records?"

"My wife has the discharge paper, I think, and I can get the records from the hospital."

"Ken, I'll go over to the hospital right now and get the records. Mary can stay here with you," Dash said.

"Wait, Dash, you'll need a release from Ken, so they'll give you the records," I said. "Give me some paper and I'll draw up something for Ken to sign."

Parsons pulled a sheet of paper from his pad where he had been taking notes. I quickly wrote out a release statement and Ken signed it.

"I'll be back as quickly as possible and that should put an end to this," Dash said. He grabbed his keys from the table and bolted out of the room.

"Now, Ken, Roland Behr was suing you about the trees you removed. Isn't that correct?" Parsons went right back to his questioning,

"Don't you want to wait to look at the records? Ken was totally unavailable to be murdering someone last night. His wife thought he was having a stroke," I said.

Parsons ignored me. "Wasn't he suing you and didn't that make you angry?"

"Right on both counts" Ken answered.

"And weren't you going around town calling Roland the Tree Nazi?"

"I don't think I was the one that invented that name. I think it was one of the boys over at Hal's store, but, yes, I used it and it kind of caught on."

Maybe it'll interest you to know that someone painted a swastika on Roland's forehead." Parsons looked like he had just scored the winning touchdown in the game of the year.

"Are you kidding? Do you think that I would do such a stupid thing over a nutty fracas about trees? I spent my life arresting bad guys and solving cases. You are way off base." Ken said.

"Being that you've been a law enforcement officer, you are proficient with a firearm, aren't you?"

"Of course I am."

"You still own at least one firearm, don't you?"

"I own a 45 caliber revolver and a hunting rifle. If you'd like to see them, stop by my house." Ken's hands were beginning to shake.

"Is my client under arrest, Sheriff?" I asked as I stood up.

"Not at this time."

"Fine. Then we'll be leaving." I took Ken's arm.

"Just don't leave town," Parsons called after us.

Once we hit the sidewalk outside the police building, I realized that Ken's car was at the inn and my car was at the diner. Dash drove off on his emergency mission with the only car available for our dramatic exit from interrogation hell.

"I'll call Rita to come get us. She's probably home worrying over my health anyway, and I haven't even had time to tell her that we got our kidnap victim back."

"And I'll try to get Dash to tell him not to return to Parsons' office. Maybe we can all meet back at my place after we retrieve our cars."

I tried to dial Dash but got no signal again. Ken finished updating Rita but left out the part about his being questioned regarding a murder.

"She's on her way," Ken said. "I thought it best to tell her about Roland Behr when she gets here. Did you reach Dash?"

"No, my cell won't work. Try yours."

Just then my cell rang. I answered quickly.

"Mary, it's Dash. Were you just trying to call? I saw your number on the caller ID. Anyway, I'm having trouble getting the records. First the hospital records department said the release wasn't proper and that Ken would have to come here himself. That damn Privacy Act, you know. So I told them I'd bring him right over and they should get the records ready."

"Good idea," I said.

"Not so good. The records clerk came back to the window and said they can't find any records for Ken Upham from last night."

"Oh, really? Dash, I'm standing outside the police office now with Ken. I walked him out when the questioning became bizarre. Rita is coming to pick us up. We'll get our cars and we can meet at my place in a little while."

"I read you, Mary. You don't want Ken to hear about no records ,right?"

"You got it. See you in a few minutes."

I clicked off and stared at Ken. Either the hospital was a pillar of inefficiency or my client was a murderer.

# FIFTY-SEVEN

Rita roared into the parking lot in a Mustang convertible. She jumped out and ran over to Ken.

"Are you okay, honey? You're still so pale." she said, motioning for us to get in the car.

"Mary, go ahead and get in while I talk to Rita for a minute," Ken said. He led Rita a few feet away and took her hand.

I couldn't hear what he said, but I could see and hear her startled reaction.

"Roland is dead? Are you kidding? They can't believe that you—"

Then I heard a long string of "shits and damns."

Fred led Rita over to the car and helped her into the passenger seat. He got in the driver's seat and pulled away from the old brick building.

"Mary, I can't believe this." Rita turned to me. "Where is Dash?"

"Oh, Dash went over to the hospital to try to get Ken's records from last night to show the sheriff that he was otherwise engaged. He was having a little trouble getting the records," I said.

"Typical, isn't it? It took me three weeks to get my last mammogram results. That's exactly why I made them give me copies of everything when we left last night. I said we needed to get them to our doctor in New Haven." Rita turned back to Ken "Now where did I put them?"

"They're probably still in your purse. That's where you put them last night," Ken said. He pulled into the parking lot at the diner next to my car. It seemed like a year since I parked the car before dawn this morning.

Rita was fumbling through her humongous bag. "Here they are, a little crumpled but intact."

She handed them over to me. I thumbed through checking the dates and times. The last entry was two-thirty a.m. on the discharge notice which stated that patient was advised to follow up with his own physician as soon as possible. There were countless entries with results of blood tests, a C-Scan, a chest x-ray, and some indecipherable doctor comments.

I took the records, jumped out of the car and waved Ken and Rita off. Then I zoomed off to Lucy's house to rescue poor Sam who had been alone for over six hours.

Dash's car was already in the driveway when I drove up. I could hear Sam barking as I rushed to the door. I opened the kitchen door and found a tidal wave of what appeared to be yarn and paper.

When Sam gets bored he always finds some new enterprise to break the boredom. This time he had trashed a kitchen rug into thousands of shreds. Mixed in with the remains of the rug were tiny pieces of paper towel along with the cardboard roller that had once housed the roll. The remains of the contents of the garbage can now lying on its side in the middle of the debris added bits of color to the heap.

Dash was standing in the doorway. He let out a low whistle. "Wow, what an amazing mess."

"At least he didn't eat the bottoms of the cupboards, thank God." I hustled Sam out the back door. He promptly relieved himself and scratched on the door to get back in where he stood proudly surveying his handiwork.

"Aren't you going to punish him? Spank him or something?" Dash said.

"It's too late for that. He won't connect it with the mess. You sort of have to catch him in the act. Besides, it's my fault for leaving him for so many hours," I said.

Dash just shook his head and wandered back to the great room. Immediately, I thought of how Carlos would have joined me in laughing at Sam's kitchen makeover. Dash's reaction was totally different.

Dash always reminded me of someone else I knew, but I never could put a face to this picture. Now it was coming to me. Dash reminded me of my brother, William. William was the middle child so he was closest to my age. I was the baby in the family with both brothers looking out for me. William in particular would often scold me for disobedient behavior. Dash had the same paternal, no nonsense attitude. His first thought was to punish my silly dog. Carlos loved a good joke, and Sam was famous for pulling laughable antics.

Dash was a good friend, but I knew for sure now he couldn't be the right guy for me. I still thought he'd be the model boyfriend my dad would love.

After a hasty attempt at cleanup of the kitchen with a broom and dust pan, I joined Dash and handed him the records that Rita had given me.

"Shouldn't we take these over to Jim right away?" Dash asked.

"Yes, we should, and we should also find out what else that inept sheriff is doing to find who did Roland in. Call Ken and tell him to sit tight at home while we try to assist Sheriff Parsons in a real investigation."

# FIFTY-EIGHT

"What did you find in Roland's house? Do you even know if he was killed out in his yard or just deposited there?"

We were back in Jim Parsons' office. While he looked at the hospital records, I had begun peppering him with the questions that rolled around in my head.

"Not that it's any of your business, but I haven't been in the house yet," Parsons snarled.

"Well, why not, Jim? Why weren't you in there the minute you got there? The killer could have been in the house for all you know. Valuable evidence could have been taken." Dash looked at Jim with a puzzled frown.

"Well, for one thing, I was busy arresting Francie and Otis Wallace out at the farm where I also had my two deputies working. Then we had to question them briefly at least and I had to call the prosecutor to get on over to our lockup."

"Instead of wasting time picking up Ken and questioning him, you could have gone right into the house," I said. "There could have been more bodies in the house, or the killer could have been holding hostages. Exigent circumstances like that would have allowed an immediate entry."

"I'm working on a search warrant now. I still have to get this over to a judge to sign, so it'll probably be tonight before I can get in there. Why is it that you two lawyers think you can run my investigation? Listen, Dash, if you're so smart, why don't you run for sheriff?'

"Good idea," Dash said. "If you or one of your officers had gone right in there, the exigent circumstances would have allowed you immediate entry without worrying about a warrant. Who knows who might have been hiding in there?"

"Well, I've got a man stationed in a car out front and the place is secured with evidence tape so whatever's there will still be there." Jim said.

Dash and I looked at each other. "We'll get out of your way," I said. "Can we get copies of those records for our file?"

"Yup. Here, just take them up to Mrs. Bradley at the front desk."

I clutched our copies of the hospital records as we got into Dash's car. "Are you thinking what I think you're thinking?" I asked.

"And what would that be?" Dash smiled.

"That we can easily get into Roland's house through the back entrance. That is if you don't mind fighting your way through the overgrowth . The sheriff hasn't stationed anyone back there. By the time Jim gets there, we'll be out. And I can use my phone camera to record whatever we find, so Jim can't hide evidence from us."

"Mary, we could get ourselves in some big trouble."

"Or we could get Ken out of trouble. Come on. Let's go."


We parked down the street from Ken's house. I remembered how Ken and I had accessed Roland's house the day we went to court.

"Just follow me between those two houses and we can cut through the easement and get right into the backyard," I said.

I motioned Dash to follow me. Soon we were facing the mess that comprised Roland's yard.

"Are those targets for gun practice?" Dash whispered.

"They sure are. Come on. Let's see if the back door is unlocked."

We made our way through the old tin cans, the weeds and God knows what else that was concealed in the brush. In another minute we were on the rickety back steps leading to the back door. Dash pulled back the screen and tried the door. It was locked and no amount of jiggling forced it open.

"So now what?" Dash asked. "Do your talents include blasting through bolt locks?"

"No, and if we make much more noise the lone deputy watching the front of the house will be back here."

"He's probably sleeping in his squad car," Dash answered.

I began walking around the back of the house. There were three windows facing the back yard. The first was a small window that looked like it was over a kitchen sink. The second and third windows were larger. I peered through the nearest one and saw overturned furniture and papers strewn on the floor. The third one had a screen that was partially unhooked and hanging slightly from the window.

"I can see the bathroom over here." I motioned to Dash.

I pulled on the screen and it promptly fell onto my foot. The window was the old pull up style. It yielded with no effort.

"I think I can get through this one. I might need a little boost," I said. "Then I'll let you in the back door."

"Are you nuts? I can't let you do that."

"Well, you're much too tall to crawl in there. We need to see what's in this house. We may not get another chance. If Jimmy Parsons decides that Ken Upham is the guy who did Roland in, you know he won't change his mind and he'll make any other evidence disappear or overlook it. Look how he screwed up on Carolyn Brousseau's murder."

"Okay, but this is against my better judgment." Dash moved under the window and gave me a boost. I grabbed the window sill and pulled myself up and jumped down, landing in an old claw footed bath tub.

"I'm coming to unlock the door," I said as I picked myself up and hurried through the house.

Even though it was still light outside, the house was almost dark. The windows were obscured with a decade of dust and grime. The weeds and overgrown shrubs obscured any ray of light coming in the front windows. I found the kitchen and opened the bolt lock and a second lock on the doorknob. Dash almost fell through the door.

"Look at you. You're covered in dust or mud or both." he said. He brushed some dust from my hair.

We started through the kitchen into the living room, dining room combination. There was an old sofa and table and chairs. Book shelves were loaded with aging books.

A small room in the back of the house was the one I had seen from outside the back of the house. Someone had thrown the contents of an old roll top desk to the floor. A chair was turned on its side and a there was a broken lamp and an overturned end table.

"Don't touch anything. There may be fingerprints on these things." I pulled my phone out of my pocket and began taking pictures of the mess. "See if you can find a flashlight in the kitchen." I said. I glanced down at some of the papers and saw they were letters that were written in a foreign language,

Dash returned carrying a large flashlight. "This was next to the back door on the counter. I thought you said not to touch anything, but we need the flashlight."

"I'll wipe it off when we return it," I said as I continued snapping pictures.

We took the light back into the living room. I began to shine it on the floor. We both immediately saw dried stains on the carpet that looked like they could be blood. They led to the front door. I turned the light back around the room and saw a flash of silver. I moved closer and saw that it was a casing. Dash started to pick it up.

"Don't, Dash. We know what it is and where it is, but we can't remove it. It shows that Roland was probably shot in here and was thrown outside into the bushes, or he tried to get out before he died. Either way, it's important to leave it where it is". I took several pictures of the casing and tried to get shots of the blood stains.

I picked up one of the books on the edge of the shelf and saw that it also was in a foreign language.

"That's German," Dash said examining the book. "We need to get out of here before someone finds out we've committed a burglary."

"Okay, but let's just see what else is in here."

I walked into a small hallway. There was a door that I guessed went to a closet. It opened but instead of clothes or linens there was a stairway.

"Shine the light here. Where do these steps go?"

Dash approached with the light and we saw that they led to a basement. I hurried down the steps. Dash followed behind me. The light exposed a large room, its walls covered in posters and photos. There were flags in a stand and other paraphernalia of some kind. My mouth dropped open when I realized what we were looking at.

# FIFTY-NINE

"Roland Behr wasn't a tree Nazi. He was a real Nazi," I said, as I walked around the basement area.

"I can't believe this. So this is what Roland's secret club was," Dash said.

Swastikas emblazoned each wall and several bulletin boards. There were German flags, pictures of men dressed in boots and uniforms. A gun cupboard held a variety of weapons. There were typed and printed slogans and pledges pinned to the walls.

"We will not be silenced. We will rise once again and show pride for our Aryan Nation," Dash read as he flashed the light over the words. "Jews do not rule America, Down with Jewish filth," covered another wall.

"This is a Nazi clubhouse," Dash said, as he continued to read the manifestos."

"This isn't something to be handled by local law enforcement. This has national implications. Who can we call?" I asked. I snapped photos of the walls with their Nazi messages.

"You're right. I know the U.S. Attorney for this area. His office is in Burlington. We were friends when I practiced up there. Let's get out of here, so I can call him."

"Better get him on this fast before Jimmy comes in here, and while you're at it, maybe he can prosecute Sherry's kidnappers. They did take her across state lines from New Hampshire into Vermont, even though it was only across a river."

We tiptoed up the steps and out the back door. Then we ran to Dash's car.

Dash used his satellite phone. It was after five o'clock but like all lawyers, the U.S. Attorney didn't keep nine-to-five hours. Dash spoke to him for ten minutes, explaining what we had seen and what details we knew of Roland's murder.

Finally, Dash clicked off. "Curtis is going to call Jimmy Parsons right now and order him off the investigation. He'll have the FBI and one of his assistants here in a few hours. I had to tell him how we got in the house and saw the meeting place. He promised not to reveal his source. He also told me that there have been rumors of a neo-Nazi cell in Northern New England. He was contacted by the rabbi from the temple here a few weeks ago complaining that there had been some anti-Jewish incidents and some members believed that there was an organization in our area."

"Curtis? That's the attorney's name?"

"Yes, Curtis Lemay. He's a real go-getter. I can't believe this has been going on right under our noses."

"You seem to be saying 'you can't believe' an awful lot lately. Well, I don't believe that no one knew about this. Everyone gossips in this village. Everyone knew who I was, what case I was handling. Your friend, Curtis, has had tips about this. The good news is Ken shouldn't be a suspect any longer. It seems Roland wasn't so interested in trees after all."

"But now I think maybe someone in our Jewish community may be suspected. Let's go back to the office and see if my mother is still there. I wonder if she's heard about this neo-Nazi group."

"If anyone knows everything, it's sure to be Daisy," I said

# CHAPTER
# SIXTY

I was surprised to see Daisy's car as we drove up to the office. I wasn't surprised that she was on the phone. We heard her as we opened the front door.

"Yes old Roland was found dead in his front yard and Dash's client is being questioned. I can't tell you who. Yes, I'll keep you posted," Daisy said as we stood in front of her desk.

"I didn't hear you come in." Daisy stood up. She looked like Sam when he's caught with one of my shoes.

"Mom, you know not to discuss office business with your friends," Dash said.

"I didn't tell Phyllis anything she couldn't read in the paper. I didn't name any names."

"Daisy, do you know anything about an anti-Jewish group in this area?" I interrupted Dash and his mother's quarrel. No sense shutting her up when we were looking for information.

"Well, sort of. Why do you want to know?"

"Never mind why we want to know about this. What have you heard?" Dash was quickly losing patience.

"Well, the Rabbi met with the synagogue board a couple of weeks ago. Mary, I'm the head of the caring committee. I make visits to people who are ill or have had a death in the family."

"Never mind that. What happened at the board meeting?" Dash asked.

"The Rabbi told us there had been some incidents. A swastika painted on the door and garbage left in the vestibule. One window was broken another time and someone pinned a note to the door saying Jews weren't wanted in the Upper Valley."

"Why didn't you tell me about this?" Dash asked. I could see that his hands were trembling.

"Because the Rabbi told us to keep it quiet. He said it was best if we kept a low profile. Some of the members repaired everything. The consensus was that if this were broadcast, then other copycat crimes would occur. Everyone thought it was just kids who didn't know better."

"I can't believe that you kept this to yourself," Dash said.

"What's happened? Is there going to be trouble?" Daisy asked.

"Not going to be. There is." I said.

"I'm going to call Rabbi Goldblatt. I want to talk to him right away." Dash went to the phone in his office.

"You can't call him now," Daisy called after him. "It's dinner time."


Within minutes Dash and I were back in his car on the way to meet with Rabbi Goldblatt.

"We need to warn him so he's prepared if the FBI decides to question his members. He may know who would have a motive to go after Roland. Maybe he even knew about the Nazi group." Dash said.

My mind was whirling. My half Jewish side was sickened by what we had seen in Roland's basement. Being raised in Miami, I had never experienced this kind of religious hatred. Of course, there are small minded people in Miami who resent immigrants, but this was a different kind of hatred, one that should have died with the worldwide pain of the Holocaust.

Now I was on the way to meet with a rabbi. I hadn't done that since I was twelve years old. For a while I attended two religious schools until I called a halt to the tug of war between my parents' and grandparents' background and decided that organized religion was not in my future.

"Mary, we're here. Come on," Dash said.

We walked up to a pretty white frame house with green shutters that looked like it belonged on the set of a movie about New England. A gray-haired man dressed in sweater and slacks opened the door before we could knock. He smiled at us and ushered us into a cozy library. Dash introduced me and I shook hands with Rabbi Goldblatt who looked a lot like my Uncle Max.

"Well, it's lovely to see you, Dash. I haven't seen much of you lately, except of course at Yom Kippur services. Is your mother well?" Rabbi Goldblatt asked.

"Yes, she's fine."

"So is this about you two, you and Mary? Maybe you have some good news to tell me."

"No, Rabbi, it's not good news. Mary is a lawyer from Miami who's been helping me with some cases. Today we uncovered something that I must warn you about. You probably know that Roland Behr is dead. He was shot and found in his yard."

"Yes, I heard. One shouldn't speak badly of the dead, but I have to say, he was an unsavory person."

"Rabbi, did you know that Roland had a Nazi group meeting in his home?"

"I didn't know that's where it was." The rabbi sighed and looked as if he might cry. "I have heard for some time that there was a neo-Nazi group somewhere in our area. We had some incidents at the temple. Some members have reported various rumors to me. I finally called on the U.S. Attorney and asked him to investigate."

"Is it possible that any of your congregation could be under suspicion? The FBI is opening an investigation into this group and Roland's murder." I asked the hard question, hoping to get Dash off the hook.

"Anything is possible. Of course, there is Franz. You remember him, don't you, Dash? Franz Goldstein? He's a Holocaust survivor. But he hardly goes out anymore."

"What about his family, his son and grandchildren?" Dash asked.

"His son works in New York and comes up here about once a month. His grandson and wife work in this area. In fact the grandson, Jeff, is one of the people that passed on rumors about a Nazi group operating in this area. He was pretty upset."

"It's up to you whether you want to give anyone a warning that they might be questioned," Dash said. We just thought it best to give you some time to prepare for what may come out of this whole event."

Dash stood up and we began to inch our way to the door. The rabbi followed and thanked us repeatedly for coming directly to him. The aching feeling in the bottom of my stomach was growing as I flashed back to Roland Behr's basement.

"Dash, can you drop me at home, please, I think I've had it for today."

I waved goodbye to Dash and hurried inside. Sam was barking as I opened the door. He had bent the bars on his crate door and was lying next to the back door.

"Bad boy," I yelled. I need that crate for traveling back to Miami. What have you done?"

Sam rubbed his big head against my legs and made his moaning noises. I realized that I was being unfair to him, leaving him holed up in a strange place.

"We've had enough of this crazy place. We need to go back to Miami. I promise, we'll go soon," I said.

I went to the fridge and pulled out some leftover chicken and ham. I made myself a sandwich and filled Sam's dish with the rest of the chicken for a special treat. I opened a beer for my special treat, and snapped on the TV. The news carried Roland Behr's suspicious death and a short blurb about a Dartmouth coed who was alleged to have been kidnapped by locals in the Upper Valley. The announcer was saying, "this normally tranquil area has been shaken by two crimes in the same week."

I was reminded to call Lillian and check on Sherry. It seemed a month since we found her, but it was less than twelve hours ago.

Brett answered Lillian's phone. Lillian and Sherry were resting. Then he lowered his voice.

"Mary, we're going to be packing Sherry's stuff in her dorm room tomorrow and shipping everything back to Miami, but Sherry doesn't want to leave until she visits that animal, Paul, in jail. Mother is dead set against it."

"Maybe Sherry needs closure, or maybe she just wants to tell him what a pig he is. Either way, maybe it's best to let her get this off her mind so she can look ahead."

"I'll tell mother what you think. She usually listens to you." Brett said.

As soon as I hung up, Dash called to say that Curtis Lemay had let him know that he was on his way down here along with FBI agents. He had decided to start this investigation himself, and would be calling on the lawyer who found Roland first thing in the morning. He also said that he wanted to talk to Ken Upham. I told Dash I'd be ready to sit with Ken.

I sat down on the comfy sofa and was half asleep when Sam began to bark and jump at the back door. "Haven't we had enough excitement for one day?" I asked as I got into my boots and coat and grabbed my flashlight. I hooked Sam's leash on him as he pulled me through the door.

As soon as we galloped into the back yard, Sam began to pull me toward the path through the woods. I really didn't want to take a hike in the dark, but I didn't have a choice. As long as I held tight to the leash, my eighty pound dog was in charge of our flight pattern.

I shined the flashlight on the semi-path through the woods that connected to Carolyn Brousseau's property. Now that Carolyn's killers were safely locked up, I wasn't worried about confronting a killer, but I also didn't think this foray into the woods was in pursuit of some wild life. Once and for all, I wanted to catch whoever had taken up residency in the Brousseau house. No one else seemed to care. I wasn't even sure why I cared. Maybe it was just lawyer's curiosity.

We came onto the Brousseau property on the side of the barn that served as a garage. I pulled Sam in that direction and eased the door open a crack. I shined the light inside the door and saw the black Subaru parked inside. "That means the intruder is at home," I said.

We approached the house. One small light was on in the kitchen. I tried the back door. It was unlocked. As we entered, Sam barked loudly and began pulling me through the kitchen. I thought I heard a door slam somewhere above us. The knife rack stood on the kitchen counter. Instinctively I pulled out a large carving knife as Sam began to pull me to the back stairway.

The bedroom doors were open and nothing looked disturbed. I walked into the hall bathroom and saw that the tub had water droplets on the tile surrounding it. At least the intruder is clean, I thought.

Sam sniffed as we went down the long hallway. He stopped at the door that was locked when I stayed in the house. I tried it now and it was still locked. Sam pawed at the door.

"Okay," I yelled. "Come out of there now. I'm armed and I've got a police dog." My hand holding the knife was shaking. What a stupid idea this was. I started to turn away from the door, but Sam jerked hard on his leash and jumped against the door.

The door flew open. A young guy stepped out. He was wearing shorts and a stained tee shirt. The stains were dark red and the idea of blood raced through my addled mind. He wore glasses. His eyes looked startled behind the glasses. All of these details were obscured by what was in his hands; the largest rifle I had ever seen.

"Don't shoot my dog," I screamed. "What are you doing in this house?" In my panic I dropped the knife.

"What are you doing in my house?" the gun holder shouted back.

"I asked you first," I said.

"Don't fool with me." The rifle pointed from Sam to me. "What police agency are you with, or are you a private investigator?"

"I'm not the police. I'm an attorney from Florida, visiting here. My name is Mary Katz. Who the hell are you?"

I'm Tom Brousseau. I own this house. You've got a lot of nerve barging in here again. I know you were using my house."

"If you will please lower that elephant gun, I'll explain why I was in your house."

I watched the man who said he was Tom hesitate and then lower the gun. If he was actually Tom Brousseau what was with the hiding in the attic and cat and mouse game he'd been playing with me?

"Okay. I'm a good friend of Lucy Stern. Her grandmother left her the house down the road. She let me use the house for a vacation and I got lost and thought this house was hers. I left as soon as I saw the mail on the hall table with the Brousseau name on it."

"That story is unbelievable. You're really here to arrest me. Tell me the truth," the man said.

"Your story is not believable. Why are you hiding in your own house, if you really are Tom. I am the furthest thing from law enforcement. I'm a criminal defense attorney. I defend people who are arrested. I don't arrest them."

Sam had begun to wag his tail. Tom, if that was his name, reached over and petted him.

"Let me get my wallet and show you some ID. Come with me". He pointed to the door he had popped out of.

I saw a stairway leading up. "That's okay. I'll wait right here," I said.

"Oh come on. This whole situation is actually funny," he said.

"Well, what are those stains all over your shirt?"

"You'll see in a minute." He started up the stairs.

I bent over and retrieved the carving knife. Then Sam and I followed him up the stairs. We entered a large attic. Windows looked out of three sides of the room. An astonishing sight explained the stains. Colorful paint-ings lined the whole room. Some were propped up on easels. Others leaned against walls or sat propped on chairs. There was a half- finished work and fresh paints on a large easel near one of the windows.

"You're a painter. I mean an artist." I mumbled

The paintings depicted autumn scenes in the area. There were also snow scenes and pictures of barns. Figures of children appeared in several of the works.

"These are magnificent. Where do you exhibit? Are you in any galleries?"

The artist was holding out some cards. "Here are my ID's . Please look at them."

"They all say Thomas Brousseau., but why are you hiding in your own house?"

"I know it seems crazy. Sheriff Parsons believes that I killed my own mother, and I think half this village does too. He questioned me even before my mother's funeral. I figured I owned the house and no one would look for me right under their noses. I guess I panicked.

" I always wanted to have my studio in this house and do nothing but paint. The whole hiding thing just sort of fell into place I thought I'd stay in the house for a few weeks and get my bearings. I thought about going to France to paint and study, but I figured the sheriff would have people watching airports. Then I started painting and I got comfortable here. I concentrated on just doing my paintings. I never had that luxury before."

"First of all, questioning you was just routine. Police always start with family members and you seem to be the only family left. Didn't Dash explain that to you?"

"You know Dash? I thought he was against me too. Half of this town hates the Brousseaus because my dad sold the mill to people who moved it to China. Everyone lost their jobs and they blamed me for that."

"Why would they blame you? You didn't sell the mill."

"Father sold it because I refused to work there and take it over. I'm not a business man. All I ever wanted to do was paint and draw. My father thought that was a waste of time."

"Okay, Tom, I have a big news flash for you. This week the killers of your mother were arrested."

"Are you serious? Who are they?"

"Francie Wallace, your family's housekeeper and her son Otis and Paul Conrad."

"I can't believe it. I knew Francie was very upset about her husband losing his job. I guess she blamed my family for his suicide but killing my mother, good God."

"I'm sure there's a lot more to their story, but you'll never find out if you don't come out of this hermit existence and rejoin the world. You could have saved yourself a year of grief. When you disappeared. it just added to Sheriff Parson's suspicion. If you had stuck around, maybe he would have found the real killers sooner. I wish that had happened because these same bad guys kidnapped a lovely young woman who I know quite well, and she almost lost her life."

"You mean Francie did that too? What about our dog?"

"What do you mean?"

"Another reason the sheriff thought I did it, you know murdered Mother, was because our dog would have barked and carried on if a stranger broke in. The dog was missing when they found mother."

"I guess the dog knew the housekeeper. Maybe now that Francie is in jail, you can find out about the dog. Can we go downstairs and continue this conversation?"

"Oh, sorry, of course we can. Come on, I'll make us some tea."

We headed down the attic stairs and the back stairs to the kitchen. Tom lit the flame under the tea kettle and produced an assortment of teas. He gave Sam a cracker and put a plate of crackers and jam on the kitchen table.

"What I don't understand is how you managed to live undetected up here," I said, "especially, when this place is filled with nosey people who know everything about everybody."

"It wasn't that difficult. It's so remote up here that no one sees who's up here. You stayed in the house without anyone seeing that you were in the wrong house. I took the car out at night and drove to different towns to shop for supplies. I got my mail at a post office box in Randolph, about forty-five minutes away, or at my friend's place on the Cape. The solitude and luxury of painting full time was wonderful."

"Was that you that took a shot at me on the road?"

"I wasn't shooting at you, just trying to scare you, hoping you'd go away."

"You were stalking me, weren't you?'

"I was trying to find out who you were. I was sure that you were brought here to investigate me. I'm sorry. I shouldn't have gone in Lucy's house. I guess I became paranoid. And when I saw Sam, I thought he was a K-9 police dog."

"You've got to reintegrate into this community if you want to continue to paint here. Start tomorrow by going to see Dash."

"Will you come with me?" Tom looked like one of my scared juvenile clients.

# SIXTY-TWO

The phone in the kitchen woke me. I reached for my alarm clock and nearly fell out of bed. The alarm clock I pictured was the one on the bedside table in Miami. I opened my eyes and remembered I was still in Vermont.

Sun was streaming in the windows and my watch said nine o'clock. The phone was still ringing as I ran to the kitchen.

"Mary, are you okay?" It was Dash.

"Yes, I was so exhausted that I was still sleeping. You'll never guess who I met last night. Tom Brousseau has been living in his house. I told you someone was in there. He'll be over to see you later."

"That's interesting. No that's bizarre. The reason I'm calling is that the FBI people want to talk to Ken Upham today. They're meeting with the lawyer who found Roland's body this morning. I guess Curtis is actually meeting the lawyer while the FBI guys go through Roland's house."

"I'll bring Tom over to your office later this morning. Have Ken come over and I'll be there while he talks to Curtis. They're not wasting any time with their investigation, are they?

"No they're not. They're appalled at the inefficiency of the local sheriff's office."

At eleven o'clock I was seated in Dash's office. Tom had finished his explanation of his weird behavior. Ken was waiting in the reception room listening to Daisy's constant conversation.

I walked out to speak to Ken when a tall man walked in. He was beginning to turn grey. The graying hair made his round face look young.

"I'm Curtis Lemay, here to meet with Ken Upham," he said.

"So pleased to meet you," Daisy jumped up from her desk and pumped Curtis's hand. "Thanks for coming to help our little community."

I wasn't sure whether she meant High Pines or the Jewish congregation.

"This is Mary Magruder Katz. She's going to be representing Ken, and this is Ken Upham," Daisy said, sounding like she was introducing guests at a cocktail party.

Just then Dash came out of his inner office. Dash and Curtis shook hands. .

"Please use the library," Dash said. "If you need me, just dial one on the intercom and I'll come right in. I have a young client in my office who needs me right now."

I led the way into the library followed by Ken and Curtis. We seated ourselves around the table. Curtis pulled a number of papers from his briefcase.

"Mr. Upham, I understand you are retired from law enforcement. As a matter of fact, I checked into your background and career and spoke to your chief in New Haven this morning. You have had an enviable career and a flawless record. Even so, I need to have you sign this Miranda rights form before we go any further."

"I understand," Ken said. He took the form and quickly initialed each line and signed it at the bottom.

"Tell me everything you know about Roland Behr, how you met him, what transpired leading up to his lawsuit, anything you observed about him," Curtis said.

Ken described in detail the problems he had encountered with Roland, even including much of the hearing in Barre on our motion to dismiss. I was impressed with the details he was able to describe.

"Mr. Upham, what was your opinion about this secret club that met at Behr's house?"

"Please, call me Ken. I never thought they were an environmental group. All the target practice that went on in his backyard was suspicious.

I told my wife it was unsafe, and I wanted to talk to Roland about it, but my wife told me not to start any more arguments with the man. I thought he might be part of some right wing militia group, but when I asked others here in the village about this, everyone said he was just a crazy old coot."

"I appreciate your input. I am not looking at you as a suspect in this case. In fact I would be happy to hear any insights or theories that you may develop as this investigation unfolds." Curtis stood up and gathered his papers.

"I'm sure Dash doesn't mind if you stay here to question any other witnesses," I said.

"Thanks, but I'm headed to investigate some other names that have surfaced. I spoke to Rabbi Goldblatt earlier today. He is bringing some of the congregants to his office today or tomorrow. One of the FBI agents will be spending the day there doing the questioning."

"Do you have a theory as to who the killer is?" Ken asked.

"Let's just say I have some ideas to follow up on," Curtis said as we followed him into the reception area.

As soon as Curtis walked out the door, Daisy looked at us with a strained expression.

"Are you okay, Daisy?" I asked.

For once she was quiet. She reached for a handkerchief in the pocket of her sweater and finally spoke very slowly. "Do you think someone in the Jewish community killed Roland Behr? If that's true, this village will never be the same."


Ken and I were standing in the driveway outside Dash's office when Ken's cell phone rang.

"Yes, Rita, I'm fine, dear. Not to worry. Mary? Yes I know where she is. She's standing right next to me. I'll tell her." Ken signed off and turned to me. "Lillian Yarmouth is looking for you. Better call her right away."

# SIXTY-THREE

## Sherry Revisited

Sherry was feeling sick again. Her ears buzzed and she couldn't shake off the feeling of being constantly cold. The Dartmouth psychologist that she met with said the feelings that weren't subsiding would take time, but would eventually be erased when she got back to a normal schedule.

Mother had already set up appointments with a medical doctor and a psychologist in Miami. Brett was getting her transcripts from the college for her to take with her back to Miami. Most of her things were packed and ready for the UPS truck to pick up at her dorm to be shipped home.

The other sick feeling she had was from the constant arguing with Mother. Sherry had decided she wouldn't leave until she went to the jail to talk to Paul. Mother was adamant that she wouldn't permit her to experience "any further trauma" as Mother portrayed this. The psychologist sided with Sherry, explaining to Lillian that it was important that Sherry have a chance to close the door on her feelings of betrayal. But still Mother would not listen.

Mary was meeting with Lillian in the coffee shop downstairs. Sherry stretched out on the bed in their little room in the inn. It was early afternoon, but Sherry felt as if she had been awake for hours. She had no energy. It was hard to believe that she had been walking to classes, riding her bike, playing lacrosse, just days ago. Now the thought of so much physical activity brought waves of nausea.

She must have slept a little because she was startled when the door opened. She looked up and saw Mother and Mary standing looking down at her.

"Hi Sherry. Sorry we woke you. How are you doing?" Mary asked.

"I've been better." Sherry answered.

"See, I told you Sherry doesn't need any more emotional events, Mary"

"Sherry, your mother tells me that you are insistent about visiting Paul at the jail. She is opposed to this, as you well know. We've been discussing this and I think you should have the opportunity to say what is on your mind. It will make things easier when you have to appear as a witness at the trial."

"What do you mean appear as a witness?" Sherry sat up and gasped to catch her breath.

"Didn't Sheriff Parsons explain to you that you would be called to testify? It won't be for a while, and I'll come back with you for the trial, if you like."

"No one told me anything about this. I'm never coming back here. That's why I want to see Paul Conrad before I leave here."

"Well, we don't have to discuss the trial now. The important thing is that your mother has agreed to your visit to the jail as long as I go with you," Mary said. "Is that okay with you?"

"Yes, you can go with me."

"Ken Upham found all the directions to the jail. It's a twenty-five mile ride from here, so as soon as you get ready, we'll get going. Ken said visiting hours are in the afternoon, but they end at four so we should go as soon as you're ready."

Sherry got up and went into the bathroom.

"Please be careful with her," Lillian said.

In a few minutes, Sherry came out of the bathroom. She had applied a little makeup but her eyes looked sunken and her cheeks were hollow. She wasn't that young innocent coed anymore.

The drive to the prison was a dichotomy of feelings. Mary kept pointing out how the hills were crimson and yellow with the changing leaves. She pointed to spectacular crimson oak trees or bright red maples. Sherry looked at them without really seeing them. She was putting all her effort into planning what she would do and say when she saw Paul.

"Are you sure that you don't want to finish college here at Dartmouth? It's such a beautiful campus and you'll be leaving friends."

"I'm sure. I'll finish at the University of Miami. I want to be where it's warm. Miami was what I thought about when I was in that cold barn. Anyway, you went to Miami and you turned out great."

"I think it's a fine university. I just want you to decide your future based on what you really want, not because of what anyone else wants."

"You mean my mother. I want to see the sun and swim in our pool and wear shorts and flip-flops, and feel incredibly warm all the time."

They drove through several small villages and turned off the state highway onto a narrow road. Mary glanced at the directions she had on a piece of paper. Soon they pulled into a parking lot in front of an old brick building.

"This is it," Mary said. "I'm going to go in with you and help you with the paper work and visitor processing, but I don't want to go with you to visit Paul. What you and he talk about is private, and I'm not about to invade that privacy. The only thing you shouldn't discuss is what you will say as a witness. It's possible that Paul will try to persuade you to help him by not telling his part in all of this; maybe by urging you to go to the sheriff and change what you have already said about Paul's part in what happened."

"I know better than that, Mary. I went through my mother's hearings after Dad was murdered. I appreciate your respecting my privacy."

"One other thing. I promised someone that I'd ask you to find out about what ever happened to Carolyn Brousseau's dog."

"What dog? What are you talking about?"

"Just ask Paul, please."


They walked into the old brick jail. In a few minutes, Sherry had signed the visitor's roster, and given the guards her purse. She was buzzed through a metal door and disappeared accompanied by a guard.

In a few minutes the guard reappeared. "Are you the lady who accompanied that young woman?" he asked.

"Yes, that's right. Is something wrong?"

"I'd say so. When she went through the metal detector, we found this under her sweater." The guard held out a large Swiss Army Knife. "She said she forgot she had it, always carries it for protection."

"Is she going to be able to see Paul Conrad?" Mary asked.

"Yes, but not in the visitors' room. She can talk to him by phone through the screen. Just a precaution."

The woman corrections officer who searched her and found the knife delivered Sherry to a dimly lit area. Prisoners were behind a screen, seated at small windows. The officer pointed to a chair at one of the windows. No one was on the other side. A few minutes passed. Then a door opened and she saw Paul being brought through the door. He was in leg chains and handcuffs. The guard who brought him in unhooked his handcuffs and cuffed one hand to the arm of the chair. The guard pointed to the telephone receivers on each side of the window. Paul picked up his receiver with his free hand.

Sherry hesitated for a minute. As soon as Paul came through the door, her heart had started beating faster and faster. She thought she might black out. How ironic that Paul was now the one tethered to a chair. She looked at the receiver and picked it up.

"Sherry, I didn't expect to ever see you here. I thought it was my public defender when they said I had a visitor. How are you?"

"Do you actually care how I am?"

"Why did you come?"

"I came because I realize that if you hadn't helped me out of that place, I would have died, so I am grateful for that."

"You have to believe that I never knew that Francie planned to kill you."

"What I can't understand is how you convinced me that you cared about me, that you loved me. I thought you were so special. I guess I am just stupid."

"You're one of the smartest girls I ever met, not silly or spoiled like a lot of the Dartmouth girls that hung at the pubs and bars. Please believe that I did have feelings for you, and not just because you were a good lay."

"Then how could you have done what you did to me? You traded my feelings for money. That's all you wanted."

"Sherry, I lied to you a lot. My parents aren't dead. Well, my mom is. My father is serving a life sentence in prison. He beat my mom to death. I was only fourteen and I had no parents left. Francie Wallace took me in. She was my foster mom, and Otis was like my own brother. They were all I had"

"I wish you'd told me the truth. I would have understood. We have a lot in common. My mother was accused of stabbing my father to death. After her arrest, I found out that he had been cheating on my mother through their whole marriage. It turned out that the woman who probably did kill him was one of his girlfriends. I thought my dad was the greatest until I learned the truth about him."

"I didn't think someone like you would understand. I guess we should have talked to each other more instead of fooling around all the time we were together."

"Maybe things would have been different, but the reality is that you allowed me to be abused by that Francie."

"Francie fooled me. She had me and Otis help her break into Mrs. Brousseu's house where Francie used to work. She said we were just going to take some stuff while no one was there, but the old lady was there and Francie shot her, and then Otis shot their old dog and buried him in the woods"

"So Francie was already in big trouble. Why didn't you go to the police, or get out of there?"

"Where could I go? And then Francie said if I told, she'd say I did the killing and I'd be in prison forever like my dad. She said they'd believe I was just like my dad."

"So why were you hanging out with me?"

"Francie had this plan that if we could get a lot of money, we could get out of the Upper Valley and get far away, before the sheriff decided to find out who really killed Mrs. Brousseau. We were thinking of going to Florida or California. Francie said a lot of girls would like to be my girlfriend, and that all I had to do was find one of the rich Dartmouth ones. Once I got one interested in me she'd grab her and get money from the girl's parents and then we'd be out of here. I never thought that she'd kill someone else."

"So I turned up and fell for all of your lies."

"Not all of it was lies. I was even thinking that I'd get my share of the money and come to Florida and maybe I'd find you there. I guess I'll end up like my dad, sitting in prison all my life."

"I told the sheriff that you were the one who got me out of that place before I was killed, so you probably won't get as bad a sentence as Francie and Otis. I'm glad I came to see you and heard the real truth from you, but I don't ever want to see you again. If you get out, don't ever come near me. Do you understand?"

"Yes, Sherry. I truly am sorry."

Sherry slammed down the receiver and walked out of the room as fast as she could. For the first time in days, the buzzing in her ears stopped.

She retrieved her purse and fled from the damp building. Mary hurried behind her.

"I found out about the dog. Otis killed it and buried it in the woods."

"It wasn't an it. It was a her," Mary said. "Do you want to talk about anything else?"

"No, I don't. I'm ready to leave for Miami. I hope we can go tomorrow."

# SIXTY-FOUR

I delivered Sherry back to Lillian, refused Lillian's dinner invitation and began the drive home. Of course, not my real home. Lucy's house was beginning to feel familiar and safe.

I thought about Miami as I drove. Sooner or later I had to return to home and work. What would it be like without Carlos dropping into the office or waiting for me at my house in the Gables; without Chicky phoning to tell me about the latest fashions? I knew my family would be around to fill those gaps. As annoyed as I got over Mother's fussing over me, I sort of missed being that center of attention. Sooner or later was becoming sooner in my mind. Could I ever forget Carlos? I hadn't been able to stop thinking about him all the time I was here, seventeen hundred miles away from him. How would I erase him from my mind when he was only blocks away. Maybe I was as stupid as Sherry had been about Paul. For all my experience judging people, I believed in Carlos, and he turned out to be a liar.

Before I knew it, I was passing the mini-mart. I hadn't seen Riley for days. I turned into the drive and parked at the gas pump. As soon as I entered the store, Riley saw me and came out from behind the counter.

"Mary, I've heard all about the kidnapping and Francie Wallace being in jail. I feel just awful that I had no inkling what she was up to. I'm the one she left the package with that your friend, Mrs. Yarmouth, came here to get. I hope you're not mad at me. I just didn't know."

I didn't even bother to ask Riley how she knew these details. Between Hal's store and this mini-mart, there was little need for a newspaper or television.

"I'm not mad at you. I couldn't share anything that was happening for fear that we'd never get Sherry back alive."

"How is she?"

"I just left her. She's doing better and getting ready to go home with her mother. Listen, Riley, I'm sure you know about Roland Behr being murdered. You'll probably hear soon enough that he was running some kind of Nazi organization at his house. Were you aware that there was a hate group like that here in the Upper Valley?"

"I know he was shot. There have always been rumors about who he really was. If you're asking if I knew he was a bigot, the answer is yes. I think almost everyone knew that. Even his wife was always quick to tell a joke about Blacks and Jews."

"What I can't figure out is how there could be an active Nazi cell operating here without everyone knowing about it. It seems like no one can do anything in secret here. Everyone knew who I was before I could introduce myself."

"It's probably hard for you to understand. You come from a big city where people are more anonymous. People probably did know more than you think. Some people definitely agreed with the distrust of minorities. They just kept it to themselves. Others may have known that Roland was involved in some ugly stuff. Try to understand that Vermonters believe in live and let live. We gossip, but we don't judge peoples' thoughts. Does that make sense to you?"

"No, it doesn't, not really; not when it is so hurtful. But I still hope you and I are friends. I want to make sure that Ken Upham is not a person of interest anymore in Roland's murder and then I want to get back to Miami, and back to making a living again. Maybe you'll even visit me there sometime."

"I'd love to, especially during the grey days of March when I tend to get cabin fever. It sounds like you're telling me goodbye. I was hoping you and Dash would become a couple and you'd stick around."

"Thanks for wanting me around. Dash is a great guy. He's just not my great guy."

# SIXTY-FIVE

I gassed up the Explorer and headed for Main Street and River Road. I realized I was just blocks from Dash's office. I pulled into the drive next to the barn and parked next to Daisy's car. Dash was sitting at Daisy's desk as I walked in. Daisy was looking over his shoulder at the computer. She hurried over to me and gave me a hug.

"I haven't had a chance to tell you how happy I am that everything turned out fine for Sherry. Dash told me how brave you were helping with her rescue." Daisy's heavy hairdo bobbed up and down as she talked.

"Mary, I'm glad you stopped in. We were just talking about you and laughing about how you smoked Tom Brousseau out. I have to admit, I thought you were overly imaginative about someone staying at the Brousseau house."

"You don't know the half of it. For a while I thought it might be you hanging out there. You and Tom have the same exact car."

"So does half the valley. A black Subaru SUV is standard here." Dash broke up laughing and then Daisy joined him. I began to giggle too.

Daisy left for a minute and returned with a tray and glasses. "I think it's the cocktail hour," she said.

She poured a shot of scotch in each glass and we all swilled it down. The warm liquid left an after- glow that even warmed my feet a little. I still wasn't adjusted to the power of the wind to envelope all of my parts. If I stayed until real winter I might develop an alcohol problem.

"Mary, Daisy and I were just discussing the feds investigation into Roland's murder. Curtis is questioning all the board members of the temple,"

"Even me!" Daisy said.

"Do you want me to sit in with you, Daisy?" I asked.

"No, one of the FBI men already talked to me. I'm worried about Franz Goldstein and his family."

"I can't believe that Curtis is going to question Franz. He must be at least 85 and he's fairly feeble," Dash said.

"Isn't he the one you said was a Holocaust survivor?" I asked.

"Yes, that's right."

"That's the reason he's a suspect. If he knew there were Nazis operating here, wouldn't that cause flashbacks to whatever he endured during the war?" I asked.

"Possibly, but I can't picture Franz being able to attack someone physically. Roland was either chased into his front yard and shot there, or his body was dragged out there. How could Franz manage that?" Dash asked.

"Mary, couldn't you represent Franz and his family when the FBI questions them?" Daisy asked.

"That might not be proper. I represented Ken."

"Ken's off the hook. He told me himself that Curtis said he wasn't under suspicion," Dash said.

"Sometimes the Feds say that, but they really don't mean it, trying to catch a suspect off guard," I said. "Maybe I could offer a limited representation just for the purpose of guarding Franz's rights during questioning. Why don't you represent the other family members, Dash?"

"I'm not the criminal law expert. If any of them get charged with anything, I'll find them permanent Vermont criminal lawyers," Dash said.

"Please, do this Mary. These are such good people," Daisy said as she poured me another hit of scotch.

# SIXTY-SIX

I was awake before six the next morning. I couldn't believe that I was again working on a case in Vermont when I should be returning to Miami.

I got up and went right to the computer and sent a long e-mail to Catherine. I told her about Sherry, the Brousseau murder, and Roland Behr. I assured her that this was the last case that I would be even peripherally involved in here, and that I would be leaving for Miami by the weekend or Monday at the latest.

I grabbed Sam and sped off to Hal's store to pick up breakfast and the morning paper. Hal was just opening the store, although I could smell that he'd been baking for hours. We bought pumpkin bread and coffee for me, and homemade dog biscuits for Sam. I dodged Hal's questions about Tom, and about the feds showing up to investigate Roland's murder.

Back at Lucy's, I spread out the Valley News to read about the murder and the full story of Sherry's kidnapping. My name was mentioned four times. The second page carried the story of Francie Wallace and Carolyn Brousseau's murder. I got two mentions in that article.

What surprised me was the sidebar that accompanied the story of Francie's arrest.

Sheriff Jimmy Parsons tendered his resignation last night to the Village Manager, stating he wished to spend more time with his family. He had two years left in his term of office. The Select Board will discuss appointing an interim sheriff to serve the two years remaining in Parson's term or until a future election.

Some citizens of the village have expressed distrust of the abilities of Parsons after Carolyn Brousseau's murder went unsolved for over one year. Many others felt that Jimmy Parsons did a good job of keeping the highways safe from speeders and drunk drivers.

Parsons was unavailable for comment prior to deadline.

With a kidnapping and two murders in the past twelve months, High Pines better get a super cop appointed fast, I thought.

I had treated myself to a New York Times and opened it to National News. Immediately an item jumped out at me. Seaside National Bank in Miami was under scrutiny from the Securities and Exchange Commission, the IRS, and the Justice Department for irregularities. Seaside was the startup bank that J.C. Martin, Carlos's father, served as a board member. I remembered that he even tried to get me to move my law office trust account to Seaside. I had a pang of regret when I saw J.C.'s name.. I had always felt real affection for him. He was a complete gentleman, always saying the right thing at the right time. I missed him.

It was time to put on my lawyer's attire and get myself over to Rabbi Goldblatt's chambers at the temple.

"I can't take you with me, Sam. I'm sorry to leave you home again," I said.

Just then I heard a tap on the back door. I saw Tom Brousseau through the glass.

"Tom, how are you?"

"I'm great, Mary. Thanks to you, I'm starting a whole new life. I came over to say thank you so much. I hope I'm not coming over too early."

"Not at all. I'm just about to leave to do some legal work. I was just putting Sam in his crate."

Sam jumped up and put his paws on Tom's chest, a greeting reserved for his closest friends. Tom rubbed Sam's chest.

"Mary, why don't you leave Sam with me? It's a shame to keep him cooped up. I'll be home all day, painting. It's so pretty that I may even set up an easel outside and Sam can romp around."

"Are you sure? Sam can be an escape artist, so you need to keep a close eye on him. You never told me where your paintings are exhibited."

"Nowhere right now. I had some exhibits when I was at the art institute and a small show on Cape Cod, but I've been out of touch as you know."

"We have a big art show in Miami every February, the Coconut Grove Art Show. I'll send you all the information and maybe you can get accepted. If you do, you can stay with me."

"Thanks, Mary. That would be great."

I snapped Sam's leash on him and he and Tom set off on the path between the two houses.

# CHAPTER
# SIXTY-SEVEN

I followed Daisy's directions to the temple. I admired the interesting building as I approached it from the parking area. It had a New England look and fit into the rural setting as easily as one of the red barns I kept passing; nothing like the Moorish architecture that older synagogues utilized, nor the stern modern looking buildings in Miami.

A group of people was standing around in the entryway. They were of mixed ages. A very frail appearing man sat on a bench. He cradled a cane in his knarred hand. Next to him sat a man around my father's age. He had his arm around the shoulder of the older man. A young couple stood nearby. I was sure these were the Goldsteins.

"Hi, I'm Mary Katz. Are you the Goldstein family?"

"Thank goodness you're here. I'm Jeff and this is my wife, Sophie. This is my grandfather Franz Goldstein and my dad, Harry. Dash Mellman said you'd be here to help us when we talk to the FBI people. How can this be happening ?"

I shook hands with each of them. Franz barely acknowledged that I was there.

"Don't be upset. This is all very routine. I will be in the room with each of you as you're called in. If I don't want you to answer a question, I'll put my hand on your arm at the same time that I object. That's your cue to stop talking and wait," I explained.

"You mean they're going to talk to each of us separately?" Harry asked.

"Yes, they have that right, and actually it gives the investigator a better idea of what each of you might be able to add."

"It's impossible for my father to be questioned without one of us with him. He doesn't always even recognize his own family anymore. We are accustomed to keeping him calm. We know how to handle him and help him listen to directions. His mind is not functioning as it used to," Harry said.

"I'm sure that the investigator will realize this, but let me sit with Franz for a few minutes and see if he can understand me," I said.

Harry moved over and I took the seat next to Franz. "Good morning Mr. Goldstein. How are you?" I asked.

Franz gave me a happy smile. "You can call me Franz," he said. He had a fairly heavy accent. He reminded me of the old people who used to live on Miami Beach when I was a young child.

"He likes women," Jeff said.

"I can see that. Franz, do you know where you are?"

"Of course, I'm at the *schul*."

"So do you know why you're here?"

"Sure. It's Rosh Hashanah. Shouldn't we go in and get our seats for the service? Why are we sitting out here?"

"That holiday was a few weeks ago. We're here today because a policeman wants to talk to us about something that happened to Roland Behr. Do you know who he is?"

"That *schtunck* ,*that gonif*. Of course, I know who he is. He shouldn't be allowed to live here."

"Okay, Franz. Do you know what happened to Roland Behr?"

"Who?" Franz asked.

"See what I mean?" Harry asked.

"I'm sure they won't speak to him for long," I reassured him. "Now do any of you have any other questions for me? I'm sure they will ask you where you were on the night of the murder, and whether you own any firearms, and whether you knew about the neo-Nazi group."

"I think this is ridiculous. They can't believe that we would actually murder someone." Sophie spoke up for the first time.

I reminded the Goldsteins that Franz had suffered at the hands of the Nazis, so it was inevitable that they would want to meet with the family.

The door to the Rabbi's study opened and a tall young woman stepped out. She ushered out an older woman. They shook hands. Harry approached the older woman and gave her a hug.

"Mildred, are you being questioned too?" Harry said.

"Please, I must request that you do not discuss anything I've asked you with the other witnesses," the tall woman said as she escorted Mildred to the outer door.

I was happy to see that the agent who was doing the interviews was a woman. I knew Franz would respond better to her.

I quickly introduced myself and explained why I was there.

"I'm Laura Morris. I'm with the FBI office serving Northern New England," she said and showed us her badge. "I'm going to speak to each of you in just a minute, but to save time, let me explain that my job is to gather as much information as possible regarding the death of Roland Behr. I will be handing each of you a form explaining your rights. If you have any questions about the form, just ask me. You have counsel who will represent you during my questions. Once you are sure you understand the form, please sign it."

"Are we being accused of something here? Are any of us under arrest?" Jeff was showing his anger.

"No, this is completely investigatory at this point." Agent Morris answered.

"Let me suggest that we get under way. I'm sure you're on a tight schedule. Why don't you start with Harry Goldstein?" I stood up and steered Harry toward the door to the study. My hope was that the whole family didn't become defensive and appear guilty of something.

We entered a pleasant room with a large antique desk and several comfortable leather chairs. The view from the large window reflected the sun on the crimson apples still remaining on a squat tree..

Laura seated herself behind the desk, placed Harry under oath, and turned on a tape recorder. "I hope you have no objection to the use of the recorder." Without waiting for an answer, Laura began her questions.

"State your full name and date of birth, sir." Laura began.

"Harry Joseph Goldstein. July 12, 1954.

"What kind of work do you do?"

"I'm a social worker. I work for the United Jewish Appeal of Greater New York."

"What are your duties there?"

"I'm in charge of overseeing several of the services run by the organization including family services, vocational services, and nutritional services."

"How long have you worked there?"

"Let's see, almost six years. Prior to that, I was employed by Vista services of New England working with families."

"Did you live in this area at one time?"

Yes, I did. We raised our children in Vermont. My wife died six years ago. I took the job in New York and moved there. It was just so difficult being here after she died."

"And where do you live in New York?"

"In the East Village, near New York University."

"When you lived here, did you know Roland Behr?"

"I knew who he was, but I never socialized with him, if that's what you mean."

"Why not?"

"Everyone knew he was anti-Semitic. He and his wife had a few friends who shared his views."

"Am I correct that your father came from Germany and was interred during the war?"

"That's a polite way to put it. My dad and my mother lost their entire families during the war, killed by the Nazis. They met here in the U.S. They didn't like to talk too much about what happened to them while I was growing up, but later when Jeff came along, he asked my dad a lot of questions and got him talking. Jeff had a school writing project. Dad agreed to speak to the students and that opened the door for him to speak out. He addressed high school classes here for several years until my mother passed away. He's gone downhill very fast. I hope you will understand that he is no longer able to converse coherently."

"I will have to judge that for myself. Right now I need to hear where you were on October Twelfth in the evening hours."

"Just a minute," I said, placing my hand on Harry's arm. "Mr. Goldstein was trying to explain something important to you. There's no reason for you to be rude. He's answering all your questions, but I expect you to respect him and the rest of his family."

"No need to get your dander up. Ms. Katz. No one's being rude. I'm just doing my job, as I assume, you are. Is your client going to answer my last question?"

"Go ahead, Harry," I said.

"I was working that night. That was our opening fund raising event. We had almost a thousand people at the Plaza Hotel. Elie Wiesel was our speaker. People were still there at eleven o'clock, and I wasn't able to leave until after midnight."

"Are there people whose names you can provide who saw you there?"

"Give or take a thousand or so," I interrupted. "Look Agent Morris. Harry was a five hour drive from High Pines. I think you can safely eliminate him from your suspicious list."

"Thank you, Ms. Katz, for your assistance, but I feel capable of making such judgments on my own. Now, Mr. Goldstein, when was the last time you were here in the Upper Valley?"

"That would have been on Yom Kippur, about three weeks ago."

"And how often do you visit here?"

"I try to get here once a month if my work allows. I like to check on my dad and see how Jeff and Sophie are doing, and to see my little grandson."

"Do you own any firearms?"

"I did, but I gave my hunting guns to Jeff when I moved down to New York."

"Okay, sir, I think that's all I need from you. Please, don't discuss these questions with other members of your family. Ms. Katz, please bring Franz Goldstein in."

Harry and I departed quickly. Once outside the Rabbi's study, Harry shook his head.

"She's some piece of work. I don't know how she's going to interview Dad."

"I'll do my best to keep everyone calm." I turned to Franz. "Come on Franz. Let's take a little walk. I want you to meet a lady named Laura. She's very pretty."

"Oh, good, I like the pretty ones," Franz said. Harry and I helped him up and Harry tucked his cane in Franz's hand.

We made our way slowly through the door.

"Franz, this is Laura .She wants to ask you some questions."

Laura turned the tape recorder back on.

"For the record," I said, Franz Goldstein is unable to sign his rights form or to understand its meaning. He has dementia and it is my hope that he will be treated very carefully."

"Are you finished, Ms. Katz?" I nodded my head.

"Hello, Franz. My name is Laura Morris. Can you tell me your full name?"

"Do you know my wife. I'll bet she'd like to meet you," Franz said.

"Franz, tell Laura your name," I said.

"She already knows it".

"Franz, do you know how old you are?"

"Sure, I'm fifty-five."

Laura looked at me. I guessed that she had never encountered someone with dementia.

"Franz, were you born in Germany?"

"I don't want to talk about that place." Franz frowned and tried to turn his back on Laura.

"Okay, we won't then. Did you ever meet someone named Roland Behr?"

"I don't want to talk about him."

"Where did you meet him?"

"In Dachau."

"Where is Dachau?"

"Back there."

"Where do you live, Franz"

"In my own apartment. I can't talk to you anymore. We're late for the service, and the rabbi doesn't like it when people come in late."

"You can go in just a minute. Franz, have you seen Roland here in High Pines?"

"Jeff said, just ignore him. Jeff said he'd take care of everything. I hate Roland, and now I don't like you anymore." Franz struggled to his feet. "Don't bother me anymore." He raised his cane and pointed it at Laura.

For a minute, I thought he was going to hit the agent with the cane. He lowered it and it was clear that he didn't have the strength to hit anyone.

"We're through here," I said. I took Franz's arm and led him from the room.

Laura followed us into the hallway. "Please bring in Sophie Goldstein."

Harry guided his father into a chair and approached Laura. "Ms. Morris, may I leave and take my father home? He seems very upset."

"Yes, you can leave, but please don't go back to New York or out of the area without checking with me. I may need to speak to you again," Laura said.

I shook hands with Harry, and motioned Sophie to follow me into the rabbi's study which was now an interrogation room.

Laura went through her routine about the rights form and the tape recorder and placed Sophie under oath. Sophie squirmed in her chair, her eyes darting from me to Laura and back again.

"Sophie, do you recall the evening of October twelfth and can you relate everything you do remember about that evening?"

"I'm pretty sure that was one of the nights that we had Papa Franz over for dinner. It was our baby's nine month birthday and Papa loves to play with the baby. It always cheers him up."

"How did he get to your house and what time did he arrive?"

"Jeff picked him up on his way home from work. The assisted living facility is close to where he works when he's not working out of our house. We're both graphic designers so we don't always have to go into the office."

"When did Franz and Jeff arrive? How did the evening progress?"

"They got home about six. I fed the baby and then we all sat down and had dinner. We had a cake and Jacob sat in his high chair with us and got the icing all over his face. It was so cute. We took some pictures."

"Yes, well, how long did Franz stay at your house?"

"We watched the Red Sox game on TV. Franz fell asleep. I guess the game was over around ten, and Jeff woke his granddad up and got him into the car."

"How far is it to Franz's place?"

"About five or six miles."

"And when did Jeff get home?"

"Jeff called from there. Papa Franz refused to settle down and go to bed. Jeff said he was disoriented and kept saying he wanted to go with Jeff."

"What time did he call?"

"I had already gone to bed, so I'm not sure. I told Jeff to bring him back and I'd get the guest room ready. Jeff said he was waiting for the nurse to come in and maybe they'd give Franz a sedative or a tranquilizer or something."

"So when did Jeff get back?"

"He called again and said Franz was very hyper even after the medication, I told him to bring him home and we'd get him quiet. I got the bed made up and they got here a little after twelve."

"So you really don't know where Jeff and Franz were for over two hours, do you?" Laura said accusingly.

"Okay, Laura, Sophie has answered all your questions very patiently. Knock off your tone," I said.

Sophie interrupted me. "Yes, I know where my husband was. He was with Papa trying to get him relaxed. Unlike some people today, we place great value on our elders. This happens fairly often. We don't just abandon him to some nurse."

Sophie and I stood up. "We're through with the questions for Sophie Goldstein," I said.

# SIXTY-EIGHT

As Sophie and I left the room, my cell phone rang. Laura followed us out. She called out to us and then her cell phone rang. I was surprised that there was actual mobile reception for both of our phones.

I glanced at my caller ID and saw that Lillian was calling. What now? I thought

"Lillian, please hold on a moment," I said, and turned to Laura. "Let's take a break for a few minutes."

Laura was looking at her phone and frowning. "Okay, fifteen minutes and then I need to interview Jeff Goldstein," Laura answered as she hurried back into the Rabbi's study and shut the door.

I motioned Jeff and Sophie to follow me out to the courtyard. The sun was actually shining and the wind had subsided. The pleasant weather was in contrast to the tense mood of the remaining Goldsteins. Jeff and Sophie sat down on one of the benches a short distance away while I went back to my cell phone..

"Lillian, is everything all right?"

"It's fine, Mary. I just wanted you to know that Sherry and I are leaving on a three o'clock flight back to Miami. Brett is driving us to Manchester, and then he's headed back to New York."

"How is Sherry?"

"She's still very quiet, but she seems much less nervous since you went with her to the jail. I just can never thank you enough for everything. I wanted you to know that I've mailed a check to your office to cover all the time you spent helping us."

"Lillian, that wasn't necessary. I'm very fond of Sherry and I considered helping her as a friend, not a lawyer."

"Mary, is there anything I can do for you once we get back to Miami? When are you coming home?"

"I don't know, Lillian. I've been away too long, but I keep getting involved in cases here."

"Maybe that's just your way of avoiding whatever is bothering you in Miami. Let me know if I can do anything for you, please."

"I will. I'll be back soon, really. Safe trip"

I put my phone in my pocket and moved over to sit with Jeff and Sophie. I was ready to admit that I was avoiding a return to Miami and to life without Carlos. I decided to set a firm deadline to start the trip back. Maybe just one more weekend here.

Jeff interrupted my argument with myself. "Mary, Sophie says that bitch Morris thinks I was out murdering Roland Behr. This is ludicrous."

"Jeff, can you find the nurse that helped you with Franz the night of Roland's murder?"

"I hope so. They're all practical nurses, not R.N's so they do tend to come and go, but Marie has been there a while and she is fond of Papa. She'll remember the problem we had with him that evening."

I glanced at my watch and ushered the Goldsteins back inside. They were an attractive couple and clearly devoted to each other and to Jeff's family. Maybe they would lie to help each other.

Laura was waiting outside her adopted interrogation room. Jeff and I took seats in front of the desk, as Laura started her spiel about rights and tape recorders once again.

Laura began with the usual questions, name, address, job, how long at the current address. Then she slid into police mode. "I know that Franz was at your home on the night of Roland Behr's murder. Did you leave with Franz sometime after dinner?"

Jeff told Laura pretty much what Sophie had told her; that Franz had been volatile and refused to go to bed or even to lie down. The night nurse named Marie had given him a tranquilizer and finally Jeff brought Franz back to his home where he and Sophie had gotten him to bed.

"Were you acquainted with Roland Behr?"

"Everyone in High Pines knew who he was. He was a scary old guy, sort of like a hermit," Jeff said.

"Did Franz know him?"

"Franz and my dad always said to stay away from him."

"That's not my question. Do you know if Franz was acquainted with Roland?"

"Papa Franz is no longer clear in his mind. In the last year, he has said that he knew Roland in Germany. We didn't pay much attention to this because we didn't know where Roland came from. There was speculation about him, but no one around here was sure."

"Your dad said that it was you who got Franz to talk about his experiences as a boy in the Holocaust," Laura said.

"He started helping me with some projects in high school and ended up making a great contribution to several history and writing classes. We even recorded a tape of his memories. His whole family was murdered or died of disease in various concentration camps. He was sent to Dachau where he was assigned cleaning work because he was young and strong. He had flash-backs for years about the atrocities he witnessed.

"One thing that I never forgot was his explaining how close the camp was to the town of Dachau. He told us that the townspeople had to know what was happening there. They could smell the human flesh being burned."

"So do you think that Franz believed that Roland was one of those people who lived in that town?"

"Objection," I put my hand on Jeff's arm. "Jeff doesn't know what someone else thought."

"Just a minute, Mary. I want to tell Agent Morris something."

Before I could stop him, Jeff waved my hand away. "Just about everyone in this community knew that Roland was a nasty guy. We all knew that he hated Jews and that somewhere in this area there was a group that was carrying out hate crimes. At first there were a couple of incidents, but those events were escalating. I'm pretty sure that the U.S. attorney's office wouldn't be here in High Pines if there weren't some hate crimes or even seditious acts happening here." Jeff was standing in front of Laura Morris.

"Jeff, please sit down," I said.

"Just one last question," Laura said. "Did you suspect that Roland Behr was a member or leader of this hate group?"

"Of course not. If we knew this, we'd have taken this knowledge to the proper authorities immediately. As it was, the Rabbi met with Curtis Lemay to let him know about the various acts occurring at our temple."

"All right, Jeff. Please write down the address of the assisted living facility where your grandfather lives and the name of the nurse that helped you on October twelfth so we can check into this further."

"Does that mean that you don't believe me?" Jeff glared at Laura.

"Jeff, it's Agent Morris's job to fact check. You and I can check with the nurse as well," I said as I gathered my file and notes. We moved quickly out of the building. I told Sophie and Jeff not to worry. Then I left the parking lot and headed straight over to Dash's office.

# SIXTY-NINE

Daisy was not on the phone for once. She came around her desk and led me into the library, explaining that Dash was in a client conference. I could tell she was eager to hear how the interviews had gone.

"The Goldsteins are very nice people. They've been through difficult times with Franz," I began.

Without divulging the content of my clients' statements, I asked Daisy if she knew that Franz had been imprisoned in the Dachau concentration camp.

"Oh, yes, I heard him give a talk at a high school assembly when the school allowed the public to attend. But did you know that Jeff and Sophie visited the camp?"

"What? When was this?" I asked.

"When they finished college and before they were married they took a few months and backpacked through Europe. They made a special side trip to Germany to see where Jeff's grandfather had been. Jeff spoke to a forum at the temple. He was pretty shaken by what he saw."

The phone rang and Daisy left to get back to her desk. Thoughts swirled in my brain. Could Jeff have actually murdered Roland as retribution? He seemed too smart to do something like that, but he did adore his grand-father This whole case brought back memories of my father talking to my brothers and me about the history of the Holocaust and his taking us through the Holocaust Memorial in Miami Beach. In our safe and diverse environment, I never gave much thought to what that era meant to Jews everywhere.

Suddenly I had pangs of homesickness for my parents and especially Dad and his unabashed love for his family. I realized I had been unfair, not letting them know where I was or how I was. I let my anger at Carlos make me act like a spoiled little girl

I was so deep in thought that I never heard Dash come into the library. He touched me on the shoulder and I jumped as if I'd been shot.

"Sorry, I didn't mean to give you a heart attack," Dash said. "Are you a little nervous after spending the morning with the FBI?"

I pulled out my notes from the interviews and gave Dash a quick version of the morning, ending with the nagging feeling that Agent Morris suspected Jeff of Roland's murder.

"We need to go over to the facility where Franz lives and start checking out Jeff's recollection of the night Roland was murdered. We need to see if that nurse still works there and what time she comes to work." I gathered my notes and picked up my file.

"I agree, but I think you need some lunch and a calming cup of tea or better yet a glass of wine," Dash said. "Curtis left a message with Daisy that he'd be stopping by around two, so let's go eat and wait 'til we hear what he has to say."

CHAPTER
# SEVENTY

Dash insisted on a fancy lunch at Simon Pearce, a restaurant and glass shop that I drove by many times in the last weeks. The décor was very New England; historic appearing wood floors and spare wooden furniture. An enclosed patio overlooked an active waterfall. Dash explained that the waterfall had powered an old mill that this building once housed. In contrast to the historic feel of the building, the blown glass vases, bar wear, lamps, cups, and plates looked totally modern in design and could have fit comfortably into any South Florida home.

We were seated in the patio section with the sun glimmering over the fast moving water below us. It had a calming effect or maybe it was the excellent glass of chardonnay. In any event, I did feel much better as we left the restaurant.

When we arrived back at Dash's office, Daisy met us at the door.

"Jeff Goldstein is here waiting to see both of you. He seems very nervous. I put him in the library. He immediately lit a cigarette. I told him no smoking here, but he ignored me," Daisy said.

We went directly into the library, now as smoke-filled as a political party meeting. Jeff was pacing to the window and back to the door. Three cigarette butts were resting in a saucer on the table and Jeff was working on number four.

"Jeff, is everything okay?" I asked, and then felt foolish for asking this when I could see the agitation pouring out of Jeff along with the cigarette smoke.

"Of course, it's not okay. That Agent Morris phoned me as soon as I got home and said she just wanted to warn me that I shouldn't leave town. She said if I did, a warrant might be issued for my arrest. This whole thing is out of control. I want you to do something. You're supposed to be representing me."

"Actually, Mary's representation was just for the purpose of your interview with the agent," Dash explained. I think a great deal of investigation would have to be done before any arrests are made, but if this escalates, of course, I will find you excellent criminal counsel. I think this is all premature."

I looked at the alarm on Jeff's face. "Listen, Jeff, Agent Morris is a young agent. I think she's just covering her ass. She doesn't want to make any mistakes. She told your dad not to leave town. She probably just forgot to tell you that at the interview. I've seen a lot of officers and they all want to appear as aggressive as possible. It's their way of keeping everyone under their control."

Dash nodded in agreement. "Curtis Lemay, the U.S. Attorney, said he'd be stopping by later this afternoon so we'll learn more about the investigation then."

"Maybe he's coming to let you know that they're going to arrest me. I didn't have anything to do with murdering Roland Behr. You believe me, don't you?" Jeff looked from me to Dash and back again.

I've heard that same question from many clients; some who are guilty and some who aren't. I gave my stock answer. "Of course, I believe you."

Dash nodded. "I definitely believe you. Now why don't you go home and get your mind off of all this. We'll call you the instant we know anything new."

Jeff snuffed out his current cigarette. "I'll be waiting to hear from you," he said. He grabbed his coat and walked quickly out of the library and out through the front entrance. We heard Daisy call goodbye but heard no answering goodbye from Jeff. We did hear his car rev up and wheels squeal as he shot out of the driveway.

Daisy rushed into the library and opened all the windows. I wasn't sure which was worse, the cold air flooding into the room or the stale smoke that Jeff left behind.

# SEVENTY-ONE

Dash picked up some phone messages and went into his office to return calls. I read through my notes from the morning interviews and thought about Franz.

It felt totally unfair after his early suffering to think that dementia was ruining the end of Franz's life. It made me realize how short life is. I wondered if I was wasting a part of mine, carrying so much anger at Carlos. I wished I could remove him from my thoughts, but he just wouldn't get out. I was able to remove his physical presence, but it was proving much harder to erase him from my memory.

I realized that Daisy was standing in front of me.

"You're lost in thought and it doesn't look from your expression that the thoughts are happy," she said. "Curtis Lemay is in the reception area. Dash said for me to tell you to come into his office and then I'll show Curtis in."

I moved quickly into the office. Dash motioned for me to sit down. "I hope Curtis has some news. If the feds arrest Jeff, this community will never be quite the same. Maybe I should call Rabbi Goldblatt. He and some of the other clergy in the area should be prepared for the outcome of this investigation. They may have to hold some interfaith sessions or something."

"Maybe Rabbi Goldblatt should go sit with Jeff and Sophie. He might be able to keep them calm," I suggested.

"A better idea. I'll call him right now. You go out and chat with Curtis while I make the call," Dash said.

I didn't have to worry about small talk with Curtis. Daisy was holding forth on the benefits of blueberries and anti-oxidants. She was giving him recipes for pies, and muffins. Curtis appeared totally enthralled. He was a good actor, but I guess all good lawyers can be good actors, even me.

"Curtis, thanks for coming over in the midst of your investigation. I know you must be anxious to get back to Burlington," I said, pretending real pleasure in his appearance.

"Actually, I'm close to winding down this investigation. I know Dash will want to hear what I've found. There will be arrests today and tomorrow. I'll be updating Jimmy Parsons since he's in charge of this state jurisdiction, even though I understand he's tendered his resignation."

Daisy interrupted to tell us that Dash had just called on the intercom for us to go back to his office.

Dash walked around his desk and shook hands with Curtis. He moved over to the small round table and Curtis and I followed. We seated ourselves around the table. An awkward silence enveloped us. Dash and I looked at Curtis. I felt curious and scared at the same time. I wanted to know what Curtis's next move would be, but if that encompassed the arrest of Jeff or any of the Goldsteins, I didn't want to hear it.

Finally, Dash broke the silence. "I hope you can share your findings with us, and I hope that you can help High Pines heal after this murder and the revelation that a neo-Nazi group has been operating right under our noses."

"Well, Dash and Mary, let me first thank you for the cooperation you and the citizens of the Upper Valley have provided to my office. It's difficult to go into a small community when we know we may have to arrest people that are a real part of the community."

My heart sank into the floor. It sounded like he was talking about the Goldsteins.

"No, thank you for coming to help us," Dash said.

Curtis drew a breath. "In this case, I think the community will be glad to rid themselves of the people who have committed and were plotting to commit more hate crimes. I believe you know that Roland Behr's lawyer was the person who found Behr's body."

"That was Christian Berger, wasn't it? I asked. I had a run-in with him when he represented Roland in the lawsuit against Fred Upham."

"Yes, that's correct. Berger was the first person I questioned. Berger was hired by Roland and his group on retainer to represent them in any civil or criminal actions. It's clear that they were anticipating legal troubles."

"This was the group that had passed themselves off as some kind of environmental group?" Dash asked.

"They didn't give a damn about the environment. They were a collection of far right crazies. Roland was a teenager in Germany during the Nazi era. When we searched his house we found scrapbooks filled with memorabilia and even a picture of Roland in some kind of uniform, sort of like a boy scout with swastikas. How he got to this country and passed himself off as a good citizen, we don't fully know, but our Washington office will pursue those answers. There's been talk for a long time about a secret report at the Justice Department."

"What kind of report?" Dash and I asked at the same time.

"It's all inside gossip so please don't pass this off as coming from me. There were a number of Nazis admitted to the U.S. after the war. Some were brought in to help with scientific work on rockets and other defense projects. But the story circulating is that a good number of Nazi war criminals were allowed to lie about their past and receive citizenship. It's possible that Roland Behr and his family fall into that category."

"So the defeated got their share of the good life. That's disgusting," Dash said.

"What about the other members of this group?" I asked,

Berger told me that Roland collected members from all of the surrounding areas.. Some were vigilante types and liked to march and play with guns, but as time went on, younger men began to join. These were guys looking for trouble; guys who resented the so-called liberals in the area."

"That's the majority who live in Vermont," Dash said.

"I understand, but there is a certain element that resent anyone with a good job and some money to spend. In bigger cities they join gangs. Up here, they decided to harass Jews. Several of them have criminal records around the state. They came from all corners of the area to meet with their hero, Roland, the true Nazi."

"Berger told you all this?" Dash asked.

"Most of it, especially when I intimated that he was the prime suspect in the murder. He got real talkative."

"I can't stand this suspense," I blurted out. "Is Jeff Goldstein a suspect?"

"No, I know who the murderers are. Jeff is definitely not one of them."

"Then why was Agent Morris threatening him with arrest?"

"I went over Agent Morris's report with her at noon today. We divided the investigation. I assigned Morris to follow up with members of the Jewish community. I handled those directly involved with Roland. I wanted to be as thorough as possible, especially knowing that this community had spent a year without closure in the Brousseau murder."

"Agent Morris alienated a number of people in the Upper Valley," I said.

"Don't be too hard on her. I know it sounds trite, but she was just doing her job," Curtis said.

Just then Daisy knocked and opened the door. "Mary, I have a telephone message for you. Can you step out here for a minute?"

"Please, Curtis, wait 'til I take care of this. I need to hear everything about your investigation."

I stepped into the hallway. Daisy handed me a long note. "Tom Brousseau called. He didn't know whether you would be here. He said a strange man was parked outside Lucy's house in a rental car. Tom saw him when he walked Sam over to get his dish and food. The man asked where you were and when you'd be back. Tom told him he didn't know. The man said he'd wait and he's still sitting out there. Tom wants to know if he should call the police."

"Do you want me to call him back for you?" Daisy asked.

"Well, he can't very well call the police. That would be Jimmy Parsons who just quit. Maybe it's one of Lucy Stern's friends. Tell you what; call Ken Upham and see if he feels up to riding by there to check this guy out. Let Tom know that you're getting in touch with Ken."

"I don't like the sound of this. When you get done here, Dash will go home with you. I don't want you to go alone," Daisy said.

# SEVENTY-TWO

I hurried back to Dash's office. I didn't want to miss a word about the murder investigation.

Dash was showing Curtis a large headed golf club. "This driver has really helped my game, not that I get enough time to play."

"Tell me about it," Curtis said as he hefted the humongous club.

"You sound like my dad," I said. "Come on, Curtis. Put the toy away and let's hear who is being arrested."

"I got a list of the group and their addresses from Berger who also told me that most of the group was upset with Roland for starting the escalating argument with Ken Upham. A couple of them thought Roland was a little off his rocker. When he filed the lawsuit and it hit the papers, the whole group went ballistic"

"That's a pretty poor pun," Dash said

Curtis smiled. "It's not exactly a joke. Travis Smith and Lewis Devore, two of the most militant of the group, reamed Roland out at a meeting shortly after the lawsuit hit the papers. Apparently, the story was even picked up by the Manchester Union Leader and by the local Fox News affiliate. Travis made some threats to Roland at the meeting. Berger said those two told Roland he was going to blow their cover by calling all this attention to himself and his demand for privacy."

"Why did Roland continue this vendetta against Ken Upham?" I asked,

"Berger said that Roland couldn't stand having anyone threaten his property rights. Roland also had some mixed up idea that his lawsuit furthered the group's cover as an environmental club."

"Anyone who looked at his decaying house and yard would know that the environment was the last thing on his mind," I said.

"After talking to Berger, I contacted Lewis Devore, and asked him to come in voluntarily for an interview about the murder. He claimed he didn't have transportation, so I sent a car to pick him up and bring him to Jimmy Parson's office. About thirty minutes into the interview, he admitted that he was a member of the neo-Nazi group. He said he knew nothing about Roland's murder. I told him that Travis was being questioned and had already told us that Lewis shot Roland."

"How did Lewis react to that?" I asked.

"He slammed his fist into the table and said Travis was a lying bag of shit. Then he told me that Travis was the mastermind who decided that Roland had to go, and that they could make the murder look like a Jewish plot by painting the swastika on Roland's forehead. Lewis agreed to help him. Travis had some other Jewish symbols that he wanted to steal to leave at the scene."

"I don't remember hearing about religious objects left at Roland's house." Dash said.

"They didn't have time to get the items they wanted. Travis thought they needed to silence Roland before he shot off his mouth. Lewis was supposed to bring a yarmulke that they were going to put on Roland's head, but Lewis got spooked when he tried to get inside the temple.

"While I was interviewing Lewis, I had my assistant pick up Travis and bring him to the office. What a piece of work he is; tattoos on all the parts of his body that showed, probably more in private areas, a shaved head and biceps the size of grapefruits."

"Did Travis make a statement? Dash asked.

"Sort of. He said he and Lewis went to Roland's house to talk him out of going any further with his lawsuit. He said the old man actually got in a fight with them and that when Roland realized that they were overpowering him, he pulled out a revolver. According to Travis, the gun went off during a struggle and Roland died instantly."

"Maybe that is what happened," I said.

"No way. Roland was shot three times. Once in the leg and twice in the back. I guess he was trying to run from Travis and Lewis, and of course, they did paint the swastika on his forehead after they turned his body over."

"So where are these two goons now?" Dash asked.

"They're sitting in Jimmy's office in handcuffs waiting for transport by the marshals to a federal holding facility"

"Isn't this going to become a state case?" I asked.

"I intend to bring an indictment to a grand jury for attempts to overthrow the government and for hate crimes. I guess I forgot to tell you that Travis lost his cool when I placed him under arrest and yelled that the Nazis in this country had lots of cells just like Roland's and that soon they would be taking over the entire country and this time they'd do everything right. He said the average citizen was sick and tired of the liberal establishment and their control of all the banks and newspapers."

"What about the rest of the members of this cell? And please, tell me that they don't all live in the Upper Valley." Dash said.

"Over the next couple of days, I plan to have all of them interviewed. There may be more arrests. Travis and Lewis live in Claremont. The members are scattered over the Upper Valley and beyond Don't worry, Dash. They're not your next door neighbors, but they're close enough to make you wonder who else might have feelings of sympathy for their hate mongering. You just never know."

I headed for the door as soon as Curtis finished

"Where are you rushing off to?" Dash asked.

"I've got to call Jeff and Sophie Goldstein, and tell them not to worry about being charged with a crime. Now all they need to worry about is whether there are any other neo-Nazis in their neighborhood."

# SEVENTY-THREE

The Goldsteins were ecstatic that they were no longer under suspicion and that the Nazi group had been uncovered. Their enthusiasm waned when I pointed out that this group was operating under everyone's collective noses. Sophie said that maybe this wasn't the healthiest place to raise their young child.

"No place is perfect. The Upper Valley looks like a very good place to grow up; that is if you like cold weather," I told her.

We told each other what a pleasure it was meeting and other platitudes. I realized Dash was standing right behind me waiting for me to hang up.

"Mother told me about the phone call from Tom and the strange man hanging out at your place. I'm going to follow you home," Dash said.

"I really don't think it's necessary. I think Ken Upham was going to ride by and see who it is," I said.

"I'll feel better if I see that everything is okay. After all the weird things that have gone on in the past weeks, anything is possible."

Dash fell in behind me in the now famous black Subaru. I was anxious to get back and retrieve Sam and have a little down time. We pulled into the familiar gravel road and as we approached the house, I saw two cars parked in the circular drive. One was Ken Upham's Lexus. The second car was unfamiliar. Dash and I added our two cars creating the look of a cocktail party.

Dash came around to my door as I got out of the Explorer. "I think that large red Lincoln is a rental car by its license plate."

"Good detective work," I said. There's a Hertz sticker on the window."

I heard Sam barking inside just as Tom opened the front door. "Mary, just a minute. I need to talk to you before you come in." Tom closed the door and joined Dash and me.

"Is something wrong? Please tell me that Sam is okay," I said.

"Sam is fine, but I better prepare you for your uninvited guest. I came back here with the dog after Daisy let me know that Ken was coming over to check out this guy. We talked to him together."

"Well, spit it out. Who is it and what does he want?"

"It's Carlos Martin. He explained that you wouldn't want to see him, but he's here to break some news to you."

"This is a crock of shit. He could have left me a message or something." I was so caught off guard by this news that I actually began to tremble.

"Mary, we'll get rid of him, if that's what you want, or we'll stay with you. It's your call," Dash said.

"Please, go in with me. Is Ken there, too?"

"Yes, he thought you might need him. He's in the living room with Carlos. Carlos is very charming and Sam is crazy about him."

"Oh, he can be charming. That's Carlos to a 'T'. I charged through the front door.

Ken and Carlos were seated in front of the fireplace chatting away like old friends. A wave of panic swept over me, or maybe it was just raw lust when I saw Carlos, so macho, so handsome. My heart was pounding.

Carlos stood up when he heard us. "Mary, please don't be angry. Don't send me away before I have a chance to tell you why I'm here."

Ken stood up and walked over to me. He put an arm around me. "I'm afraid Carlos has some bad news. Let him explain. We're all here for you. Carlos, this is Dash Mellman, an attorney and friend of Mary's. Dash and Tom and I are going to be in the kitchen when you need us." Ken led the way and Tom and Dash followed him.

"Mary, please sit down," Carlos said.

"Thank you, I'm fine. Just tell me what was so important that it required a trip up here. How did you find me, anyway?"

"Catherine had to tell me and Lucy gave me all the directions. Carlos crossed behind the sofa and stood in front of me. "Your father has had a heart attack. I'm here to help you get home to Miami as quickly as possible."

Carlos reached out and steadied me.

"Is he, is he?" I couldn't get the awful word out.

"No, no, he's alive, but it's serious. They're going to do surgery the day after tomorrow. Your mother needs you. Your brothers and their wives are with her at the hospital, so I knew I was the one who had to get up here and tell you in person."

"When did this happen?"

"Yesterday early morning. Around six o'clock"

"Why didn't Mom call me?"

"You didn't exactly leave her any contact information and her hands were full. She got your dad to the hospital in Boynton Beach. His cardiologist in Miami arranged for his transfer by helicopter to the University of Miami hospital. Jonathan called me to help. Your brothers didn't know how to reach you either, and they were all too upset to think clearly."

"Well, I appreciate your going to all this trouble. I'll get packed and start back at once."

"I have all the arrangements made. Here is your plane ticket. I'll drive you down to the airport in Manchester. That's where I flew in. I'll help you pack your car and as soon as I get you to the airport, I'll bring Sam and your car back to Miami."

"How soon does the plane leave? I can't ask you to take that long drive back."

"The best reservation I could get you is tomorrow morning at eight. Nothing else connects tonight. Don't worry about the drive. You didn't ask me. I want to do this for you."

I sat down on the sofa. My legs felt like they were made out of water.

Carlos sat down next to me. "I'm going to get you something to drink. Are you all right? Something else, Mary, I need to talk to you about why I lied to you. I know it's not the time right now, but please promise me that you will give me a chance to talk to you, to explain everything to you. There are other reasons why you are so needed back in Miami."

Carlos left the room. The room seemed to be whirling around. A thousand thoughts rushed at me. No wonder I kept thinking about Dad the last two days. I pictured him working at the market late into the evening after my grandfather died. I remembered Mom yelling at him that he was eating at odd hours and trying to get him to eat healthy. I remembered him saying that he had three kids to educate and he was going to be sure we had what we needed. I thought how he looked when I passed my driver's license exam after he spent countless hours teaching me to parallel-park.

I remembered his last birthday when we had a family picture taken, and how he said he couldn't believe he had three attorneys as his kids. He said, "Mary I can understand. She always loved to talk your ears off, but how did I fail Jonathan and William?" I remember Mom laughing and how he put his arms around her.

I raced into the hallway and dialed Mom's cell phone but got no answer. Next I tried Jonathan and then William with the same result. So I started again with Mom and left each of them a message with the phone number here. I apologized for not being there and told each of them I'd be back tomorrow. I looked at the plane ticket I was still clutching and read off the flight number and noon arrival time.

When I returned to the Great Room, Carlos was holding out a glass of wine. Tom, Dash, and Ken were standing together.

"I know about Dad, and I'm going to take Carlos up on his offer to take my car and Sam back to Miami. I'll be leaving early tomorrow, and I won't get a chance to tell people here good-bye, so I hope you'll do that for me," I said.

"You'll get a little chance to see some of them," Ken said. "I took the liberty of telling Rita. She and Hal and Margaret are coming over with dinner. There's going to be plenty so everyone plan on staying for dinner."

"That's so thoughtful. All of you have been good friends while I've been here."

"This is what friends are for. We're used to helping each other," Dash said. "But Mary, I'm not going to be staying. Walk outside with me. It's best if we say good-bye now."

"Please, I want you to stay," I said.

Dash had already started into the hallway, so I followed him. We headed out the front door and into the driveway without speaking. Dash opened the door to his car and then turned back to me.

"I'll miss you, Mary, but I watched you and Carlos and I can see there is a magnetic attraction between the two of you. I just want you to know that if you ever change your mind and want to come back here, you've got a job and someone who cares about you right here in High Pines. Also, yesterday I sent a check to your office in Miami to cover the work you did while you were here."

"That's not necessary. I enjoyed working with you. I wish you'd stay to dinner," I said.

"I feel a little uncomfortable with Carlos giving me the eye every time I talk to you. I'll be thinking about you and hoping that your dad is up and about very soon."

"Thank you for everything, Dash. Say goodbye to Daisy for me. You're a great guy. I know you'll meet someone as special as you are."

"I thought I had," he said and put his arms around me. Then he jumped in his car and sped away.

"If you'll excuse me, I'm going to start packing," I said when I returned to the house. "I'll load up my car and just take an overnight bag on the plane, if you don't mind driving back with a stuffed SUV, Carlos. I tried to get Mother or my brothers and no one answered their cells. Where do you think they are?"

They're probably at the hospital and either they don't want to disturb your dad, or they can't get cell service in some parts of the hospital. I don't mind taking your things back for you. Can I help with anything?" Carlos asked

"Yes, thanks, let's get Sam's crate in first. And fold the back seats down."

Carlos followed me out to my car with the crate. "Mary, who is this Dash guy?"

"You have no right to ask me about any of my friends, Carlos. Dash is a good lawyer who I worked with while I was here. He's a good friend."

"I could see that when he gave you that very long embrace."

"You were spying on me? I can't believe you. I'm grateful that you came all this way to help my family, and I'll always be glad to help your family, but that's it. You gave up any right to pitch one of your jealous Latin machismo tantrums when you lied to me to sneak out with Margarita. Nothing has changed about our now non-existent relationship."

"I wasn't spying on you, exactly, and I'm glad you're willing to help my family. Just give me a few minutes to explain to you why I was having dinner with Margarita that awful night."

"You'll have plenty of time to talk to me while we drive down to Manchester in the morning. For now, I have packing to do, and cleaning up Lucy's house and visiting with friends before I leave, along with worrying about my dad. He's always been the super strong person in our family. He has to get well."

"He is strong. I know he's a fighter. He'll fight to regain his health. I don't have to stay for dinner here. Why don't I just leave you to do what you have to do. I can come back later to see if you need any help."

"You can stay for dinner, of course," I said as I hurried back inside.

"It is so cold here," Carlos said as he followed me in and retreated to a seat near the fireplace.


I sorted through laundry, throwing towels into the washer and trying to put the kitchen back the way it looked when I arrived here. It seemed impossible that I'd been here only a few weeks. I had begun to feel completely at home in this house.

I put my boots and sweaters in the car along with books, and the few things I had bought at the flea market. The car was looking crowded already. Sam followed me in and out of the house for a while. I realized he was out of sight and hurried through the house looking for him. It only took minutes to spot him sitting next to Carlos in front of the fire. Carlos was rubbing his head and Sam was making his contented purring noises. It hadn't occurred to me that Sam missed having Carlos around. Carlos was a part of his everyday life since February. Maybe Sam felt as abandoned as I felt during the week before we left Miami.

The front door opened interrupting my thoughts. Rita, Margaret and Hal came in carrying bags and trays. Luscious smells filled the front hall. I hugged each of them.

"Now, Mary, you just sit down or keep doing whatever. We are going to lay out this spread and then we're all going to sit down to supper and some good cheer for you to take back with you." Margaret said. The three of them bustled around the kitchen while I watched them and thought about how lucky I was to have a whole group of new friends.

We ate the delicious stew and salads from Hal's store, a spaghetti casserole and an apple pie from Rita's freezer and wine from Ken's cellar. Hal repeated the story of my stay in the wrong house, for Carlos's entertainment. The laughter and companionship drove thoughts about Dad out of my mind for a little while. It seemed strange to have Carlos sitting here chatting with my new friends. I couldn't help looking at him and seeing that he was looking back at me most of the time.

Everyone helped clean up the kitchen and empty the refrigerator. Hal promised to contact the caretaker that looked after Lucy's house and to double check that he cleaned the house thoroughly of any leftover dog hair.

As everyone gathered in the front hall for goodbye hugs, Ken pulled me aside.

"You'll never guess what news I have," Ken said. Since he was wearing a dazzling grin, I knew it couldn't be bad news. "Your friend Riley Simmons and two of the other selectmen from the village called me to come to a meeting. They've offered me the job of acting sheriff until they do a thorough search. They said if I will accept the job, I can reorganize the office as I see fit. What do you think?"

"I think it's a perfect idea. It'll be good for you and great for the village. You should take it," I said. "What does Rita think?"

"She thinks it's what I need. She knows I've been restless since we've been here, and she saw how I plunged into finding Sherry Yarmouth."

"You better keep me up to date on what's happening here," I said.

Tom gave me a hug and thanked me for ending his hermit existence and promised to keep painting. He retrieved a package he had stashed in the hall closet on his way in. "This is for you and Sam," he said. Then they were all gone as I stood alone in the driveway waving.

As I walked back to the door, wet white flakes swirled around the light over the front door settling on my eyelashes.

"Is that actual snow?" Carlos asked.

He was standing looking out the front door. I had forgotten that he was still there.

I quickly addressed the problem of where he was going to spend the night. Much as the sight of him still activated that fluttering feeling in my heart and elsewhere, I was not about to have his company in my bed I knew I had to be strong and resist going back into our relationship.

"Listen, Carlos, there's plenty of room for you to stay here tonight, especially since we have to be up early and on the road. There's a bedroom and bath suite at the end of the hall upstairs. I still have the last things to put in my suitcase. As soon as I walk Sam, I'll be packing and turning in."

Carlos looked away but I still saw his face turning red that was the sign that he was losing his temper. The he sighed and grabbed his duffle bag and moved toward the stairs. I turned away quickly not wanting to dwell on the look of resignation on Carlos's handsome face.

I grabbed Sam's leash and took him around the backyard quickly. The snowflakes had stopped, but the autumn winds were freeing the last of the beautiful leaves from their summer home. The bare branches stood out against a red nighttime sky.

Sam and I retreated to our bedroom and locked the door.

# SEVENTY-FIVE

I set the alarm for five, but I was wide awake long before it rang. I remembered the package that Tom handed me and went to unwrap it. It was a gorgeous painting of Sam looking out at the hills behind Tom's house. What a terrific reminder of the Upper Valley, I thought

I hurried into jeans, a Miami- weight shirt, and threw my leather jacket over it to withstand the Vermont weather.

Carlos must have heard me rumbling around. He soon joined me carrying his duffle bag into the front hall. "Looks like you couldn't sleep either," he said.

"Carlos, what about your rental car?" How will you return it?"

"Your friends, Ken and Rita, offered to come get it and drop it at the Hertz place over the river in New Hampshire. I gave Ken the keys and paperwork last night. You made some great friends here."

We were silent as we loaded the last of my things in the car. I ran Sam around the backyard one last time and loaded his food, water and dishes. Sam jumped into his crate in the car while I took one last look through the house.

By five a.m., we pulled away from the house, the dark gravel road, and High Pines. I showed Carlos my collection of maps to guide him on his trip back.

"Not to worry," he said. He pulled out a AAA triptych and a list of dog-friendly motels along the route. "Marco ran around helping me get ready. He wanted to come along and help with the driving, but I wanted to come alone."

"I guess it pays to have a lot of cousins," I said. "There's a diner close to where we get on the freeway. Let's stop for coffee and rolls."

We were underway again, fully awake after our caffeine break. Carlos was still shaking his head over the lack of *café cubano* in the area.

We rode in silence for a few minutes. Carlos broke into my thoughts about my dad.

"I forgot to tell you that your mother has been staying in Miami Beach with one of her old friends, Janet Cole. She couldn't go back and forth to Boynton Beach. Your brothers wanted her to stay with them, but she didn't want to stay at Jonathan's because his boys are super busy with sports and Randy has her hands full running to the hospital with Jonathan and then home to drive the boys. William lives too far away in Fort Lauderdale, so Janet insisted that she stay there. My mother invited her to stay with them in the Grove, but I think she felt uncomfortable because of our—situation."

"Maybe she'll stay with me in Coral Gables once I get the house open again."

"I think your mother would like to be living in Miami again, but she won't upset your dad, especially now with his surgery and all."

"I wish they'd move back," I said. I realized that we were making small talk as the miles passed.

"Mary, can I please explain to you what I've wanted to tell you ever since you sent your ring back?" Carlos asked. He looked over at me. "Even if you say you don't want to hear, you're a captive audience so you'll have to listen."

I didn't answer. I was afraid to hear some excuse that would sound like a blatant lie. Then I knew I would close the door on Carlos for good and forever.

Carlos took my silence for acquiescence, so he began to talk at once.

"You know my dad is on the board of directors of Seaside Bank. In fact he was one of its founders."

"What does that have to do with you and Margarita?" I asked. I felt a combination of impatience and jealousy at the thought of Margarita.

"Just listen, please. My dad has had a number of business deals over the years. His part ownership in the cattle ranches in Argentina had stopped being profitable, so he was looking around for some new income when some acquaintances came to him with the idea for a new bank. They made him a proposal for a salary and bonuses for every account he brought in with deposits over a hundred thousand dollars.

"Dad and Mama live a rather extravagant lifestyle as you probably noticed, so he was ready to jump into a deal that would bring in substantial income."

"I just saw something in the New York Times about Seaside Bank being investigated. They mentioned your dad's name as one of the directors," I said.

"Yes, that's correct. Dad started working with the investors. He put some money into the deal himself. As you're probably aware, he and my mother know a lot of people in Miami and South America. Dad started selling potential customers on moving money to the new bank. Sometime during that first year, he found out that some of these people were not honest businessmen. Some of them were using the bank to launder dirty money, but he didn't want to lose his own investment in the bank and he was getting a wad of bucks for bringing in these customers."

"I still don't see what this has to do with Margarita. I feel bad about your dad but this explains nothing about you." I was sure Carlos could tell how annoyed I was.

"Give me a chance to tell you the rest of this, please," Carlos said.

"By the time the bank was in its second year, Margarita and I were married. She spent a lot of time at my parents' condo in Miami and the condo in Marco Island. I later learned that she asked a lot of questions about Dad's business.

"Apparently, she also eaves dropped on Dad's conversations with Mama and she even listened in to his phone conversations on an extension. She put things together and figured out that he was into some questionable things. She also knew who several of the customers were and started checking into their backgrounds.

"Things got worse when I asked her for a divorce. She was out of control spending money on clothes and a new car, and running around with a group of women who were part of the wild South Beach club scene. She wanted a lump sum payment in return for the divorce. I gave it to her and thought we were through. But it wasn't long before she was back asking for more. When I said no, she told me what she knew about my dad and threatened to go to every federal agency, if I didn't pay her off."

"My God, she was blackmailing you."

"Exactly. Things got worse at the bank. The president and the treasurer started advising customers to invest their money in some wild investments. Some clients of the bank were honest people who had placed a lot of money in the bank and trusted the officers. Several lost their life savings by following this bad advice. My dad wasn't personally involved in that investment advice, but he is a director of the bank.

"Then the bank made some questionable loans to businesses that may not have been legitimate. I just learned some of this in the past few months."

"I take it that Margarita made more than one blackmail demand."

"Oh, yes, she had her hand out more and more often. You saw her with Marielena, Mama's cousin, at my house one night. She came there to say she had overdrawn her bank account and had some big credit card bills. She wanted my help in paying the bills. I think she brought Marielena along so I wouldn't lose my temper and throw her out."

"Did Marielena know about your dad and the blackmail scheme? Marielena and your mother are like sisters."

"I don't think so. I just think she thought I should give Margarita dollars for divorcing her, but I'm not sure."

Our conversation stopped for a minute while I directed Carlos onto the highway to Manchester after we passed through a toll booth.

"The night that I told you I was going to a business dinner, Margarita had made a huge demand. I gave her a deal on the condo in my new building, as you know. You were already angry about that. Well, she wanted to live there rent free and without the maintenance fees. That was the last straw. I went to my dad and told him what Margarita knew and what she was extracting from me in return for her silence. Of course, he was furious and totally embarrassed. That was when he told me all the other things going wrong with the bank. He said there were feds all over the bank looking at records and that it was very possible that he and the other directors would be indicted in the future. He told me not to give her another penny; that it didn't matter anymore. The cow was out of the bag."

"I think you mean the cat was out of the bag; that's the expression."

"Whatever. I told her to meet me for dinner the night I told you I was busy. She expected some cash. But I was there to tell her that her game was over.

"I picked that restaurant so I wouldn't bump into any of your friends or I guess I should say our friends. I thought if I met her in a public place, she wouldn't cause a scene. I was wrong on both scores. You turned up there and saw me and Margarita screamed at me and then tried excessive crying. I finally paid the bill and walked out. I had no idea that you saw me in that restaurant. Then I got your ring delivered by the messenger. I made a mess of everything. If only you would have listened to me. Instead you ran away. Mary, I never would hurt you or lie to you, I was just trying to protect my parents."

"Oh, Carlos, what a mess. You should have told me all of this weeks ago, before that evening in the restaurant. Why couldn't you have confided in me? Maybe I could have helped your dad before everything escalated."

"I didn't want you to think that my dad was some kind of crook, and that you were getting involved with a family of thieves or something."

"So when you said you might be asking me to help your family, this is what you meant. Of course, I'll represent your dad, if he wants, or I'll help him find counsel that he feels comfortable with."

"What about us, Mary, you and I? Can you forgive me?"

"Right now, Carlos, I have so much on my mind about my dad. It's hard to think about the future. Let's both get back home to Miami and talk some more. Hey, turn here. This is the exit for the airport."

Carlos made a sharp turn that threw me against him. He put his arm around me and I felt total confusion. I had been working all these weeks to forget Carlos; to put everything about him out of my mind, and now here I was snuggled against him, the smell of his aftershave filling my senses. I wished the ride to the airport wasn't over.


The early morning light illuminated a cloudless sky. The sun was actually emerging on the horizon. Northern New England looked to be getting a beautiful day. I had mixed feelings as we pulled up to the departure deck of the airport. I was eager to get back to Miami to see my family and be supportive. I missed my office and my house and Catherine and the warmth that encouraged blossoms all year round. Yet a part of me felt a tug pulling me to the Upper Valley and its variety of characters, its mountains, and history. I wondered if I'd ever return here.

I realized the car had stopped and Carlos was pulling my carry-on case out of the back. He walked around and opened my door. I stepped out and ran around to the back of my SUV to tell Sam goodbye.

"Be a good boy, and don't cause Carlos any grief," I said as I opened the door of his crate and kissed his long nose. He licked my cheek and nuzzled his head against me for a minute. I closed the crate quickly before I changed my mind and leaped back in the car.

I came back to the front of the car and fished my boarding pass out of my purse. Carlos put my bag down next to me and before I knew what was happening, he held me close and kissed me. That was the moment I knew that I couldn't survive without more of those kisses Being close to Carlos was like a drug that made me euphoric.

I kissed him back and then we stood and looked at each other for a long minute.

"Safe trip, *mi amore.* I'll bring Sam directly to your house as soon as we get to Miami. If you need me just call my cell phones. I hope you still remember the numbers," Carlos said.

"Yes, I do. Why don't you call me when you stop for the night? I'll give you an update on my dad, and I think I'd like to hear your voice tonight."

"I will. I hope we never have another night where we can't hear each other or touch each other, Mary." He held my hand for a second and then turned back to the car.

"I picked up my bag and went through the revolving door into the airport on the first leg back to my old life.

CHAPTER
# SEVENTY-SIX

I slept on and off during the flight. I was jarred awake by the voice of the flight attendant announcing our landing in ten minutes in Miami. I looked out the plane window into brilliant sun. The plane was following the ocean and beach south, passing Palm Beach, and Fort Lauderdale. I began to pick up landmarks. There was Carlos's new condo tower, there was the endless traffic on Interstate 95. In another minute I saw downtown Miami with its cluster of office towers. I could pick out the performing arts center with its unique roof. The plane turned sharply west and we glided toward Miami International Airport.

Suddenly, I couldn't wait to free myself from this metal box and be home again.

I grabbed my bag from the overhead compartment, almost bopping the passenger in front of me. As I came through the long walk connecting the plane to the terminal I felt the heat of midday Miami. I wanted to cover myself in it.

Once in the terminal, I heard the babble of twenty different languages and saw hurrying passengers in an array of colors from white, to tan, to brown and black skins and I knew I was home again.

As I moved quickly toward the front exit, I heard a familiar voice. "So you finally got here, little sister." There was Jonathan waving and calling to me.

He grabbed my bag with one hand and hugged me with his free arm.

"I am so glad to see you. How is Dad?"

"I'm glad you're here. Mom can't wait to see you. Dad is holding his own. The doctor thinks he's strong enough to have the surgery soon, maybe even tomorrow. We told Dad that you'd be here today. He grumbled that it was about time, but you could see how happy he was"

I hurried to keep up with Jonathan's long strides. Soon we were getting into his car in the parking garage, and then pulling out into the traffic on the Palmetto Expressway, but I didn't even mind it as long as the sun sprinkled my face with freckles of warmth.

"We're going directly to the hospital, aren't we?" I asked.

"Of course," Jonathan said. He looked over at me. "My God, Mary, I never knew your skin was so white. We better get you some sun before people think you're from Minnesota or Canada or something"

I pulled out my cell, turned it on and got immediate service. What a luxury.

"I need to make this call," I said apologizing to Jonathan.

"I dialed a familiar number and in a minute I heard J.C.'s baritone voice. He sounded so much like Carlos.

"J.C., it's Mary. I just got back in town. Carlos told me everything about the bank. I'm so sorry that you have to go through this."

"Mary, how good you are to call. I feel ashamed that I ever got into this mess. I'll be over at the hospital later to check on your dad," he said.

"Listen, J.C., I will give you all the legal help I can, but please don't talk to any law enforcement. Just tell them your lawyer, Mary Magruder Katz must be present at all interviews."


So like I said at the beginning, I went out to dinner one night and it changed my life. I made lots of new friends, saw another part of the country, lost a boyfriend and got him back, and learned how much home and family mean to me. Now if I can just get Carlos's dad out of trouble and my dad well again. I'll let you know how it all turns out.

17576977R00173

Made in the USA
Middletown, DE
31 January 2015